Acknowledgments

From idea to book, the path to publication for *Dead Girl Walking* has taken twenty years. There are many people who helped along the way that I'd like to thank: my first critique group, which saw the first version of this book (formerly titled *Turn Left at the Milky Way*) in 1988—Micqui Miller, Eloise Barton, Barbara Woodward, Nan Finch, and Dorothy Skarles; talented author Julia DeVillers, who while at a SCBWI conference in the early 2000s offered great critique suggestions and encouraged me to keep working on this book; the wonderful authors in my face-to-face critique group—Patti Newman, Erin Dealey, and Connie Goldsmith; and my savvy editors—Andrew Karre, who came up with the idea of turning this book into the first title of a series and to add dark villains, too, and Sandy Sullivan, who improved the final draft. Thank you everyone!

DEAD GIRL
WALKING

Linda Joy Singleton

Woodbury, Minnesota

First Edition
First Printing, 2008

Book design by Steffani Sawyer
Cover design by Gavin Dayton Duffy

Flux, an imprint of Llewellyn Publications

Library of Congress Cataloging-in-Publication Data
Singleton, Linda Joy.
  Dead girl walking / Linda Joy Singleton.—1st ed.
     p. cm.—(Dead girl series ; #1)
  Summary: When Amber, a smart, middle-class, high school student, is hit by a truck, she meets her deceased grandmother in a dreamlike place, then takes a wrong turn and awakens in the body of a wealthy, beautiful, popular classmate with serious problems.
  ISBN 978-0-7387-1405-9
  [1. Identity—Fiction. 2. Death—Fiction. 3. Future life—Fiction. 4. Family problems—Fiction. 5. High schools—Fiction. 6. Schools—Fiction.] I. Title.
  PZ7.S6177Dec 2008
  [Fic]—dc22

                                                    2008012991

Flux
Llewellyn Publications
A Division of Llewellyn Worldwide, Ltd.
2143 Wooddale Drive, Dept. 978-0-7387-1405-9
Woodbury, MN 55125-2989, U.S.A.
www.fluxnow.com

Printed in the United States of America

"I am so dead!" I groaned when the road ended at a decaying graveyard.

Slapping the steering wheel of my mother's third-hand Toyota stung my palm and solved nothing. This could not be the right road. Where were the perfectly mowed, ginormous lawns and elegant homes of Gossamer Estates? Obviously I'd made a wrong turn, which—considering the importance of today—could be the most disastrous wrong turn of my life.

"Amber, um, are we lost?" asked a timid voice. Trinidad Sylvenski had been so quiet I'd almost forgotten she was in my passenger seat. Her slim shoulders hunched over as she peered out the window. She was a new student at Halsey

High so I didn't know her well, but if my career plans worked out we'd soon be better than best friends.

"Lost? Absolutely not." An aspiring entertainment agent could never admit fear in front of a potential client. I flashed a grin that the book *The Cool of Confidence* promised worked in any stressful situation.

"Are you sure?" Trinidad bit her peach-shimmered lip. "You hit the steering wheel kind of hard and you seem really tense."

"Me? Not even." Another book, *Positive Persuasion,* advised to always put forth a positive attitude. "I know exactly what I'm doing. Could you hand me the map?"

"Sure. Here." Trinidad's whispery speaking voice was a huge contrast to her powerful singing voice. I'd only heard her sing once, but that's all it took to be blown away. Finding raw talent in my own school was an amazing stroke of luck. I'd expected to wait years—well, at least until college or an internship—to make my mark in the entertainment-agency biz. According to my books, an agent's age wasn't a factor; preparation and persistence mattered most, along with the ability to jump at an opportunity.

Checking the lavender-scented map printed in purple calligraphy, I could find where we wanted to go (Jessica Bradley's house), but not where we were (creepy graveyard). Like it was a wicked algebra problem, I knew the mysterious X answer but not the formula to get there. But I kept smiling, like I had everything under control.

"Shouldn't we turn around and look for Jessica's street?" Trinidad asked.

"Excellent idea. But we probably should call to let her

know we'll be late." And to get directions out of this God-forsaken dead end. Trying to remember all those confusing turns made my head ache.

"Use my cell." Trinidad fished inside her dainty silver clutch bag and withdrew a rhinestone-decorated phone. I tried not to drool as she flipped it open.

"Oops." She frowned.

"What's wrong?"

"No power. Guess I forgot to recharge my battery—again. You got a phone?"

Don't I wish! But there was no extra money for frivolities (that's what Mom called anything I'd wanted ever since she had the triplets). So I had no phone, no car, no college fund—stuff that was handed to other kids like candy on Halloween.

I started to confess my non-phone status when I remembered that Mom always left her phone charging in the Toyota. It was a business phone, only to be used for emergencies. Well, this ranked as an "emergency" to me.

Only when I checked the cell, take a guess…

Full battery. But no signal.

"Is your phone dead?" Trinidad's voice quavered.

"No, I just can't get reception inside the car. Not a problem. The signal is sure to be stronger outside. Once I get a signal, I'll call Jessica and we'll be on our way."

Trinidad stopped biting her lip and smiled in a stunning display of white teeth and dimples. With my guidance, that mega-smile would shine from CD covers someday. Assuming we ever made it out of here.

Stepping out of the car, I searched for signs of life or

even a street sign. But all I saw was a creepy landscape of headstones guarded by a rusty iron fence that stretched for miles. There wasn't a breeze, as if the wind couldn't find its way into this desolate place. I hated roads that ended when they weren't supposed to, but mostly I hated my sense of direction. It was like a metaphor for my life; even when I thought I knew where I was going, something usually happened to spin me the wrong way.

Today was supposed to have been my Big Chance.

Invited to a party by *the* Jessica Bradley. Not the most popular girl at school (that would be Leah Montgomery), but Leah's best friend—which would give me a toe upward on my career staircase. This was not about becoming popular. I mean, I'm not that shallow. It's just that my *Networking Works!* book said making it in Hollywood was all about connections. No fakeness allowed; just enhance your opportunities by getting to know influential people.

Jessica and Leah reigned as school glitterati. But even more important, Leah's father, as part-owner in Stardust Studios, had music industry connections.

This is how I wrangled an invite to Miz J's big party:

I was wandering around the halls, my arms wrapped around a huge HHC (Halsey Hospitality Club) gift basket to welcome the school's newest student, Trinidad Sylvenski. When I'd started the club my freshman year, we had three members. I was a senior now, and we still had three members. Everyone loved the baskets, but passed on joining the club. So our trio of membership included my best friends, Dustin Cole (a computer genius) and Alyce Perfetti (Diva of Basket Design), plus me.

It was part of my role as Official New Student Greeter to give Trinidad her "Hello Halsey!" basket. Lunch period was almost over when I finally found her leaving the cafeteria with Jessica. As I joined them, I overheard Trinidad say she couldn't go to Jessica's party on Saturday because her car was in the shop.

Be bold and take command of fortuitous opportunities (advice from one of my books).

I wouldn't have had the nerve to say even one word if Leah was around. Blonde, beautiful, and rich in all definitions of the word, Leah Montgomery was a goddess among high school students. Whenever I got near her, all my confidence drained to painful envy. Fortunately, according to rumors, Leah had already cut school with her boyfriend.

Jessica recognized me—or perhaps my basket—right away. She told me she admired the work I did with the "basket club" and that it was "just so sweet" of me to welcome Trinidad. Then both she and Trinidad oohed over all the goodies inside the glossy, wrapped basket: snacks, fruits, coupons for local businesses, a "Welcome to Halsey!" booklet, and a cute stuffed toy of our school mascot the Halsey Hippo.

Before my fear gene could kick in, I told Trinidad, "You need a ride on Saturday? No prob. I can drive you."

"I couldn't let you do that—" Trinidad started to say, at the same time that Jessica said enthusiastically, "Oh, sure! What a great idea. And Amber, why don't you stay for the party? We'll be making plans to raise funds for a charity food drive and you can help. Of course we'll have plenty of food there, too. Our caterer is totally brilliant. Come to my house this Saturday at noon." Then she bestowed a map with directions upon me like a queen offering crown jewels to a mere peasant.

Here it was: Saturday, 12:07 P.M.

And Trinidad and I were hanging with ghosts in a graveyard.

I walked around with Mom's phone held high above my head, checking for a signal. Around the car it was a total dead zone, but as I neared the tall, wrought iron cemetery gate, I got one bar. Excited, I lowered my arm—and the bar vanished.

"Amber, is the phone working yet?" Trinidad hung her head out the car window, her snaky black braid swaying inches above the ground.

"Almost," I rang out confidently. "I'll have a signal any minute now."

"I hope so. I skipped breakfast so I could pig out at the party and I'm starving."

"I won't be long," I assured her, but with less confidence.

Waving the phone, I rushed around searching for a signal. Dead air everywhere except by the cemetery gate. Even there, the bar only flashed for a mega-second. Then I slipped my arm through a gap in the gate; two bars flashed. Hmmm... the strongest signal was inside the cemetery. I stretched my arm up, the metal fence digging into my skin, and was rewarded with one more bar. Almost a full signal!

Now if I could press a few buttons, activate the speaker function, I'd be able to call Jessica. If she couldn't offer directions, I'd try Dustin. He was always at his computer, a click away from Google.

My arm ached but I kept stretching, contorting my fingers around the phone. A thumb tap and the screen lit up. All I had to do was hit seven digits and—

I dropped the phone.

"No!" I screamed, leaning forward and banging my head on the gate.

"What's wrong?" Trinidad called from the car.

"Nothing. Everything is fine!" I rubbed my head. "I'll just be a bit longer."

"Hurry, okay? This place gives me the creeps."

Me, too.

"I have it all under control," I shouted. Damn, my head hurt. "Why don't you listen to your iPod? I'll just be a few minutes."

I looked back to see where the phone had fallen—then slapped my hand over my mouth to muffle my gasp. Instead of falling straight down, the phone must have bounced off a shrub, then rolled down the slanted embankment of what was once a paved driveway. I could see a corner of it, poking up from behind a broken concrete slab. Totally out of reach.

Oh, whoops, I thought. Mom is going to kill me.

I had to get her phone back.

Even though the rusty gate appeared dilapidated, the lock was shiny new. I tugged and rattled and whacked, but it wouldn't budge. There were no breaks in the wrought iron fence. The only way over was to climb. Impossible. The gate was at least ten feet tall, twice my height, and gym was my worst subject.

Then I got this horrible flash in my mind. Of Mom's face when I tried to explain how her phone had gotten into a locked cemetery. That was scary enough to jolt me with a burst of Super-Amber Energy.

Sucking in a deep breath, I reached high and grabbed an iron bar. I managed to grasp another bar, then another, until my feet dangled a few inches above the ground. But my arms were already giving out. So I kicked out with my right leg in a pathetic attempt to swing myself up. Clunk! My leg banged against the gate. I cried out in pain and my hands slipped. I landed flat on my butt.

Diagnosis: Bruised, a little battered, but not giving up.

I thought how girls like Trinidad and Jessica would just shrug off the phone loss. "I'll buy a new one," they'd say. Easy for them, I thought. It would be heaven not to worry about money and wave credit cards around like magic wands.

My life had almost been like that two years ago. I was the adored only child of professional parents and we lived in a condo by a lake. But when my parents decided to have a baby, they sold the condo and moved into boring suburbia. Mom quit her job, so money became tight. When I found out my parents had spent my college fund on fertility treatments, I walked around with the words "No Future" written in lipstick on my forehead. And I kept asking, "Would you like fries with that?" My friend Alyce accused me of being overly dramatic, and I never argued.

I couldn't count on anyone for my future. Except me.

So I brushed off my dusty backside and looked around. A ladder would have been nice, but no such luck. I spotted an old board propped against a scraggly oak. Gravel crunched under my open-toed sandals as I carefully pushed aside weeds. The board was filthy with bugs, moss and gross droppings I didn't even want to think about. I brushed off a corner with leaves, then dragged the long board through the weeds and propped it against the gate.

I half-walked/half-crawled up my makeshift ladder. When I reached the top, I swung up and straddled the curved iron saddle-style, with a leg dangling on each side. Holding tight, I huddled there for a moment, breathing hard.

When I could breathe normally again, I lifted my head to look around. Not so bad, even kind of cool if you were into old tombstones and monuments shaped like angels, saints and temples. There were no flower vases or other offerings from loved ones. Obviously this cemetery was so old even the loved ones were dust and bones. If Alyce were here, she'd snap pictures for her "Morbidity Collection." She gathered images of the grim side of life, and aspired to be a famous starving artist or get rich from publishing a best-selling photo journal.

But morbidity was not my idea of fun—and the ground seemed so very far away. On the cemetery side there were sharp chunks of concrete from a crumbling sidewalk. Jumping into the cemetery would be suicide. Mom could save up to buy another phone, but I couldn't buy a new body at Wal-Mart.

Defeated, I prepared to climb back down. But my leg swung too hard and banged into my board-ladder. The board wobbled, slid sideways, and landed on the ground with a poof of dust.

Now what was I going to do? Stranded high on the gate, I slumped against the cold iron. I'd lost my Big Chance. I'd never make it to Jessica's now, and she'd think I was a loser. Trinidad would never accept a ride or anything else from me.

Diagnosis: Depressed and ready to give up.

I should just jump, end it all now—except I hated messes and really hated the idea of ending up a concrete pancake. I could wait for Trinidad to notice I was in trouble or jump to the softer ground in front of the gate. If I landed on my ample butt, I had a fifty-fifty chance of survival.

I had almost worked up the courage to jump, when I heard a sound that would change the direction of my life forever.

Mom's cell phone!

Ringing!

Startled, I whipped around on my narrow perch toward the sound. Bad move. My hips shifted and swayed. I lost my balance. My leg shot out from under me, my hands slipped then flailed in empty air.

I was screaming as I fell toward the concrete.

When I opened my eyes, my first emotion was surprise. Somehow I had missed the concrete and landed in a scratchy bush.

Good news: I was alive.

Bad news: The bush was full of stinging nettles.

Pain kicked in like stabbing knives. I jumped away from the bush. Quick body inventory: no broken bones, but the mint-green shirt I'd bought with hard-earned babysitting money was mortally wounded. And tiny red bumps swelled in an ugly mass of welts across my arms and legs.

I couldn't dwell on it, though, with the phone ringing.

Was it my parents? Dustin or Alyce? Psychic police coming to my rescue?

Hobbling and itching, I eased my way down the sloping road. As I grabbed the phone, the ringing stopped with a silence more painful than the stinging nettles. The signal bar flickered on and off. For better reception, I needed to move higher. An angel statue atop a steep granite podium with stairs looked promising. When I reached the angel, the sun peered through dark clouds and Mom's phone flashed on. This had to be a good omen from the heaven—or from my Grammy Greta, who I often sensed watching over me.

Before I could dial an SOS, the phone rang again.

I hit the green answer button. "Who is this? Dustin? Mom, Dad, whoever—you have to help me!"

But the voice that replied wasn't familiar. Or human.

"Good afternoon, I'm calling from Ledbottom Mortgage International," droned a computerized recording, "and I can save you a ton of money by offering you a limited low rate to—"

I. Could. Not. Believe. This.

Punching disconnect, I started to call Jessica when I heard a scream. I looked over at the car and saw Trinidad yanking off her iPod and rushing toward me. She'd finally noticed I was in trouble—but too late.

"Ohmygod! Amber!" She stared through the gate incredulously. "What are you doing?"

"I have a phone signal." I waved the phone feebly.

She gaped at my ripped, dirty clothes and the outbreak of red bumps. My too-curly brown hair was a disaster, too. I must look ridiculous, perched on the angel's halo with my arms stretched out like a giant bird. Not the professional image I preferred.

"I'll call my friend Dustin," I said quickly to cut off any more questions. "He works part-time for a locksmith and can unlock the gate. I'm sorry we'll be late for the party, but we should make it in time for dessert—which is always the best part of a meal, anyway."

"Uh … sure. The party." She nodded at me like she was afraid to make any sudden movement that might send me completely over the edge. She reached down and plucked a leaf off her silver crossed-strap sandals. "Um … I'll go sit in the car and listen to my tunes until you're … um … ready."

Sighing, I leaned against the angel's stone wing and called Dustin.

"Hey Amber." He picked up right away, his monotone hinting at distractions. I imagined his gaze glued to one of his monitors as he swiveled in his chair, kicking aside discarded papers and snack wrappers in his self-named "Headquarters," walled in with bookshelves overflowing with science fiction and political novels.

"Dustin, thank God you're there!"

"Where else would I be? Wassup?"

"Me." I stared far, far down to the ground. "Don't ask."

He asked anyway, and I told him.

"Okay, stop laughing," I said. "This is serious."

"Sure, sure," he said, still chuckling.

"I mean it. Trinidad thinks I'm crazy."

"Aren't you? But in an interesting way."

"Thank you very much for being so sympathetic." My arm ached from holding the phone at an awkward angle.

"Oh, I'm completely sympathetic, but you have to admit it's hilarious. Someday you'll laugh about this, too."

"Never. Stop laughing. Hurry and get me out of here!"

"Yeah, yeah. Already leaving my room and heading outside. Getting in my car. Starting the engine. Be there in twenty minutes."

"You know how to get here?" I asked, astonished.

"Sure, the old Gossamer Cemetery. Used to be a historical landmark until *they* shut it down and rerouted the roads when *they* put in the Gossamer Estates." *They* referred to politicians or the word that Alyce coined and Dustin preferred: "Corrupticians." He loathed politicians and commented regularly on anti-government blogs.

Dustin kept talking as he drove, spouting street names that meant nothing to me.

Fifteen minutes later he arrived in his Prius. He simply walked over to the fence and pulled a huge key ring (bounty from his part-time locksmith job) out of his pocket. He tried over twenty keys before there was a click, and the cemetery gate opened.

Trinidad applauded. "That was amazing."

"I told you Dustin would get me out." I gave Dustin a quick hug. "Thanks for being my hero. If I ever win the lottery, I owe you half. Now we can head on to the party."

Dustin just looked at me with a pitying expression. He didn't make any jokes about my lack of direction or my appearance. But his gaze said it all—with footnotes. His blatant pity made me angry and tempted to point out his mismatched brown and black socks. But I'd never sink that low, especially since he worked so hard to hide his secret. He was colorblind.

"Do I look that bad?" I grimaced at my ripped jeans and dirt-stained shirt.

"Bad would be a compliment."

"He's right." Trinidad pointed to my arms. "What are all those bumps? A rash?"

"Nettles." I rubbed my itchy arm. "Ouch."

"You should see a doctor," Trinidad said sympathetically. "You better get home right away. A party is no big deal—we can go some other time."

"We're going. I'm fine." I made myself stop scratching.

"You're going to a party looking like that?" Dustin asked with disbelief.

If we were alone, I would tell him honestly how important this party could be to my future. I might never get a chance like this again. Maybe he read my mind, because he sighed and offered to lead us to Jessica's house. "I'm not risking your getting lost again and ending up on one of those missing-persons TV shows," he said.

He also gave me the shirt off his back—literally. "It's too long for you, but at least it's clean and the sleeves will cover your bumpy arms."

"Thanks, Dustin. You're the greatest." I rose on my tiptoes to give him a kiss on the cheek. Well, the chin, actually since I couldn't reach his cheek. He blushed. We'd tried dating once, but it felt like dating my father. Dustin was unusually mature—like someone in his forties rather than seventeen, as if he'd aged in dog years.

The drive to Gossamer Estates was amazingly quick. I'd been much closer than I'd realized, only missing Jessica's street by one left turn. Her home wasn't a house—it was a gleaming white stone mansion with perfectly groomed lawns, shrubs shaped like animals, and a spouting, Grecian-styled fountain at the center of the circular driveway.

Dustin gave me a thumbs-up as he drove away.

I won't lie and say I felt comfortable surrounded by wealth and elegance. But I could get used to it. Although if I lived in a house this big, I'd probably get lost on my way to my own bedroom, which meant a lot of walking—and I hated any form of exercise.

My smile was wide and confident as Trinidad and I climbed a mountain of polished granite steps. But once I reached Jessica Bradley's door, my hands started to shake.

To hide my nervousness, I silently did a ritual that always calmed me: Grammy Greta's Good Luck Chant. My grandmother had been gone for only a little over a year, but I still missed her so much. Thinking about her made me sad, but happy, too, because she'd been so great. She'd said I could achieve anything, if I worked hard and listened to my heart. A week before she died, she told me she'd had a premonition that my dreams would come true.

"Impossible," I'd argued, because I'd just found out that my parents had used my college fund for fertility treatments. They'd promised to pay it back, but the cost of raising triplets was insane.

"Believe," Grammy Greta told me. "I have a direct line to wisdom on the other side, and know that great things are in your future."

Great things? Did she mean I'd get a scholarship to a prestigious university and become a successful entertainment agent? That I wouldn't be stuck living at home forever, taking care of the triplets or flipping burgers?

Then Grammy handed me a rainbow woven bracelet like something you'd pick up at a dollar store. "This is a lucky bracelet," she said with a mischievous wink. "Twist it three times and repeat the magical chant."

"What chant?" I'd asked, playing along.

She leaned so close I could smell her wintergreen mouthwash. When she whispered a familiar poem about a bear in my ear, I tried not to giggle. Only Grammy would choose such a corny chant: "Twist the bracelet twice to the right then once to the left, and seal the luck with a kiss."

I felt really stupid kissing a bracelet, but I did it for Grammy.

Then she reminded me that this was our secret and not to tell anyone.

"I won't tell anyone," I promised, "except Alyce."

Grammy chuckled. "Of course. Don't tell anyone except Alyce."

When we hugged, I had no idea it would be the last time I hugged my grandmother.

Now as I stared down at the bracelet I smelled roses—Grammy's perfume. I turned my bracelet to the right two times, the left once, whispered the chant, then turned my back to Trinidad so she wouldn't see when I sealed the magic with a kiss.

And it was the craziest thing—but I imagined I heard Grammy's voice saying "believe." I felt my courage rising.

After that everything was a glamorous blur.

A maid ushered us into an imposing "foy-yay" with gilt-framed portraits, a standing coat rack, and an elegant oval wall mirror. She checked our names off an official list, then escorted us across a gold-flecked marble floor, past a formal dining room with a crystal chandelier the size of a refrigerator. A curved mahogany staircase arched overhead.

The maid's heels made hollow clip-clip sounds on the tile while my sandals clunked and left a dirt trail. Please, no one notice, I prayed.

We were led to a garden patio with lovely hanging flower baskets and golden crepe streamers. Round tables with white tablecloths and glowing candles were arranged on the faux-grass lawn. Buffet tables oozed with exotic delicacies and a sparkling pink punch waterfall. Way cool!

A band played on a cement podium where a few kids danced. Most guests were my age, but there were token adults, too. Everyone was talking and laughing in cozy groups, or sitting at the tables with heaping plates of food. I recognized some kids from school, either because we'd shared classes or I'd welcomed them with a HHC basket.

"Trinidad! Amber!"

I turned and there was Jessica Bradley, gorgeous in a sapphire-hued sundress that enhanced her blue eyes and smooth olive skin. Waving her multi-ringed hand, she glided over to us and air kissed our cheeks. I almost pinched myself to make sure I wasn't dreaming. This so felt like some glam moment from a movie.

"You made it! I'm so glad," Jessica said with a sincerity that put me at ease. Well, almost. I was more used to family parties held in a crowded living room. A mansion, maid, caterers ... *Wow!* Why couldn't my real life be like this?

"Hi, Jessica," I said, scratching covertly. "Sorry we're late. It's not Trinidad's fault. I made a wrong turn and—"

"No need to explain." Her black curls swayed as she shook her head. "Everyone is late. It's unfashionably rude to come on time."

"Anything not to be rude," I joked.

Jessica turned to Trinidad. "You look great—that's a Kiana original, isn't it?"

"Yeah," Trinidad replied. "Kiana is so new. I can't believe you recognize her work."

"I know all the designers that matter. I almost bought a similar outfit but they only had it in yellow, which is tragic on me. Looks fabulous on you, though, and I love the glitter strands woven in your braid."

"Thanks." Trinidad flashed her future-diva smile, seeming totally at ease.

"Amber," Jessica turned to me. "You…um…have such an original style. I'd never be brave enough to wear a guy's shirt, but it looks so…unique on you."

"Uh…thanks." I think.

"I'm so glad you came. Not just because you brought Trinidad—which was incredibly sweet of you. With all your basket club experience I'm sure you'll bring lots of creative ideas to our charity planning committee. It's important to collect food for starving kids. I feel it's our duty to do all we can. Don't you?"

"Of course."

"I'm going to introduce Trinidad around, since she's new. Amber, feel free to hang out and help yourself to the buffet." Jessica waved toward a table heaping with assorted dishes and platters. Then she rushed off toward this blond guy named Tristan I recognized from my trig class—an arrogant jerk who kept trying to cheat off my tests.

I poured a drink from the pink punch fountain and wandered around, smiling and reminding classmates who I was. I received blank stares. I never had trouble talking with Alyce and Dustin, and wished they were here. But they scorned "society"; this was definitely not their kind of party. I wasn't sure it was mine, either—although the book *Becoming Your Destiny* advised to embrace new experiences.

The buffet was a delicious new experience. I nibbled on spicy chicken legs and oriental noodles while looking around for a friendly face. Across the lawn, in a gazebo, I spotted Trinidad with Jessica and some of her crowd. I started to go over until I noticed that the chairs were full. Could be awkward. So I plopped down next to a chatty woman with silver-blue coifed hair. Leisl, as she asked me to call her, was Jessica's great aunt. After twenty minutes listening to her stories, I escaped to the dessert buffet.

Confession: I have a passion for chocolate. I crave, obsess, lust for chocolate—which is why my clothes are double-digit size. It's a sinful obsession, a constant struggle. Once I start eating chocolate, abandon all hope. I can*not* stop.

"Try the pecan truffles."

I turned to find a medium-tall guy with tight brown curls and hazel eyes. Why was he so familiar? He must go to my school, although I couldn't think of his name.

"Okay," I answered, putting a pecan truffle in my mouth. Rich milk chocolate and crunchy nuts. The candy melted in my mouth.

The guy was nodding, and chewing on his own chocolate pecan. He pointed at a dish heaped with white squares dimpled with red specks. I nodded too, swallowed the chocolate bliss, and tried one of the white squares.

I moaned in delight. "Oh, this is *soooo* good."

"A true chocolate connoisseur."

"These desserts are amazing. So many in one place!"

His gaze swept the table. "Thirty-seven plates with approximately twenty-five candies on each plate, adding in variables of size, equaling approximately—"

"Nine hundred and twenty-five candies," I finished.

His hazel eyes widened, clearly impressed.

"I'm a math geek," I admitted.

"You, too?"

"Math just makes sense."

"When not much else does." He nodded.

"And being good with numbers will come in handy when I start my—" I covered my mouth, shocked that I almost confessed my secret ambition to a near stranger.

"Start your what?" He tilted his curly-brown head.

"Nothing."

"Come on … you can't leave me hanging with an unknown equation. I won't be able to sleep tonight trying to figure out the answer."

I laughed, liking him even more. He had quiet dignity and intelligence; someone who could be trusted. Glancing around to make sure no one was watching, I lowered my voice. "I'm going to be an entertainment agent—dealing with diva personalities, contracts, finances."

"You'll be great at it, I can tell."

"You think?" I asked, ridiculously pleased.

"Definitely. But why an agent? Most people want to be the next American Idol, not a person behind the scenes."

"Because I've always loved music and...well, I don't know why I'm telling you this...but to be honest, I have zero talent. I can't sing, act, or dance. But I like to help people and I recognize talent when I see it."

"Sounds like a cool talent to me, more exciting than selling cars like my dad—which is what my family expects."

"But is it what *you* want?"

"No, but I don't know what I want—except more chocolate." He licked caramel off his lip and gestured at the dessert table. "There are nearly a thousand candies to choose from. What next?"

"I have no idea."

"Let's try them all."

I summoned restraint and shook my head. "I have to stop. Or I'll regret it later."

"Why? Chocolate is the best thing about this party. Or at least it was." He flashed this really sweet smile that lit up his otherwise average face. Um, was he flirting with me?

I glanced away, my heart fluttering a little, and pointed to a dish of black-and-white striped chocolates. "Okay...just one more. But which one? These look like zebra candy."

"Zebra candy?" He chuckled. "Good name."

"Do you have a name...I mean, I know you have a name, everyone does, what I mean, is what is it?"

"Eli. And you're Amber."

My cheeks burned. "Do I know you?"

"When my brother and I left this boring private school and started at Halsey, you gave us a cool welcome basket."

"I did?" I studied him, but drew a blank. "I'm usually good with names, but I don't remember—"

"I get that a lot when I'm with my brother." He reached out for one of the black-and-white striped chocolates. "Try a zebra. They're actually called domino dips, but zebra is better. That's what I'll call them from now on."

He lifted the "zebra" to my lips. I got that fluttery feeling again, and hesitated. Then I opened my lips slightly, curling my tongue around the candy. Sweet milky chocolate swam around my taste buds and slid down my throat.

"Good?" he asked softly.

"Ummm," was my answer.

Our eyes met over the dessert table. We shared a moment of chocolate understanding. As cliché as it might sound, it was like we were the only ones at the party. The band's music faded so all I heard was the quick beat of my heart, accompanied by the melting richness of chocolate.

Then he glanced down and flicked off some candy that had fallen on his black slacks. His elbow bumped against the table and dishes rattled. He rubbed at the spot on his slacks but that only blobbed it even bigger.

An odd look crossed his face. "I—I've got to go."

Before I could even ask what was wrong, he turned and disappeared inside, through the French doors.

Why had he left? Had I done or said something to offend him?

Disappointed, I turned back to the dessert table.

And reached for chocolate.

3

With Eli gone, the glamour faded from the party.

I just wanted to go home—which surprised me. What happened to all my ambitions to make connections with influential people? In theory this sounded easy enough but up-close-in-action, it felt dishonest. I'd check with Trinidad and see if she was ready to leave.

As I neared the gazebo, I heard someone say my name. Curious, I paused behind a large floral arrangement. Peeking through the orchids, I saw Trinidad with Jessica and some of Leah's crowd: Kat, Tristan and Moniqua.

" . . . almost didn't come but Amber drove me," Trinidad said. She was sitting so close to Tristan that he practically shared her chair. What was that about?

"Is Amber the freak in the hideous guy's shirt?" Kat asked with a derisive laugh.

Didn't Kat remember two years ago when I'd welcomed her with a HHC basket, and she'd told me I was the nicest girl in the whole school? Guess not.

"Yeah, that's her," Jessica said.

"Ewww…fashion nightmare." Kat's blonde ponytail flopped across her shoulder as she crossed her long denim-clad legs, her shiny cowboy boots glinting with rhinestones. "When she first walked in, I thought she was, like, a street person. I wasn't sure whether to call the cops or give her money for decent clothes."

"Donate money for the fashion impoverished," Jessica joked. "Our next charity project."

"Waste of time," Kat said. "She's obviously a lost cause."

"Amber's nice," Trinidad put in defensively. "It's not her fault she's wearing an ugly shirt. She looked good when she picked me up, but then her shirt was destroyed when she fell in the cemetery."

"Cemetery! Are you serious?" I recognized Moniqua's voice because she always laughed loudest when I stumbled in gym. While Kat could be annoyingly "catty," Moniqua was just plain mean.

Trinidad had the decency to look ashamed. "Can we discuss something else? I shouldn't have said anything."

"But you did and now we have to know," Moniqua urged. "What was she doing at a cemetery?"

"Um…I don't think she'd want me talking about it."

That's for sure, I thought.

"But it's only to us." Kat patted Trinidad's hand. "Trust

me; we'll keep any secret you share. Is it something illegal? Was Amber performing a satanic ritual?"

"Nothing like that! Well ... maybe I do need to explain." Trinidad glanced uncertainly at the others, then shrugged. "We're all friends, so it can't hurt ..."

No! I almost rushed over and clamped my hand over Trinidad's mouth. But it would have been too late anyway. Trinidad proved that singing wasn't her only talent—she made my humiliating experience sound like a macabre adventure in stupidity. She laughed along with her new friends ... while I died inside.

"I'm not surprised she screwed up," Tristan said as he scooted closer to Trinidad. "Amber is in my trig class and she keeps trying to cheat off my tests. Why did you invite her, Jess?"

"She's was all 'I want to help.' So what could I say?" Jessica spread out her arms like a shrug. "She practically got on her knees and begged me. You know what they say about charity starting at home."

"You're *sooo* nice," Kat gushed. "Leah would never invite a loser to her party."

"Leah isn't here, and she hasn't returned my texts or emails." Jessica pursed her lips spitefully. "I heard she and Chad ditched school, but you'd think she'd at least tell me. I don't know what's with Leah lately. She's been so ... distant."

"Not with Chad, I'll bet," Kat said, giggling.

"I couldn't care less what they do. And Leah isn't the boss of me, so if I want Amber on the fundraiser committee, she's in."

Moniqua groaned. "She's so pathetic, though, how can we stand her?"

"No worries," Jessica said cheerfully. "Amber can do all the messy stuff like painting signs."

"Our own geek slave." Kat giggled.

"That doesn't seem fair." Trinidad shifted uncomfortably in her chair. "But I guess Amber won't mind since she volunteered to help. She'll be great on your committee."

"Yeah, a great bore." Tristan snorted. "Really, Trinidad, how did you survive being stuck with her on the drive here? At least you won't have to go back with her. I'll give you a ride anywhere you want."

"Ooh!" Kat clapped her hands. "Tristan and Trinidad, even your names sound like you were destined to meet."

"What do you say, Trin?" Tristan smoothly slipped an arm around Trinidad's tiny waist. "Ditch the loser and I'll drive you home in my Hummer—eventually."

"You have a Hummer? Wow…that's way cool. But I don't know…I mean…I'll have to check with Amber first. She's been awfully nice to me."

"She's always nice in this earnest, revolting way," Moniqua complained. "Makes me sick how she doesn't have a clue what's really going on. Her basket club is a big joke. She takes it seriously, but everyone is laughing at her club. Basket Cases, we call them."

"Maybe inviting her was a mistake." Jessica frowned. "But she's so eager to please. We'll keep her busy and out of our way."

Out of their way? Like I was a disease!

Shame washed over me and I blinked back tears. I'd

27

been so looking forward to this party. I'd used my babysitting money to buy my now-ruined shirt, and I'd prepared a list of fundraising ideas to impress Jessica. I endured getting lost, scaling a cemetery gate, and itchy nettles.

And for what?

Utter humiliation.

I wanted to turn invisible and slink away. But I couldn't abandon Trinidad, no matter how much she deserved it. Anger pushed me out of hiding. I stepped away from the potted plant, where anyone could see me, then stomped over to the table.

Folding my arms across my chest, I faced Trinidad.

"I'm leaving," I said in the calmest voice I could manage.

"So soon? Is something wrong?" Trinidad pushed Tristan's hand off her arm and stood. "Amber, are you sick?"

"Oh, I'm sick all right. Of fakeness."

"What do you mean?"

"I'm not anyone's 'geek slave.' Go home with him." I pointed at Tristan, not wanting to say his name.

"Were you spying on us?" Tristan narrowed his eyes.

I glared, holding tight to anger so I wouldn't cry.

"You heard us?" Jessica sounded a little scared. "We were just messing around. I'm sorry, we didn't mean—"

"Save it, Jess," Moniqua interrupted. "Don't apologize to her. Eavesdroppers hear exactly what they deserve."

"Yeah," I agreed sadly. "The truth."

Then I left the party.

I could hardly see out of the windshield through my tears.

To shut off my thoughts, I amped my radio full blast and sang at the top of my lungs. I didn't even know the words to the song, so I messed up the lyrics...like I'd messed up my life. I hoped a truck would smash into me or a bolt of lightning would strike my car. But there wasn't a cloud, much less a lightning bolt in the sky, and all the trucks on the road were wise enough to avoid me.

It was almost a surprise to make it home safely.

Only I couldn't bring myself to get out of the car. Why bother? My life was over. The fact that I was still breathing was a cruel irony.

There was no going forward or backwards, only sitting here in limbo land. I couldn't bear to talk to anyone, so going into the house was out of the question. Mom would take one glance at my face, know I was upset, and pepper me with questions. Then she'd tell my father and insist we discuss it over a family meeting.

So I just sat there, with the car running, drowning in dark, hopeless thoughts. I glanced down at my lucky bracelet, tempted to rip it off my wrist.

Lots of luck it brought me—all of it bad.

By Monday morning, whispers and gossip would have spread around school. Basket Case...Basket Case! Is that really what everyone thought of my club? Of me? Were Alyce and Dustin my only real friends? Was everyone just laughing like I was a pathetic joke? I could never return to school. I'd have to transfer to another school or drop out. But dropping out would mean never going to college and having a big career. If I asked Mom about home schooling she'd just say no, because she was already crazy busy raising the triplets. So what could I do?

I couldn't just leave school—yet how could I stay?

Hearing a car, I looked up at the mail truck slowing in front of my house. The mail lady, Sheila, saw me and waved. She and I had gotten to be friends after I'd sent off tons of scholarship applications that sent me rushing out to meet the mail truck daily. But I didn't want to talk to her today and hear about her chronic back pain and how her sister's husband was in jail again. So I hunched down in the car and prayed she'd leave.

Sheila waved again and called out my name.

Just what I didn't need.

But she kept shouting for me, and if I didn't go over my parents would come out of the house. I wiped my tears, arranging my hair so it partially hid my face. Then I walked over with a fake smile.

"Amber, check out my new wheels!" Sheila said happily.

"You finally got a new mail truck?" I said with forced cheerfulness. "Cool."

"Isn't it a beaut? Except that it's a manual and the gears are all wonky. I'm still getting used to it. But hey, enough about me." She reached for a letter on her lap. "I have good news for you! That scholarship you were waiting for!"

They're probably rejecting me, I thought, but I didn't want to ruin Sheila's upbeat mood. So I kept on smiling and took the letter.

"Well, open it up!" Sheila urged.

I hesitated, then shrugged and ripped into the envelope.

The opening lines jumped out at me: *Congratulations! We are happy to offer—*

Ohmygod! I got the scholarship!

Next thing I knew I was jumping and crying for joy. Sheila laughed and congratulated me, and then said she had to finish her route. I heard an awful clunk of gears as her car jerked forward, tires squealing.

I read the letter, then read it again. *Congratulations! We are happy to offer you a scholarship to a California State University of your choice. We have evaluated your application...*

I'm sure my eyes were as big and round as all those lovely zeroes. I nearly fell to my knees and kissed the pavement.

Totally, totally amazing! All my dreams come true and folded neatly into an envelope. Grammy Greta was so right. I did have a future—and a great one! I could go anywhere and be anything I wanted.

I was hugging the letter, poised to rush into the house and tell my parents the good news, when I heard an engine roar, the screech of wheels, and a scream.

Then Sheila's brand new mail-mobile, which was careening out of control in reverse, ran right into me.

And I died.

Golden light shone so brightly my eyes should have hurt, yet they didn't. Nothing hurt.

I didn't even itch!

Surrounded by the dazzling clouds of light, I felt incredible, amazing joy. I wasn't anywhere in particular, yet I was somehow everywhere, which made no sense at all.

Dreaming. Yeah, that had to be it. Floating, flying, sweet dreams soaring. There was music, too, an orchestra of crystal-pure angelic music. And when the clouds cleared, a woman glided toward me with arms outstretched, smiling wide. A smile I loved dearly and had never expected to see again. Not on Earth, anyway.

Could that mean I was ... ?

"Not quite," Grammy Greta told me, squeezing my hands and peering deep into my heart. Strangely, she had no wrinkles and her hair was dark brown, not silvery gray. She wore beige slacks and a striped shirt with a cat embroidered on the pocket. Not the starchy yellow cotton dress I'd seen her wearing at her funeral.

Funeral...buried in the ground...over a year ago.

I blinked at Grammy, then looked down at myself, searching for some clue to what was going on. I was still me, in ripped jeans and Dustin's baggy shirt that barely covered my nettle bumps and reddened scratches. I ran a finger along an old scar on my right thumb, where I'd been snagged by a hook on my first (and last) fishing trip with Dad. The scar felt real and so did I—yet how could that be?

"Am I dreaming?" I lifted my gaze from my hands to Grammy's beaming face.

"Dreams and reality are elementally the same."

"I don't get it...but it doesn't matter. If this is a dream, it's a great one and I'm in no hurry to wake up. Oh, Grammy, I've missed you so much!"

"I've missed you, too." When she squeezed my hands she felt real and alive and wonderful.

"How is this possible?" I asked, marveling at the misty ground swirling around my very ordinary sneakers, scents of mountain and ocean breezes, and the amazing woman standing in front of me. "I can't believe we're together. I never thought I'd see you again."

"But I've never been far away, and I see you all the time. Remember the card you received on your birthday with no signature?"

"Sure. The cute black dog on the front looked exactly like Cola. I tacked it on my bulletin board. I couldn't figure out who sent…" I stared at her widening smile. "You?"

"I was only the messenger." She nodded. "It was his idea."

"His? You mean … Cola?"

There was a sharp bark as a furry black dog sprang out of nothingness with the bouncing energy of a puppy. He scampered over to me, red tongue lapping and his black whip-like tail wagging.

If being with Grammy Greta was a shock, seeing my favorite (dead!) dog was absolutely mind-boggling. Until now I'd thought it was a dream, but dreams didn't come with doggy breath and barking. Cola looked so healthy! When he'd died at the old age of nineteen, he'd been blind and lame. Now his black eyes shone with lively mischief. His tongue tickled my face when he slurped a doggy kiss.

"Cola!" I wrapped my arms around his soft warm neck. When I brushed against his luminous gold collar, sparks sizzled like an electric halo. Vivid images circled around Cola's neck as if my touch had pushed a remote control button and switched on a holographic TV. The cinematic collar reeled with pictures and garbled sounds. I tried to focus on the images but it was all a blur. Then abruptly the spinning stopped. The collar stilled to a plain gold band.

"What kind of collar is *that?*" I jumped back, the buoyant ground swishing cloudy puffs around my ankles.

"It's not a collar. Cola's Duty Director notifies him of new work assignments."

"Work … you mean my dog has a job?"

"Why does that surprise you? Animals are very spiritual creatures and have evolved to a higher plane than humans. Cola was honored with the position of Comforter. Usually that work goes to cats or ferrets, but Cola showed outstanding empathetic abilities."

"He always did seem to understand me." I nodded, patting his head. "What does he do?"

"Comfort people when they're alone and frightened. Comforters take the form of beloved pets, to help as a soul embarks on its final journey. Cola joins the person, usually in a hospital bed, offering love and companionship until their wait ends. I'm very proud of him ... and of you, too."

I continued to pat Cola's furry head as I met my grandmother's tender gaze. There was so much I wanted to say, so many things I'd longed to tell her.

"It's all right, honey," she said softly. "I already know."

"Even about my scholarship?"

"Yes. It's a wonderful opportunity."

"Except how can I ... I mean ... the mail truck went out of control. What happened?" I spoke with no fear, only confusion. "I was sure the truck would hit me, but I feel okay and nothing's broken. My nettle bumps don't even itch."

"They will when you return. But for now you're in a neutral state. I brought you here in that instant before you were struck."

"So the mail truck did hit me?"

"Yes, but only your body." She nodded. "I couldn't bear to watch you suffer, so I bent a few rules and brought you here."

"How? Are you and Cola angels?"

"Far from it," she said with a chuckle. "I manage a complicated network of volunteers—some living and some moved on. My job comes with certain abilities—like the power to bring you here. I'm so proud of you, honey. Watching you read that scholarship letter was one of my proudest moments."

"You saw that?" I asked, pleased.

"I wouldn't have missed it for the worlds! I helped make it happen. Not that you wouldn't have done it on your own, but a persuasive voice in the right ear can speed things up."

"I've heard that advice before." I snapped my fingers. "I read it in *Create Happiness Through Happen-Ness*."

"That was some of our guide-writers' best work," Grammy Greta said, nodding. "You know what they say about great books."

"Actually ... I don't."

"Great books aren't written, they're relayed." She glanced down at my wrist. "I'm pleased to see you wearing the lucky bracelet."

"I always wear it." I caressed the rainbow cloth. "But it wasn't lucky today."

A screech echoed in my head with the blur of the mail truck careening toward me. But I pushed it aside, detached and emotionless, as if it had happened to someone else.

Around me clouds shifted in purple and silver hues, and I glimpsed a panorama of brilliant green meadow, shady trees, sparkling water, and a distant shore where figures waved. I had a strong sense of knowing them ... yet I couldn't possibly.

"Tell me, Grammy. What is all this?" My fingers curled

in Cola's silky fur as I regarded my grandmother solemnly. "Heaven?"

"Close, but not exactly. It's more of a moment, a transition in time, than a specific location."

"I don't understand, but it's nice here with you and Cola." Cola perked up at his name, his collar flickering with quicksilver images. I scratched his head, which made him thump his back leg in his usual way. "You're such a good boy. And I'll bet you're a great Comforter."

"He's the best," Grammy said.

"I always wondered what happened to animals. What about my cats Snowflake and Pinky?" I looked around. "Can I see them, too?"

She shook her head. "There isn't time."

"Why not?"

"While time has little meaning here, it's ticking away on Earth. But before you go, I must warn you about Dark Lifers."

"What are they?"

"Dark souls who can steal energy and human bodies. They can't stay in a host body longer than a full moon cycle, so they go from body to body, causing trouble."

"Can't you stop them?"

"I have to find them first—and travel between our worlds is difficult." She frowned. "Regretfully, I've put you at risk by bringing you here. For a few days you'll have an afterglow that will attract Dark Lifers. They may try to touch you to feed on your energy. If you see one, call me by doing our lucky ritual and I'll send in the Dark Disposal Team. You have nothing to fear."

"I'm not afraid, but I'd like to help you. What do Dark Lifers look like?"

"Like ordinary people—Earthbounders—except for their gray fingernails and a shadowy haze around their hands. Their touch can be painful and their lies even more dangerous. So avoid them and stay safe." She gave me a sad smile. "You have to return now."

"Now?" I frowned. "But I don't want to leave you. Can't I stay longer?"

"Sorry, hon. But that's not possible. You have a wonderful life waiting for you. That scholarship is going to open up fantastic opportunities."

"As an entertainment agent?"

"It's entirely up to you."

"But things have a way of going the wrong way for me. Making connections, making friends, is harder than I expected." I winced as the words "Basket Cases" replayed in my head. Trinidad would never sign on with a loser. "Grammy, can't I just stay here? You said I could decide what I wanted, and I want to be with you."

"Are you sure?"

"Of course."

She gazed at me in a way that made me think I was forgetting something important. Then she spoke in a tone so soft I had to lean forward to hear. "What about your family?"

Her question struck me with a jolt like lightning. I'd been so happy to see Grammy and Cola, I'd completely forgotten about Mom, Dad, Cherry, Melonee, and Olive.

"Look here." My grandmother reached down to touch Cola's collar.

The collar sparked with life and colors, reeling with sound and shining rays of live video onto Grammy's open hand. When I peered closely at her palm, it was like viewing a TV screen. Memories flashed by. Birthdays, holidays, ordinary every days. Camping trips, school plays, holding the triplets in the hospital after they were born, Mom and Dad taking me on a special dinner because I was the Big Sister now.

There were scenes of my friends, too.

My kindergarten best friend, Lola, sharing one of her prized naked Barbies; reciting Australian words over the phone with my online pal Emily; giggling as I taught Alyce some of these words ("tacker," "bikkies," "dunny"); screeching through a red light when Dustin tried to teach me to drive; staging a vampire neck-bite for Alyce to paint; a school play where my family and friends filled an entire row and applauded like I was the leading lady rather than the ass end of a costumed donkey.

The palm pictures faded, but their applause sang in my ears.

"Still want to stay with me?" Grammy asked gently.

I remembered the hurtful things I'd overheard at the party, which had sunk my self-esteem like tons of gravity. But a different kind of gravity, a foundation of real friends, supported and grounded me. Not fake Jessica and her crowd, but people I could count on—like Dustin, Alyce, and my family.

A lump ached in my throat. "They'll miss me if I don't come back."

"Yes," she said simply.

"But it's so hard … I hate leaving you."

"'Hate' is a four-letter word and it's strictly forbidden here. Take heart, Amber; our parting will be short. What will seem like a very long life to you is a blink in time here." She reached down to pat Cola's head. "We're always here for you."

Clouds thickened around me. "So how do I get back?"

"See that path up ahead?" Grammy Greta pointed and bright bulbs of light lit up a winding pathway. "Follow the path to an area of velvety darkness illuminated with shooting streaks overhead that are as dazzling as the Milky Way. It's very beautiful, but don't linger. Make a left turn."

"A left turn? At the Milky Way?"

"Right," she said. "Be happy, Amber."

"I'll try," I promised. Then we hugged—for the second "last" time.

Cloudy puffs under my feet pushed me toward the road of glowing lights. I was moving—not exactly walking, but almost floating through a fine mist that sparkled like body glitter. When I reached a burst of brilliant light, I hesitated. The light beckoned, offering a glorious glimpse of deep green trees against a sapphire-blue lake, with waving figures on a distant shore. I was tempted to follow the light—until I thought of my friends and family.

So I surrendered to the flowing current that pushed me forward, and entered a darkened tunnel. Darkness faded like a segue in a movie, from night to dawn, and overhead I saw a dazzling light show—like crystal shards of stars sprinkled across a glittering path. The stars shone brighter: glowing, waving, inviting.

"Like the Milky Way," I murmured.

I replayed my grandmother's directions to a fork in the starry light path, hesitating for only a moment to look each way.

Then I turned right.

Slowly, I swam back to consciousness.

When I tried to open my eyes, agonizing pain crashed into me, and I realized I was back on Earth.

"Grammy, take me back!" I wanted to scream. "I've changed my mind!"

The pain was too much, overwhelming, concrete buildings exploding with shards of piercing glass, slamming onto me, torturing. I couldn't take it. *Please let me go back where nothing hurt and everything was perfect.*

My head floated, thoughts drifting and nausea and pain attacking my body. I sensed movement, someone bending over me...a prick on my arm and...

More nettles, I thought, as I sank into darkness.

When I awoke next, I heard a mechanical hum of machinery and distant murmurs. I smelled an odor like disinfectants and starchy sheets covering me. I vaguely saw pale light streaming underneath a door, and heard voices whispering outside. I tried to lift my head, but pain exploded. Moaning, I sank against a cool pillow. Weak, dizzy, utterly helpless.

Ohmygod! I was in a hospital! My condition must be serious! How badly was I hurt? I could barely move, although

I was able to wiggle my toes and fingers, so I wasn't paralyzed. I'd expected some broken bones (I mean, I'd been hit by a truck), only I didn't feel any casts. But the pain was beyond miserable.

How bad were my injuries? Had I been disfigured? What if my face was horribly scarred? I'd seen an episode on Oprah once, where this supermodel was crushed so badly she didn't have a nose or half of her mouth.

What if that happened to me?

How could I have a public career with a scary face?

Panic gave me the strength to lift my head. After the dizziness passed, I blinked and my vision cleared. I struggled through the pain to click on a bedside light.

When I looked down at my left arm and saw the tube poking from my arm, I almost threw up. It was all so real now, and my heart rate increased to frantic beats on the monitor. My hands were pale ghosts that I didn't recognize. My arms seemed unusually thin, too. As if I'd been ill so long I'd wasted away. Not the way I'd hoped to lose weight.

And where were all the nettle bumps? My skin was pale and smooth, with no rash or bruises. How long had I been hospitalized? My visit with Grammy had seemed as short as a brief nap, but if my nettles had already healed, it must have been a long time.

Days, weeks... a month?

Grammy Greta said time ran differently between worlds. Had those brief moments with her passed by in weeks on Earth? Had the school year ended? Had I missed my finals? Had my class graduated without me?

I spotted a mirror on a tray just a reach away. But moving my body hurt so much … I couldn't … too hard. Still, I struggled through waves of dizzy pain, gasping for each ragged breath as my fingers touched the edge of the tray.

The heart monitor quickened: *beep, beep, be careful,* it seemed to warn. Still there was no turning away. I had to know … was my face scarred and disfigured? Worse than scared, fingers trembling, I lifted the mirror.

Then I screamed and screamed and screamed.

The face looking back at me wasn't mine.

It belonged to Leah Montgomery.

"LEAH!"

An elegant blonde woman I'd never seen before rushed toward me in a cloud of lavender perfume. She pushed aside a table to sit beside me, her diamond necklace glinting, tears streaming a pale trail down her rouged cheeks.

"Oh, Leah," she sobbed, clasping my hand. Her hand on mine felt wrong, like we were both made of plastic and none of this was real.

I'm not Leah, I tried to say, but her lavender fragrance caught in my throat. I gasped for breath.

"Leah, you're awake! Thank God! At last!"

Not Leah. You've made a mistake.

"Leah, baby!" Trembling, she wrapped her arms around me. "You can't imagine the hell I've been going through since Angie found you yesterday. You wouldn't wake up! I've been frantic with worry that my baby girl was gone forever."

I struggled to speak, my throat burning, suffocating.

"Are you all right, darling?" the lavender woman cried.

I might be if you'd let go, I wanted to say.

"Don't exert yourself." Her hold eased as she studied me. "You're looking better already, and you're going to be fine. That's all that matters now."

No it's not, because I don't even know you.

Shaking my head was a big mistake. Blinding pain exploded. I sagged back against the pillow and fought to speak, but only spit out a pathetic croak.

"Honey, are you trying to tell me something?"

Duh! I'm not your honey or anything. But I couldn't do more than moan. My energy faded. I wanted to sleep.

"Leah! Stay with me!" Hands gripped my shoulders, shaking. "You've made it this far, you can't go back into a coma now. Don't you realize what a miracle it is you woke up? They told me you didn't want to live, which was utter nonsense. What do those quacks know? Thank God they were wrong! Don't you ever do anything like that to me again."

She hugged tighter and my throat burned like I'd swallowed flaming coals.

"That's it, honey. Keep those pretty blue eyes open."

Not blue eyes. Brown. I opened my eyes wide.

"You can't imagine the horror I've gone through since your accident," the woman prattled on. "Your father blames me, and perhaps he's right, so from now on things will be different. I vowed that if you got well, I would change, join one of those twelve-step programs, and I sincerely mean it this time. Oh, Leah, my dearest daughter."

Lack of breath battled with the desperation to explain that I wasn't her dearest anything. I had to make her understand that she must be in the wrong room, or needed glasses. But my body wasn't cooperating. When I spit out "Not Leah," my words croaked in garbled demonic language.

"What's wrong?" Her eyes almost popped out. "Are you having an attack?"

I thrashed in bed, pointing at myself and shaking my head. Unbearable pain made me gag, jerk erratically, and even drool a little.

"Someone help! My daughter is in trouble!" The woman let loose with an ear-piercing scream that would have knocked me flat if I weren't already lying on my back.

The door burst open with blinding light and a swarm of green-garbed figures. Noisy voices swelled like an attack of hornets. I closed my eyes, sinking into blissful sleep.

When I opened my eyes again, the empty room was dark except for ghostly lights from shadowy machinery. Rhythmic beeps echoed my own heartbeat.

Is it *my* heart, though? I thought with growing panic. Am I even me?

Of course I'm me, I reasoned. I had thoughts and memories that were all about me. Being anyone else would be insanity. I was a lot of things—scared, confused, hurting—but I wasn't crazy. The whole looking in a mirror and seeing

Leah Montgomery (I mean, Leah of all people!) had to have been a hallucination.

Well I was awake now, so I'd just look in the mirror and prove that I was still me.

Only when I reached for the mirror, I stared down in horror...

At a stranger's hand. Not mine.

My own fingers were chubby, tanned sausages; these fingers were as thin as French fries, and too soft to have ever washed dishes or changed diapers. Also, Grammy's lucky bracelet was missing, replaced by a plastic hospital bracelet inscribed "Montgomery, L."

Abso-freaking-lutely impossible.

My identity shouldn't be like a tough question on a pop quiz. I knew who I was. Amber. Not Leah. So why did I look so different?

Possible Answers:

a) I'd looked into a trick mirror.
b) I was asleep and having a horrible nightmare.
c) Lavender Woman was part of a twisted conspiracy.

I was leaning toward "c" because LW was definitely *not* my mother. Theresa Borden was soft-spoken, with a gentle touch and a fresh herbal scent from working in her garden. Mom hated cooking but loved baking pastries, so she often had dough on her hands and flour sprinkled on her dark chestnut hair. She wasn't complicated. She was just Mom.

Childishly I thought, *I want my mommy.*

Well, why not? I'd call home and ask Mom or Dad to come get me. I'd explain how I'd been dead for a little while, had this really cool talk with Grammy, and even got to pet Cola, but on the way back something went horribly wrong and I didn't look like myself anymore. My parents were always solving triple-type problems from Cherry, Melonee, and Olive. Admittedly, my problem was more complex than locating a missing pacifier and dodging projectile spit-up, but my parents would know what to do. They would make everything okay.

I winced at the tube in my arm as I reached for the phone. Not so easy, I realized when the heart monitor sped up. My head didn't feel so good, either—my brain was like a pinball machine with steel balls ricocheting around.

Still, I persevered, until my hand clenched the phone. My brain might be fuzzy, but fortunately my fingers knew the routine. I punched in my home number and waited for the familiar ring. Instead there was a click-click sound, then a young, uptight-sounding woman droned, "Community Central Hospital. May I help you?"

"Yes!" I croaked. It sounded like "uh."

"How can I assist you?"

"Call." This came out like a crow saying "caw."

"I see that you're calling from Room 289. I must inform you that this is a restricted line, so if you're attempting to make an outgoing call, you'll need proper authorization."

"What the hell are you talking about?" is what I wanted to say, but it came out like a crow caw again.

"I regret that I cannot be of further assistance. Please contact your floor nurse or your physician." The phone went dead.

She didn't sound like she regretted not helping me. But that was the least of my problems.

I wanted to cry, but that would hurt too much. What was wrong with my throat anyway? Had I damaged my lungs in the car crash? I remembered the sound of gears grinding and the squeal of tires, but I had no idea what happened to my body afterwards. Impact with a truck had to be pretty serious, and seriously not pretty. But this body didn't seem broken or even bruised. Mostly my head hurt. Even thinking about my head hurting hurt.

My thoughts and memories were the only part of me I recognized. Had the accident done so much damage that I'd needed plastic surgery? I imagined a doctor wheeling my body into the emergency room, taking one horrified look at my broken everythings and declaring my only hope was a total body makeover. But why an entire new face? Especially one that belonged to someone else?

When I looked in the mirror again, there was Leah.

To make sure it wasn't a trick mirror, I angled the glass at the bed and saw a bed. I angled it at the metal tray and saw a metal tray. I angled it back at my face ... and Leah was still there, her eyes mirroring my fear.

Not a hallucination.

Not a nightmare.

Not me.

But Leah? I mean, *Leah Montgomery!* At school I was so awed and intimidated by her that I avoided getting in her way. She wasn't mean like Moniqua or sarcastic like Kat. Leah was loved and feared; aloof, controlled, royalty. Her power went beyond beauty and wealth. Leah possessed that elusive "X Factor." That mysterious quality I'd sensed in Trinidad that separated ordinary people from extraordinary stars.

Kids around school bragged about their "Leah Moments." Like Hollywood celebrity sightings, Leah Moments usually began in mundane ways. "I'd forgotten a book, and while I was getting it from my locker, Leah came over and told me she liked my shoes and asked where I'd bought them."

"Her pen dropped on the floor, and I picked it up for her and she thanked me!"

Or sometimes it was just a casual brush with Leah fame, like pulling into her parking spot as she was leaving.

I had had a Leah Moment a few months ago. Unfortunately, it had not gone well. Since extreme humiliation was not something to brag about, I'd never told anyone about it...well except Alyce. (I mean, I had to tell my BFF Alyce everything). Here's what happened.

The office secretary told me about this new student, Margrét from Iceland. So Alyce created an amazing basket, which I couldn't wait to deliver. Inside the basket were snacks, coupons, school newspapers, spirit banners, and an adorable stuffed puffin (Iceland's unofficial mascot). Margrét squealed excitedly over the basket and hugged the toy puffin. Then she went into the restroom, and I noticed she'd dropped the puffin. So I picked it up and as the restroom door opened, I tossed it to her. "You forgot your puffin."

Only, you guessed it—not Margrét.

Leah Montgomery caught the puffin with a pinched,

puzzled expression. She shook her golden head and said, "I don't think so."

"Sorry," I murmured. "My mistake."

"Obviously."

"I thought you were someone else."

"Oh?" She arched her blonde brows. "Who?"

"Not actually someone else, that's not even possible. What I mean is..." Under Leah's glacial stare my brain froze. What had I meant to say? Something clever and witty, like my book *Celebrities Are People, Too* advised. But my mind blanked.

Afterwards, I would torture myself by replaying this scene in my memory. Leah's hair flowed symmetrically like a waterfall, spilling golden waves over her slim shoulders. She wore a chic red-belted dress, a cropped jacket, and open-toed, gold-heeled sandals. Her makeup glowed with glossy peach lipstick and a luminous glitter trail across her dusky eyelids. Everything about her seemed so perfect... making me feel less than adequate. That's my only excuse for fumbling my words, rambling on like an idiot, saying something lame about puffins and baskets.

"Whatever." Leah held the puffin's black tail delicately, with two French-tipped fingers. "I believe this is yours."

Before I could even say "thanks," she'd tossed the toy back at me and turned to join her groupies, who suddenly appeared out of nowhere. She whispered to them, pointing in my direction, and they all convulsed into giggles.

Humiliated, I shoved the fuzzy puffin in my backpack and took off running. After only one or two wrong turns, I reached my next class just as the bell rang. And the puffin remained tucked away in my locker for a month.

Now I was living the ultimate Leah Moment. There could only be one Leah Montgomery and I was definitely *not* her. I had to tell someone, but who would believe me? I didn't know what to believe myself. Except I had a sick feeling this was all my fault. "Turn left," Grammy had told me.

Instead, I'd turned right and landed in the wrong body.

I didn't just look like Leah.

I *was* Leah!

When Leah found out that I'd shanghaied her body, she was going to be supremely mad. Hmmm...where exactly was Leah? If I was in her body, was she in mine? Was this like that movie where the mom and daughter switched bodies? Or were Leah and I both sharing this body? Like a two-for-one body offer.

Leah, I thought, *raise our hand if you're in here with me.*

Nothing happened.

"Leah," I whispered in that awful croaking voice. "Where are you?"

The heart echo quickened and each beep slammed me with new fear. I looked at myself—or well, Leah—and tried to understand how my body wasn't my body. It just didn't make sense. You couldn't change bodies like switching a TV channel.

This. Could. Not. Be. Happening.

Yet it had happened. And until I figured out to make it un-happen, I was stuck looking like the most beautiful and popular girl in school.

Alyce is going to die when she sees me, I thought. Except I'm the one who died ... or did I?

Desperately, I wished I could talk to Alyce. She believed in all things weird and could come up with an explanation for my body change. But if calls were restricted from this room, how could I reach her?

Maybe a nurse could help.

Struggling through waves of dizziness, I pressed the "call" button. Then I sagged back against my pillow, breathing heavily and dizzy.

The door opened and a light flashed on.

"Are you all right?" a soft voice asked. A nurse in a flowered uniform hurried to my bed. "It's good to see you awake," she said cheerfully. "How are you feeling?"

"Awful," I groaned.

"No surprise there," she said, patting my hand.

I longed to ask so many questions: why my throat burned, how long I'd been here, what was wrong with me, where my real family was, and if there was any special meaning for the horned snake tattoo on her wrist. But I was so damned weak.

"Can I get you something? A glass of water?"

I pointed at the phone.

"Sorry sweetie, but it's not allowed."

I mouthed, "Why?"

"For one thing, you can't talk."

"I-I can ... whisper."

"For another thing, it's not allowed."

I shook my head and pointed at the phone again.

"Would you like me to call your mother, Leah?"

"No!" I croaked. She meant the Lavender Woman.

"Then what do you want?"

To be myself and wake up from this nightmare. But that was impossible to explain, so I just leaned back wearily. Tears burned my eyes and I didn't even have the strength to stop them.

"Don't you fret, honey." The nurse reached to smooth back some loose hair from my forehead. She wasn't much older than me, yet she seemed motherly, making me miss my own mother even more.

"You're just making things hard on yourself," she added. "You have so much going for you. I just don't get it. Someone like you shouldn't be here."

Someone like me? I didn't understand the disappointed look she gave me, and anxiety knotted in my gut. "Wh... Why?"

She bit her lip, hesitating as if she wasn't sure what she should tell me. In her hesitation, I sensed pity. Ohmygod! How bad were my injuries? I didn't seem to be missing any body parts and wasn't paralyzed, so what was wrong? What was too terrible for her to talk about?

"Don't you remember what happened?" she asked, glancing behind as if afraid someone might overhear.

I shook my head, then gestured to the phone again, pleading with my eyes for her to help me.

"I can't," she said softly. "I'm so sorry. They don't trust you after what you did."

"W-What?" I cried, fear mounting.

She looked over her shoulder again, then seemed to

reach a decision. She bent down, so close that her ponytail brushed my neck. "You can't make calls or talk to anyone outside your immediate family because you took all those pills," she whispered. "You tried to commit suicide."

Suicide! But I would never ... I mean ... *never!*

Sure, I'd had self-pitying moments when I threatened to do something drastic, but I never meant it. End my life? No way! I had so much to live for: best friends, family, college, career, and the unknown super-hot guy I would marry. We'd have only one child—boy or girl, I wasn't picky. Being an "Only" had lots of perks, which I'd enjoyed until the triplets came along, and I wanted that for my child. I had all these huge plans for my career, too, complete with sketches I'd drawn of the fabulous Malibu beach home I'd live in with an entourage of "my people," which would include a personal assistant, hair stylist, chef, and nanny. It was exciting to imagine myself as a top-flight agent, giving advice, counseling clients, and watching a spark of talent skyrocket into stardom. Also I'd be invited to A-list parties, where dessert tables offered oh-so-delicious chocolates.

Yeah, life was going to sweet.

So suicide? I don't think so.

Of course, while all these thoughts raced through my head, I watched sorrow play across the nurse's face as if her heart was breaking for me. And I remembered that this wasn't about me. I wasn't the one who'd attempted suicide.

That was Leah.

And she'd nearly succeeded.

Um … not good. Definitely not good.

Not being myself anymore—at least on the outside— was terrifying. Like when I'd been trapped in my sleeping bag at fourth grade science camp. My hair had snagged in the zipper. I screamed, squirmed and yanked, but I was totally stuck. It took two counselors to unsnag me, and eventually the bald spot grew back. But I never forgot the suffocating panic of being trapped.

This was worse.

I couldn't unzip my way out of this body. I wasn't me, yet I wasn't Leah, either. A non-person, that's what I was—except on the inside I felt like the same Amber Borden. Whatever equaled identity was beneath the skin: fears, hopes, feelings, and memories. I knew who I was—but how could I convince anyone else? Especially as a hospital prisoner with no phone privileges and zero strength to get out of bed? I had to figure out a way out of this mess … but I was just too tired.

So instead of coming up with a plan, I went back to sleep.

My dreams danced to soul music, soaring with no boundaries. Free from restrictions, I flew backwards into memories.

Zoom in, camera-like, to the rustic lake community of Sutton Pines, to a shady tree-lined street winding into the paved driveway of 43 Molly Brown Lane. Flowering bushes and a brown picket fence welcome visitors into a cozy, two-story, wood-sided house. Pan up to the round attic window, and close in on two thirteen-year-old girls huddled around a plain brown box. Oh, how well I knew that private attic hideout and those girls—and especially that box!

The box was the result of whispered secrets and hard-earned babysitting money. Alyce and I had conspired for weeks. When the package finally arrived, I snatched it up and immediately called her. She came over ASAP, bursting into my bedroom. We couldn't wait to open our prize.

"Will it work?" Alyce asked as I ripped off the paper.

"It better for $49.95!" I told her.

"I can't believe we're doing this!"

"Why not? You thought it was a great idea."

"But now I'm not so sure," she said, gnawing on her black-polished pinky. "Maybe it's too unnatural…shouldn't we be satisfied with what nature gave us?"

I nailed her with a dead-on stare. "Are *you* satisfied?"

"No, of course not." She frowned at her chest. "A's are good when it comes to grades, but not bra size."

"Exactly. B-minus isn't that great either."

"So open the box already!"

Holding my breath, having no idea what to expect, I pushed back cardboard flaps, tossed aside bubble-wrap, and pulled out our very own, guaranteed-to-add-two-cup-sizes-or-your-money-back, "Mammo-Glamm."

Unfortunately it wasn't very glamorous. Hand-size plastic pink paddles connected by a coiled spring. We read the directions over and over, then practiced extending our arms straight out, grasping the Mammo-Glamm between our palms and then pumping in and out. After six weeks we only gained sore muscles—without enhancing even one measly cup size! Our pathetic little boobies remained pathetic and little. And the Mammo-Glamm Company never did refund our money.

Dreams shifted as I drifted back to consciousness. Tossing from side to stomach then back to side, I couldn't get comfortable. Something hard and round poked my chest—two somethings actually. I reached up to push away these annoyances, and found them attached.

"What the—!"

Memory crashed in like a ceiling of bricks. I longed to go back to my dream, to be flat-chested and happy Amber.

Before I could sink too deep into depression, I heard a snicker, and looked over at the foot of my hospital bed. I saw a skinny blue-eyed boy, about nine or ten. His curly, dark-blond hair was pulled back under a blue bandana, and he wore a leather jacket and baggy black jeans.

He was a stranger.

But then so was I.

"Why you touching your boobs?" His cynical, crude tone seemed at odds with his young face.

"I wasn't," I retorted. From the inside, Leah's voice didn't sound as sweet as I remembered.

The boy crossed the room to stare down at me. His scowl gave a strong hint that he didn't like me very much. Who was he anyway?

"I know you don't want me here, so just tell me why and I'll get out," he said bluntly.

I cringed under those hate-filled blue eyes. "Why what?"

"You know."

"Yeah, like not."

"Liar! You can't fool me. I know all your tricks."

I almost snapped back angrily, until advice from *The Bait of Debate* popped into my head: *To succeed in a confrontational situation, project calmness and curiosity.* "I don't understand," I said. "Who are you?"

He snorted. "Acting dumb isn't gonna work."

My throat burned, so I just shook my head.

"Come off it, Leah."

"I-I'm not ... not her."

"You're so full of it, and you look like crap." He reached out for a plastic pitcher of water and poured some into a glass, then handed it to me. "Here."

My hand shook as I took the glass and lifted it to my lips. Cool water eased some of the pain but I still ached with confusion. I couldn't figure this kid out. He seemed to hate me, yet he offered me water.

"Thank you," I whispered.

"Since when do you thank me?" He took the glass back

and set it down on the tray. "Usually it's 'get lost, vermin' or 'bug off, brat.' You must really be sick."

You have no idea, I thought wearily.

He plopped down on the corner of the hospital bed and pulled out a shiny pocketknife. It was larger than his hand, with a wicked etched dragon design. I recoiled, afraid he'd flip out a menacing blade and stick me, but he just idly rubbed his thumb over the etched dragon.

"Dad's pissed off, and Mom's freaking out more than usual," he said, gazing down at the dragon.

"Dad? Mom?"

"Well...duh. They're so messed up it's pathetic."

"Your parents?'

"Duh. Who else?"

"Do I know them?"

"Ha! The whole poor pitiful Leah act, like that's going to work. Faking a lost memory won't get you out of trouble."

His chilly expression was similar to the cringe-worthy stare Leah had given me during the "puffin" incident. "You're her...Leah's...brother?" I guessed.

"And her memory returns," he mocked. "Hallelujah! It's a miracle!"

I took that as a "yes." Obviously Leah and her brother weren't close, but this hostility seemed extreme.

"I won't ask where you got the pills," he said accusingly. "I already know."

"What pills?"

"The ones you swiped from Mom's bathroom cabinet."

"I did not!"

"Did, too. I just wanna know why."

I shivered under my blankets. "Why what?"

"Why you took the damned pills?" He balled his fists, his knuckles showing blood-red tattooed symbols. "I just don't get it. You got everything, so why try to check out?"

Good question, I thought, and wished I knew the answer. Why would Leah throw her perfect life away? Well she could have it back. Wealth, beauty, and popularity sounded cool in theory, but I'd rather return to my own imperfect body.

"I already know more than you think I do, so there's no reason to lie." He clutched the knife in his fist, glaring harder. "Why take the pills?"

"I didn't."

"Stop freakin' lying."

"I—I'm not."

"Is this about Chad? 'Cause he cheated on you?"

"Chad?" I tried to place the familiar name.

"Your boyfriend," he said sarcastically. "Okay, act dumb and don't tell me anything. I'm used to being ignored. No one gives a crap about me. I should thank you, I guess, 'cause you've screwed up more than me now. Dad's so pissed at you, he's eased up on me. I should have been the one taking pills, the way Dad's always on my case. You can do anything you want, and they give you everything. I get crap."

"S-sorry."

"Like you care," he snarled. "Save it for Mom or Dad or your posse of dumb girls." Then he jumped up and strode out of the room, nearly bumping into a tall, dark-blond man in a tailored suit with dark gray tie.

I looked up at him, questioning. "Dad?" I guessed.

But I was very wrong.

"Do I represent a father figure to you?" the man asked, pulling up a yellow plastic chair. He flipped open a notepad and jotted something down. "Typically patients refer to me as Dr. Hodges. I'm intrigued you called me 'Dad,' as I bear no resemblance to your father."

Oops. Calling a shrink "Dad" was a bad move.

But when he'd walked into my room, carrying a briefcase and looking like an important businessman, I'd assumed he was Leah's father. I'd already met her mother and her brother, so "Dad" was the next logical visitor. Dr. Hodges didn't even look like a shrink. No beard or dignified glasses; instead, he had acne scars and large ears that poked out from thinning brown hair. Kind of like a grown-up nerd.

"Let's just talk about anything on your mind." He bit the end of his pen and tilted his head expectantly, clearly waiting for me to say something fascinating.

"Um…" I blinked. "My memory is fuzzy."

"That's perfectly understandable."

"Do I know you?"

"Do you think you should know me?"

"Yes… I mean, no… I don't know." My head started to ache and I leaned wearily against my pillows.

He leaned forward, his pen sticking up between his fingers. "You're making remarkable physical progress."

"I don't feel—" I paused to swallow "—remarkable."

"It takes time to recover, but I can assure you your prognosis is highly encouraging. You're going to be just fine."

I shook my head, despair washing over me. How could I ever be fine again?

"Don't think of me as your doctor, consider me your friend." Dr. Hodges leaned forward, his tone intimate like we were best friends. "How are you feeling?"

"My throat… hurts."

"Then by all means, let me offer you some water." He reached for the pitcher on my table and poured a cup.

I accepted the cup, soothed by the cool liquid. "Thanks."

"You're very welcome. I'm here to help you."

"Really?" I bit my lip and blinked back tears. Since I'd woken up, almost everyone had treated me with accusations and hostility. I desperately needed someone who cared enough to listen.

"I'll do everything in my power to help you through this," he said kindly. "I know it won't be easy, but trusting me is your first step to recovery. It's natural to experience initial resistance, but you'll quickly discover that I have your best interests at heart. I assure you that anything you say to me will be completely in the strictest of confidence."

"I'm afraid…" I hesitated. "You won't believe me."

"Belief begins with your willingness to trust." He gave my hand a reassuring pat. "Let me help you. Tell me everything about the real Leah Montgomery."

"I—I can't."

"Refusing to cooperate reinforces negative behavior and hinders recovery."

I sighed, too tired to pretend. "I'm not…not who you think."

He showed no surprise, although his expression softened sympathetically as he wrote quickly in his notebook.

"I only look like Leah."

"How do you usually look?"

"Like Amber."

"Who is she?"

"Me. I'm Amber, not Leah."

"You have an alternative personality called Amber?"

"No. I am Amber."

"A nickname?"

"No. Just me." My words trailed off in a whisper and I wasn't sure he heard me as I added, "I'm in the wrong body."

"I see." He straightened, his gaze sharpening with interest. Finally, I was saying something fascinating and had his full attention. But did he believe me?

"Rest assured, I am completely on your side and will guide you through this traumatic time." He leaned forward, writing in his notebook. "Are you experiencing feelings of detachment, as if you're physically inhabiting an unfamiliar body?"

I wasn't sure exactly what he meant, but it was close enough, so I nodded. My head throbbed and it hurt to talk. Everything was so complicated. I didn't know how to say the right things. Dr. Hodges sounded sincere, like he truly understood and wanted to help. With his support, I could sort out this mess and return to my real family. He'd said he was my friend, and I really needed one right now.

"This could be one for the case books," he murmured with a bright light in his gaze. Not the heavenly kind of bright light; more like the kind of flashing lights that go off when a game-show contestant wins a jackpot.

Instead of being reassured, I had a bad feeling that I'd just made another very wrong turn.

No one else came to visit, except a different nurse who gave me pills that dissolved the boundaries of reality. I escaped into a sleep so deep that the rest of the day was a blur. If I had bad dreams, I didn't remember them.

Gradually, voices crept into my consciousness. I was aware of lights and movement and a strong scent of lavender. I resisted waking, not remembering exactly why this was a good idea, just feeling safer in sleep. But cool hands were lifting me…

I fought the hands, instantly tense with fear.

"Leah, honey," a woman's soft voice pleaded. "Don't make this so hard."

My eyes jerked open. I stared into the stranger face of Leah's mother.

"Go away," I told her.

But she didn't, and neither did the male nurse who stood beside her with a wheelchair. They wanted to take me somewhere unknown. No! I wouldn't go with them. Leaving would take me further from my family. I couldn't let that happen. I had to make them understand who I was. But I couldn't find the words, and crumpled inside. Instead of speaking rationally, I lost it and burst into tears.

"I-I want ... my-my mom."

"I'm here, sweetheart."

Soft hands reached for me, but I pushed them away.

"NO!" My shout slammed painfully against my throat. "You're not my mother—I don't even know you!"

"Leah, don't be like this."

"No! I'm not Leah. Can't you see?"

"I can see you're sick, but I'll help you get better."

"I want to ... to go home," I sobbed.

"That's where I'm going to take you, if you'll just get into the wheelchair—"

"No, no, NO! I want my real mom!"

I wrenched away from her, intense pain hammering my head. I could endure the pain, but not being taken somewhere my parents couldn't find me. This was all so wrong! I just wanted to climb into my own bed in my own bedroom and feel Mom's comforting arms around me. I'd been holding onto hope that my family would rescue me, or that I'd wake up suddenly to find myself in my own body.

If I left, I might never find my way back home.

"Leah, be reasonable," the woman begged. "You know very well I'm your mother. You must stop talking like this ... it's not safe. You're only making things worse."

"It can't get worse."

"Oh yes it can—horribly." She pursed her lips and lowered her voice. "Be a good girl and get into the wheelchair. Please, Leah."

"Don't call me that! This is all a big mess and I can prove who I really am if you just get me a phone. I'm not your daughter."

The nurse narrowed his gaze at me, moving around a small table to stand beside the mother. He never took his eyes off me as he whispered to her, "Mrs. Montgomery, would you like me to call Dr. Hodges?"

"That won't be necessary," she told him, lifting her shoulders and chin and speaking with refined authority. "I can handle my own daughter. We'll just need a private moment together, if you don't mind."

"Is that wise?" The nurse shot me a suspicious glance, as if I might grow fangs.

Mrs. Montgomery waved her hand, diamonds sparkling off the overhead lights, and insisted that the nurse leave. Once the door was shut and we were alone, she bent over me with an anxious expression. "Leah, you have to cooperate."

I pursed my lips stubbornly.

"I realize you're punishing me, and I'll admit that I

may deserve it, but this is not about me. I'm fighting for your life and I can't do it alone. You have to help, too."

"Give me a phone."

"You think your friends can help you more than I can? Well, you're totally wrong. I'm the only one between you and a long, unpleasant stay in a mental hospital."

"Mental—" I gulped. "—hospital?"

"That's what your doctor recommends. He thinks you're deeply disturbed and need months of psychotherapy." Her fingers trembled as she grasped my hand. "Is that what you want?"

I shook my head, fear rising like waves threatening to drown me.

"Then behave sensibly. It took all my resources to get the authorization to have you released into my care, but if you don't cooperate, they'll send you away for a long time and I won't be able to stop them. Dr. Hodges has this ridiculous notion that you have multiple personalities and he wants to study you in a confined environment. Your father was ready to go along with this plan, but I insisted that all you need is your mother."

"I'm ... I'm not crazy," I whimpered.

"Of course you're not. But whatever you said to Dr. Hodges convinced him that you have disturbing mental issues and could be a danger to yourself and others."

I bit my lip, tasting salty tears. My nightmare was careening out of control, spiraling down a black hole. Mom, Dad ... where are you? Please come get me and make everything better.

But it was the other mom who brushed away stray hairs

from my face and squeezed my hand. "Don't be scared, Leah."

"I'm not Le—"

She didn't let me finish. "You don't have to be brave for me. I know you so well, even if you don't think I do. I realize I've been emotionally unavailable, but I'm changing. You'd be proud of how I stood up to your father, just like you've always wanted." She paused, looking down at me as if she expected me to congratulate her.

I closed my eyes, wishing this unreal world away.

"You're my miracle." She spoke gently, still stroking my hair. "You came back from that coma even after the doctors said you were gone forever. I will not let them take you from me. But you have to do two things right now."

I arched my brows, silently asking, *What?*

"First, I want you to climb into this wheelchair so I can get you out of this place. Second, it's imperative for you to behave normally. No more wild talk about not knowing your own family or they'll lock you away. Can you do that?"

I stared at her through eyes that weren't my own, shuddering at the threat of a locked room in a mental hospital. I'd seen movies about mental wards with electric shocks and straitjackets, where even the sanest person turned into a drooling zombie. If I told the truth, I was crazy. But if I lied and pretended to be someone I wasn't, I was sane.

Swallowing hard, I met Leah's mother's gaze.

Then I nodded.

8

I realized later, when I woke up in a beautiful and unfamiliar room, that despite my agreement to cooperate, the "vitamins" Mrs. Montgomery instructed the nurse to give me before leaving the hospital were in fact sleeping pills. I vaguely remembered half-crawling into the wheelchair— embarrassed because the nightgown was open in the back and I was mooning the male nurse—then I was out.

The silky, butter-yellow sheets were a definite improvement over the starchy white hospital sheets. And the four-poster bed with its frilly lace canopy was right out of the "Cool Stuff I Can't Afford" magazines I flipped through when no one else was around. Oooh, so very luxurious. Unfortunately I couldn't enjoy myself. I just wanted out.

For a desperate moment, I prayed that this was all an outrageous prank. I was the unknowing victim on an extreme reality show like *Punk'd*. Any moment, Alyce and Dustin would pop out and shout, "Gotcha!"

Only when I glanced down at myself, and saw wavy blonde hair over an elegant, ivory satin nightgown, reality slapped me hard. No matter how many times I wanted to believe this wasn't happening, it was.

Emotionally I was a wreck, but physically I felt better. Sleep had cleared the cobwebs from my brain and I could move my arms with only minor pain. I tested my legs, wiggling one and then the other. Not bad, just a little stiff. I drew back the gauzy bed curtains, pushed away a satin comforter, and slowly lowered my legs to the plush carpet.

This exertion was more tiring than I'd expected. I paused to catch my breath. Then I lifted my head and looked—really looked—around the spacious room. Despite the utter mess of my life, I couldn't help but be awed.

Way gorgeous room! Ornate white-gold vanity dresser, entertainment center with everything electronic imaginable, oil paintings by famous artists I'm sure Alyce would know, an L-shaped dark gold couch, and lace-draped picture windows. I had a wild urge to fling open the closet, check out the drawers, and try on all Leah's clothes. You can bet she'd have an amazing wardrobe: designer everythings from oh-so-fab stores where under normal circumstances I couldn't even afford to window shop. But these were far from normal circumstances. I was still reeling from the weirdness of being Leah.

A full-length mirror seemed to beckon from across the room.

Like a sleepwalker, I moved toward the mirror.

And I studied Leah.

She looked unusually pale, and younger than I remembered from school. Even without makeup she was stunning: slim, with wavy white-blonde hair and exotic long-lashed blue eyes. Her creamy skin was flawless, free of the pimples that plagued me whenever I was on my period. Her slender arms tapered down to elegant French-tipped nails, and underneath the silky nightgown, tiny, cherry-red polished toenails poked out.

Leah's body was firm like she worked out, but soft like she never really worked. No scrubbing bathrooms or scouring greasy pans for these baby-soft hands. Leah probably had a housekeeper to clean her messes, a cook to fix her meals, and a personal fitness guru to firm her perky assets.

Thinking of assets . . . okay, I'll admit it, I was curious.

Before I could decide if there was something voyeuristic about what I was going to do, I slipped off the fancy nightgown and stood naked before the mirror.

Not bad, Leah, I thought.

The breasts were amazingly perfect, defying gravity and deserving of applause. But were they real or surgically enhanced?

Upon closer inspection, I found faint shadows of twin scars. And while they looked natural, when I touched them they felt hard and unyielding, like if I did jumping jacks, they wouldn't bounce with me.

Leah looked amazing with or without clothes; tight

butt, zero cellulite on firm thighs, and long, athletic legs. A tiny diamond glittered from her pierced belly button, and further down I saw proof that Leah was a natural blonde. The small puff of blonde hair curled in a unique shape. I knew some girls shaved down there, but shaving it into a heart? Now that was just … weird.

Whoa, Leah, what other secrets have you been hiding?

As I stood naked, staring into the mirror, the enormous reality of my changed life crashed into me. I was looking at myself … except I wasn't myself … not anymore.

Maybe never again.

Ohmygod! Leah freaking Montgomery! That was her, now me, in the reflection: breathing, feeling, living in this body.

And all because I had a crummy sense of direction.

Don't panic, I told myself just as I was doing that very thing. Hyperventilating would solve nothing. I had to solve this problem—my entire future depended on it. In math, every problem has an answer; X always equals something. And my self-help books stated that there was a solution to every problem. But I didn't know of any books that offered advice for this situation.

Thinking logically … I'd gotten into this body, so there had to be a way out. But even if I found it, how could I make sure Leah and I returned to our own bodies? What if I ended up in a worse body—like someone in prison or really old with wrinkles? Leah and I needed to swap back with each other. Only I didn't know where she was, or even if she was alive. What if she was gone forever?

The pale ghost in the mirror reflected terror.

I sucked in deep breaths and released them slowly, struggling not to lose whatever remained of me. I wasn't sure I could hold it together any longer, and was raveling at the edges of despair—when I noticed something in the mirror that gave me new hope.

On the dresser behind me.

A phone.

No uppity switchboard witch stopped me from making this call.

As I waited for a ring, excited/scared/hopeful thoughts scattered through my head. How would my parents react when they heard my voice? What did they think happened to me? Did the triplets miss me? Who was feeding our cat while I was gone?

It was almost noon. Dad would be at his job, but Mom should be home preparing triple lunches (unless she was running errands or meeting with her Moms & Multiples playgroup.)

If Mom answered, she'd be so relieved to know I was okay that she'd start crying, and she wasn't the crying type at all. My father was the emotional one, although he always hid it by saying he had allergies. If he answered, he'd want to rush right over and take me home. Mom knew how reckless Dad got behind the wheel when he was in a hurry, so she wouldn't let him drive alone. But then who would watch the triplets? Probably Dilly McCurry, who lived next door and often babysat when I wasn't around.

All these things whirled through my head while I waited for the first ring.

Pick up! I thought, amazed that calling home could be so terrifying. I mean, I was just calling Mom and Dad. So why was my heart racing? My family loved me unconditionally, and they'd support me no matter what.

Another ring. My palms started to sweat.

Had one of the triplets tossed the phone in the toilet again?

Another ring. Maybe this phone wasn't working right. Or I'd dialed wrong. Lately I had the worst luck with phones. I should hang up and try again—

"Hello?" a woman answered abruptly, in a voice I didn't recognize.

"Um ... I must have dialed wrong," I said, ready to hang up and try again.

"Whom were you trying to reach?"

"My par ... uh ... the Bordens. Sorry to bother—"

"This is the Borden residence."

"Is it?" I sagged against the dresser with relief. "Can you put Mom on?"

"Who? I don't think I heard you right." She sounded tired, as if I'd woken her from a nap.

"My mother," I said impatiently.

"You have the incorrect number."

Ah ha! Now I knew that voice. The formal way she said "incorrect" rather than "wrong" triggered a pleasant memory of being little and playing wild animals with my cousin Zeke at a family wedding. Less pleasant was the memory of the six-hundred-dollar wedding cake we'd knocked off a table. My aunt never did forgive me, and neither did her oldest daughter—the bride.

"Aunt Suzanne!" I cried, wondering what she was doing at my house, but not really caring because that wasn't important. Connecting with someone from my family made me giddy with relief. "Could you get Mom or Dad for me? I really, really need them."

"Who is this?" she demanded sharply.

"You know . . . Amber."

"Amber who?"

"Borden, of course. Your niece. Come on, Aunt Suz, stop kidding around."

"I never kid around." There was a pause, then my aunt spoke with brittle coolness. "I don't know what sick game you're indulging in, but if you ever have the audacity to call again, I'll contact the police."

"But Aunt Suz . . . I mean . . . I'm sorry." Instantly I realized my mistake. No wonder she didn't recognize my voice. Not only did I look like someone else, but I sounded different, too. "Wait! Don't hang up! You don't understand. Let me explain!"

"I have no intention of holding a conversation with someone with no consideration for a grieving family."

"I didn't . . . I mean . . . grieving?"

"Do you have any idea what the family is going through?"

"No . . . I don't. What's . . . What's going on?" I asked, gripping the phone tight and starting to tremble.

"I'm not going to discuss personal issues with a stranger."

"But I'm not a stranger! I'm your . . . I mean, I'm a friend . . . yeah, I'm Amber's friend Leah." I thought fast.

"We're so close, we call each other's parents Mom and Dad."

"Then you should know this is not a good time to call."

"Where's Mo...Mrs. Borden? I really need to talk with her...uh...about Amber."

"My brother and his wife aren't available. They're at...at the hosp—" Her voice cracked and broke into sobs, which really shocked me because I hadn't seen Aunt Suzanne cry since the cake incident, and that was from anger. This felt sad.

"What hospital?" I asked in a small, scared voice.

"Community Central. They're with Amber...saying good-bye."

"Good-bye? You mean...Ohmygod!" I fell to my knees, squeezing the phone.

"Didn't you know? About the accident?" she asked in the kindest tone I'd ever heard from my stern aunt.

"The mail truck?"

"So you do know. It was so utterly senseless and tragic."

"But I'm...Amber's going to be all right? Isn't she?"

There was no answer.

I swallowed hard. "Is she...still..."

"She's alive...but in a coma," my aunt finally said, her voice heavy with sorrow. "There's no brain activity and she's not expected to recover. Her body is being kept alive for the organ donation. But once that's resolved, she'll be...I'm sorry, but I can't talk about this—"

The phone went dead.

9

I listened to the dial tone for long minutes, my head spinning.

Brain dead? Donating organs—from *my* body! What did they think? That I was dead?

Well, I really would be if I didn't stop them.

I had to go to Community Central right away and rescue myself. If I could stand near my body maybe I would automatically revert back to myself. If that didn't work, I'd concentrate real hard and pray to God and Grandma. There had to be some way to reverse this mix-up. And I had to do it before The-Body-That-Was-Formerly-Amber was sliced and diced into ready-to-share pieces.

Don't get me wrong, I'm all for organ donation. It's a

great program that helps lots of people. This girl I knew, Betina Cortez, was alive because of an organ transplant. After I'd welcomed her to school with an anime-themed basket, we sat together at lunch and she'd confided all about her operation.

That night I'd gone home and asked my father if he would give me a kidney if I needed one. "Right or left?" he joked. Then, because he always made a lesson out of everything, he pulled out his driver's license and showed me his signed donor card. I pulled out my own license and showed him my signed card. He patted me on the back and said, "That's my Ambaby." (A goofy nickname . . . don't ask!)

But no more crying or feeling sorry for myself, I vowed. I was getting out of here. Only when I tried the door—it was locked.

Unbelievable!

What kind of family locks their daughter in her bedroom? Totally barbaric! I mean, what if I had to go to the bathroom? Did they expect me to use a bedpan or resort to something worse?

I pounded on the door and screamed, "Let me out!" over and over. My voice cracked, but fury gave me energy. After about five minutes, I heard footsteps.

"Shut up, Leah," the brother ordered. "I'm watching a DVD."

"Open the door."

"Forget it."

"Come on . . . " What was his name, anyway? "Let me out and I'll shut up."

"No can do. Doctor's orders."

"That's ridiculous! Why can't I get out?"

"They're afraid you'll try again ... you know, to kill yourself. Mental cases can't be trusted," he added with a snicker.

"I'm not mental! You don't understand!"

"I understand a lot, and know better than to trust you."

"Why are you being so awful to me?"

"Payback, dear sister."

"But ... But I need to use the bathroom. If you don't let me out it could get ugly in here."

"What's the problem? Use your own bathroom. Man, you really are psycho." Then I heard his footsteps fading away.

That's when I discovered that the door I thought was a closet actually led to a spacious bathroom—with gold-flecked tile on the double-sink, a glass-encased shower, and a deep spa tub. A plush white bathrobe hung on a wall hook, next to a cupboard filled with rolled towels and a wide array of bath products. On the opposite wall was an enormous walk-in closet, with a warren of shelves full of folded clothes, rows of name-brand shoes, and racks of designer clothes.

Again I wondered, why would someone with this princess life try to kill herself? What more could she want? She already had a great body, mega-popularity, and the financial means to get into any college she desired. Sure, her family wasn't perfect, but then whose family was? Her brother was an obnoxious gangster punk, but at least Leah only had to put up with one sibling—not triplets.

So why attempt suicide? It just didn't make sense. Could it have been an accident? Although how could anyone *accidentally* swallow pills? Maybe it was something more sinister? Did Leah have an enemy who stealthily slipped her an overdose?

Doubtful. Even in my wild "dramagination," as Alyce called my exaggerated ideas, I didn't think Leah's suicide was a murder attempt. Her brother said she'd stolen the pills, and even her best friend Jessica mentioned that Leah had been acting distant. Plotting her own death, I thought grimly.

No one tried to kill Leah ... except Leah.

I really did need to use the bathroom. Shutting the door behind me, I sat on Leah's porcelain throne, my thoughts shifting to my own problems. Top of my "Do or Die" list was to get myself over to Community Central Hospital right away. Since I was in Leah's body, there was a good chance she was stuck in mine, waiting for me to arrive so we could switch back. We'd laugh, hug, and say how happy we were to be ourselves again. We'd become best friends forever. Key the sappy music for the Disney version of a happy ending.

Or the music could be a funeral march.

The diagnosis of "no brain activity" was scary. How long did my body have? I could almost hear the death beep as the life support machines flat-lined. There was no chance for a body switch minus one body.

And I wasn't sure of anything ... except fear.

When Great Aunt Mariah died, her son paid over ten-thousand dollars for a polished-mahogany, satin-lined casket, and my parents freaked at the huge cost. They vowed that when it was their time to go they'd skip the fuss and get cremated. Is that what they planned for me, too? If Leah was lurking inside my body, she'd better speak up soon or we'd both be toast.

I walked to the cordless phone, my lifeline to the outside world, and tried to decide who to call. I didn't have the courage to try my parents again. What about Dustin or Alyce? They'd do anything for me—but what if they jumped to the wrong conclusions like my aunt, and hung up before I could explain? My friends wouldn't recognize this voice, and if they did, they'd think I was Leah Montgomery. Alyce classified Leah as a "celebrasnob," and would rather snap pictures of rotting bones than waste a minute with "populosers." And Dustin turned into a tongue-tied fool whenever he tried to talk to girls (excluding Alyce and myself).

Even if I did call Dustin or Alyce, it was doubtful I'd reach them. Cell phones weren't allowed inside the hospital—and that's where my friends would be, sitting with my parents around my comatose body.

Waiting for me to die.

My stomach rolled. I was sure I would barf. I hung my head over the toilet, but only choked out dry heaves. Trembling, I stumbled back to the ornate canopied bed and sank on the satin comforter.

Don't panic, I ordered myself. *There has to be a way out.*

But nothing made sense, only nonsense, and I couldn't think of any solution. I needed someone to talk to—a trusted friend who'd drop everything to help me.

Grabbing a pillow, I hugged it to my chest, rocking back and forth. I didn't know what to do or who to turn to or anything. I'd lost everything I cared about—my family, my friends, my future—and now I was losing my mind.

Miserable hot tears streamed down my cheeks, blotting like scars on the silk pillow. Nothing seemed real anymore—only despair.

I recognized the warning signs of self-pity. I was sinking deep, but what the hell? I didn't care. Why should I? No one cared about me, not the way I was now. This body wasn't even me—why couldn't anyone see that? It was like being adrift in a beautiful yacht with no other passengers. I was my own universe.

Alone.

A metallic jiggling was coming from the door.

Before I could react, the door flew open and I stared at a heavenly vision as astonishing as my grandmother, but way better looking.

The tall, dark-haired, hot guy stepped forward.

And offered to rescue me.

10

I confess … I drooled a little.

But with tears still damp on my face, I was sure my rescuer didn't notice the drool—although I absolutely positively for sure noticed every minute detail about him.

Over six feet tall, broad shoulders, long lean legs molded into perfectly fitted jeans and tender blue eyes fixed on yours truly. He was familiar, the way you recognize a famous actor or rock idol. But it was more than that. My inner math geek added it up—the hair, the face, the body: Chadwick Rockingham, Junior—son of Chadwick Rockingham, Senior, owner of the largest car dealership in the county. Two years ago, I'd welcomed him to school with a basketball-themed basket.

"You okay, babe?" he asked in this deep voice that shivered me from head to polished toenails.

Babe. So intimate, so seductive, and so not the sort of thing guys ever said to me. Usually it was, "Hey, help me with this math problem?" or "Could you get me one of those cool welcome baskets for my girlfriend?" When I complained about this to Alyce, she theorized that I was the clichéd Girl Next Door: admired and liked, but never lusted after.

Well, sometimes a girl could use a little lust.

"I was out-of-my-mind worried when I heard you were in the hospital," he went on, kneeling on the edge of the bed close to me. Ooh, he even smelled nice, like musky aftershave and peppermint.

Chad Jr. was Leah's boyfriend—off limits, untouchable, not available.

Unless you happened to be Leah Montgomery.

"Can't you talk?" he asked with deep concern as he knelt at my bedside. "Leah, tell me you're okay."

"Ooo-kay," I repeated in a daze.

"You sure? You're not like yourself."

"I ... um ... I'm not?"

"You need to get some color in your face and fix your hair."

My hand flew to my hair, and I wondered if I could figure out how to style Leah's hair and apply her makeup. I was the low maintenance type—just a dab of lip-gloss, and a quick brush through my curly hair before I captured it back with a hair clip. Leah's silky locks hung limply around my shoulders.

"Still, you look good to me." Chad leaned closer to me,

which made me a little dizzy. "I was going crazy not being able to be with you."

"You were?" I asked, breathlessly.

"All I could think about was you, but your parents wouldn't tell me anything, except that you had some extreme flu."

The flu? Was that the official story? Leah Montgomery will be temporarily absent from life due to illness—a much more acceptable excuse than attempted suicide.

"When I tried to see you, they wouldn't let me in. Your father said you were highly contagious, but I figured he was lying, blowing me off because he doesn't trust me around you."

"Should he?"

He chuckled. "Definitely not."

"You don't seem very dangerous," I couldn't resist saying. Immediately I wanted to slap my mouth shut when I realized how flirty that sounded. I knew better—really I did—yet my ridiculous thudding heart drowned out that logical voice in my head. Instead, another voice said that I might not get another chance like this with someone like Chad, so why not have a little fun?

"Seriously dangerous—at least when I'm with you," he said with a wicked grin. "That must be why your door was locked. But a lock won't keep me out."

I had a feeling they'd locked the door to keep the "crazy girl" in rather than to keep anyone out. But why spoil this intoxicating moment with awkward details?

"I've missed you so much," he told me, folding his strong fingers around my hand.

"Wow ... uh ... Really?"

"It's been hell, not knowing what's going on with you. But you're fine now and that's what matters. Real fine," he whispered huskily as he stared at me in this intense way. "You make me so crazy."

"A good crazy?"

"Very good. Oh, Leah, I freaked when I heard you were sick, but everything is all right again, now we're together."

Be still my raging hormones. I almost forgot who I really was. Girl-Next-Door types didn't make guys like Chad crazy. It just didn't happen in the hierarchy of high school. Not because I'd inherited Dad's large nose and Mom's flat chest; it went deeper than appearance. It was a caste system, like where people in other cultures believe they evolved from lowly insects into human beings. In my school caste system, Leah was a goddess, while I was an invisible worker ant.

So when Chad bent over and kissed me, I didn't pull away. Whoa baby, he knew what he was doing.

A kiss from Chad was like eating only one potato chip when you wanted to rip open the whole bag and devour them all. When he pulled away, I was ready to grab him back for more. But then he asked a question that changed everything.

"Want to get out of here?"

Instantly, my sanity returned.

"Out of here? Hell, yes!" I exclaimed, feeling suddenly foolish for going gaga over a kiss. I didn't even know Chad, and it was Leah he liked anyway. Still, escaping with him wouldn't exactly be a hardship.

"So let's get moving," he told me.

"But how can I leave without being caught?"

"The same way I got in. Locked doors can't stop me," he said with a confident wink. "There's always an angle, and I know them all. When I heard you were released from the hospital but they wouldn't put through my calls for you, I waited for the chance to come over. Then I snuck through the back door."

"No one saw you?"

"Only Angie, but she's cool with me and won't say anything."

I almost asked who Angie was, but that might make Chad suspicious. As long as Chad believed I was Leah, he was my one-way ticket out of here. I'd pretend a little longer; at least until I could get back to my own body.

"Turn around," I told him as I got off the bed.

"Why?"

"So I can get dressed."

"Since when did you develop modesty?" Chad's intimate, flirty tone gave me an uneasy feeling he'd spent more time with Leah's naked body than I had.

My cheeks grew hot. "Please turn around," I said firmly.

Chad shot me a puzzled look, but did as I asked.

I searched the first drawer in Leah's dresser and found stacks of folded socks. Another drawer scored an orderly selection of lingerie. I walked into the spacious closet filled with rows and rows of brand-name fashions, and finally chose a pale blue T-shirt and a pair of hip-hugging, sequined jeans. It felt strange wearing someone else's clothes—almost as strange as wearing someone else's body. The simple act of slipping on jeans and a shirt felt unnatural, as if my brain was disconnected from this body.

"You can look now," I told him.

His eyes darkened as he smiled, then whistled low.

"Does that mean I look okay?"

"Totally irresistible," he said, slipping an arm around me and kissing my neck. Shivers tickled my skin. "What's the hurry to leave, anyway? I could lock the door and—"

"No!"

"It wouldn't take long—"

"Not now. It's too soon."

"It's been too long for me, and I thought you'd feel the same way." He blew on my neck and I felt so dizzy I could hardly breathe.

"Um..." Deep breath. "We should...uh...go now."

"Whatever you say. We can make up for lost time later. And don't forget your purse again. It's over there, by the hamper."

"Uh...thanks." I bent over to slip the strap of a small red vinyl purse over my shoulder. It was surprisingly heavy for a micro purse and I wondered what Leah kept inside. But that was the least of my concerns, and could wait.

Right now, I was getting out of here.

Thanks to Chad, the door was no longer locked. As I stepped into the hall, I was dizzy with freedom. But scared, too. Everything was still so confusing. When I looked down the unfamiliar hallway I hesitated, uncertain. To the left was a long hall, and to the right, a staircase.

I started to turn right, but Chad grabbed my arm. "Where're you going?"

"Um … outside?"

"You'll never make it if you walk past your parents' room. The door is open and I heard the TV blaring, so your mother must be in there."

"Oh … yeah. I'm all for avoiding her."

"We'll cut through the kitchen and then go around the garage," he said.

I nodded, as if this made perfect sense. Then I followed him to the left, relieved to see a curved wooden staircase as we turned a corner.

"Shh. Be real quiet." He put his finger to his lips. "Hunter is playing games."

Hunter who? I almost asked. But I stopped myself and just nodded, as if I knew exactly who Hunter was and why he would prevent me from leaving. Tiptoeing down the stairs, we came out into a tiled hall with a high ceiling. Again I had no idea which way to go, so I followed Chad.

Electronic beeps blasted as we passed what I guessed was a game room. Chad put his finger to his lips in warning. I nodded, moving as silently as possible considering that my legs were still rubbery. We made it through an enormous kitchen and out a back door without being stopped.

The sunlight was so bright that I squinted and shaded my eyes with my hand. I paused to catch my breath, inhaling freshly mown grass. Straightening, I glanced around at a driveway leading up to a garage the size of my entire house. Bigger, actually.

"Where's your car?" I asked Chad.

"My car?" He wrinkled his brow and shot me another one of those puzzled looks. "Don't you mean my bike?"

"Bike?" I asked, surprised that he hadn't shown up in a hot sports car.

"Duh. You know I drive a motorcycle."

"Oh, yeah. Your bike." I smiled nervously. I'd never been on a motorcycle before, but I could give it a try. "Is that what we're taking?"

"After the stink you made last time you rode with me and a bug smashed on your neck? We're not trying that again. Besides, my GSXR 1300 is so powerful, everyone would hear it and know I was here. I walked over."

I frowned, trying to remember the distance between Leah's neighborhood and Community Central Hospital. Too far to walk, for sure.

"Why are you just standing there?" he said impatiently. "You want to get caught?"

"No, but I'm still tired. How far will we have to walk?"

"Walk? You can't be serious." He laughed like he was playing along with a big joke. Then he reached for my purse, rifled through it and brought out a key ring. "We'll drive like usual."

Then, before I could say anything, he'd pushed a button and the garage door rose up, revealing a hot blue convertible and a gray SUV. He clicked another button and the convertible's lights flashed.

"Come on," he urged, handing me back the purse.

"But won't Mrs. Mo … my mom get mad if I take her car?" I asked nervously.

"Why would we take her car? We're going in yours."

Chadwick Rockingham, Jr. wore that puzzled look again, but now it was mixed with a cocky grin that spread into adorable dimples when I asked him to drive. I bet Leah never let him drive. He suggested we go to our "usual place," but I could guess what usually happened in their "usual place," so I shook my head.

"That's not a good idea. I'm . . . um . . . still kind of weak."

"Where do you want to go?" He slipped into the driver's seat and started up the engine. "If you're hungry, we could get something at the Club."

The Club? As in the Courtyard Country Club. Only elite and wealthy people were members. I'd imagined lunching there with my clients some day.

I shook my head regretfully. "I'm not hungry."

"So where do you want to hang? We can't go to my house 'cause my brother has his geek friends over making some dumb school project, and I know they annoy you."

I shrugged, afraid of saying something wrong. But with my real body lying in a coma, I had to take a risk. "Let's go to the hospital."

"Huh? You're kidding, right?"

"I'm serious. I need to go to the hospital."

"But you just got out."

"Not that hospital."

His rubbed his chin, clearly puzzled. "Babe, you're confusing me. What's up?"

"I need to see someone at Community Central."

"Who?"

"A family friend," I invented. "It's really important I see her … before it's too late."

"Intenseness." He slowed the car at a yield sign, glancing over at me. "She must be really sick."

"You have no idea." I sank against the leather seat, exhausted and scared. My entire life (and Leah's) hinged on getting to the hospital.

He shrugged. "Hey, whatever you want works for me. On to the hospital."

"Oh, thanks!"

"You'll be thanking me all right," he added with a wink. "But that'll be afterwards when we go to our place."

"Um … okay," I agreed. Not my problem. By then I'd be myself again and Leah could take care of Chad in their "usual" way.

I leaned back into my seat, falling into fatigue and closing my eyes as Chad talked. It was easy to listen to him, as he had a way of talking that made even boring topics like golf sound exciting. His idol was Tiger Woods, and he was being groomed by a professional coach and already competing in golf tournaments.

"This tournament will be my first televised one, and first place is fifty big ones. Just wait, babe, I'm turning pro."

"Cool." We turned on Mercy Avenue, a few blocks from Community Central. I tensed, clawing the leather seat. Getting closer. One more turn and we'd enter the hospital parking lot. But what would I find there?

Best scenario: I rush into a hospital room where my family and friends are gathered around my body. "I'm back!" I shout. Even though I look different, they recognize me. A magical switcheroo happens and I leave Leah's body and wake up instantly in my body. Leah returns, too, and she's be so grateful that she offers eternal friendship and promises of music-industry connections.

Worst scenario: I rush into a room where my family and friends huddle together, crying over my lifeless body. The doctors have pulled the plug, and Amber Borden was pronounced dead.

Not gonna happen, I assured myself. I'd think positive, just like all my books advised, and have my happy ending.

As we pulled into the parking lot, my stomach knotted. I glanced down, startled again to see Leah's pale slender fingers clenched in my lap. We held each other's hands, unified in this soul-reversing mission.

"You okay?" Chad asked when he killed the engine.

"I'm working on it."

"Hospitals suck," he said, frowning. "You sure you want to go in there?"

"It's something I have to do." I unfastened my seatbelt.

"Then go for it. I'll wait here."

My courage faltered a little. "Won't you come with me?"

"Sorry, Babe, but hospitals smell so . . . I don't know . . . antiseptic. When my Uncle Sid was dying, all I could think of was how the room smelled. Uncle Sid was not a sweet-smelling guy, always cracking jokes about his farts or blowing smoke rings. But being in that hospital room was weird . . . too clean smelling . . . like he was already dead."

"I understand how you feel. This isn't easy for me," I admitted.

"So don't go."

"Or you could go with me."

"What's the point? I don't even know your friend."

"But you . . . I mean, she might know you."

"Lots of people know me cause of school and stuff. Doesn't mean I know them or want to."

"You might be surprised. You could wait in the lobby."

"Or not. I'll be here when you're done." He reached into his pocket and flipped open his cell phone. "I got some calls to make."

Thanks for nothing, I thought angrily.

Grabbing Leah's purse, I slammed out of the car. Being angry made it easier put aside my fears. I didn't know whether I'd find my body alive or dead, or if my own family would know me. But at least I knew the layout of this hospital. My sisters had been born here and were so small they had to stay two more months. Funny, how I'd resented their interrupting my life, then.

Now I'd give anything to see them again, hold their warm chubby bodies and tickle their little feet until they giggled. Did they realize I was gone and miss me? Or had they forgotten I existed?

Despite still being weak, I hurried up the steps and through the automatic doors. The main desk was obscured behind a long line of people waiting their turn. Everyone looked anxious and frustrated, except a security guard dozing against the wall by the bank of elevators.

Now what? I wondered. If I went in line, it would take an hour or more to reach the front desk. So how was I going to find my room?

Glancing down at Leah's purse, I had an idea. Sure enough, inside the purse was a pretty pink monogrammed wallet with ninety-eight dollars in cash plus a generous selection of credit cards. Fanning out the credit cards, I picked a shiny gold MasterCard. Then I went into the gift shop and ordered their biggest, most extravagant floral basket for Amber Borden. How ironic that my first gift of flowers was coming from myself.

"Please deliver them right away," I added as I forged Leah's name on the credit slip.

Then I pretended to leave, but ducked around a pillar. I hid my face behind a magazine as I waited in a hard plastic lobby chair.

I was beginning to think the gift shop would never deliver the flowers when I saw a girl my age, wearing a candy striper uniform, carrying my basket toward the elevators.

The security guard, a skinny guy wearing an oversized uniform, roused from his half-slumber. He eyed the pretty candy striper, a flirty smile brightening his face as his pale hand snaked out to punch the elevator button.

My magazine slapped to the floor as I jumped up and dashed toward them. The elevator dinged its arrival, and I dove inside a second before the doors slid shut.

There were only two of us in the elevator, but Ms. Candy Striper didn't notice me since her face was blocked by the enormous bouquet. I followed the flowers and Ms. Candy Striper off at the third floor. At the Intensive Care Unit, she slipped through a glass door marked "Restricted Area. Immediate Family Only."

Well, family definitely included me. So I pushed through the glass doors.

The world hushed to soft voices and a low buzz of machines. The smell of flowers was replaced with antiseptic odors and something darker: an aura of despair, hopes dying.

I passed a waiting room with two couches, several orange plastic chairs, a TV with a darkened screen, and blinds shut over two windows. Fears and prayers weighed heavily in the air and breaths were held, hoping. I held in my breath, too, anxiously looking for Mom, Dad, Dustin or Alyce. But I knew no one.

Hurrying down the corridor, I caught sight of the flowers as they turned a corner. My attitude was casual, like I belonged here, and no one noticed me. When the girl stopped at a desk, I ducked behind a corner wall, eavesdropping.

"Delivery for Borden in Room 311."

"You can't go in that room," a thirty-something guy wearing scrubs said as he came up beside her. He reached for the flowers. "But I can take them for you."

"Will you?" She dimpled. "That's so sweet."

"Smells nice. Too bad the patient can't enjoy them."

"That's too bad." The candy striper lit up as she checked the guy out. Even in loose scrubs, you could tell he had a mega-hard body. Instantly Ms. Candy Striper lost her boredom. "Are you a doctor?"

"An intern."

"Cool. So what's wrong with—" She checked the paper. "—Amber Borden?"

"Car accident, severe head trauma." His mouth frowned, but his eyes shone with interest as he checked Ms. Candy Striper out. Apparently he liked what he saw, because he didn't rush away. "Poor kid was only seventeen."

Was? I thought, rigid with fear. *As in past tense?*

"So terribly young," the girl replied in a tone clearly meant to let him know she was old enough for anything he had in mind.

"She's been in a coma since Saturday."

"Will she wake up?"

He shook his head gravely. "It's just a matter of time."

"That's horrible!" Miss Candy Striper's hand fluttered to her ample chest. The intern's gaze followed and lingered. "Her family must be devastated."

"Yes, they just left. Her parents and friends have been

here every day." He leaned in for a closer look at her cleavage. "Nice of you to be concerned for a stranger."

"I can't help but care about people, even if I don't know them." Her tone implied an intimate hope to know him better. "My ex-boyfriend hated my volunteering here. But it was the best way I could think of to help other people. He'd complained that I should spend all my time waiting on him."

"What a jerk."

"Yeah. That's why I dumped him."

"Good for you. You're better off without him."

"Yeah, he was all into himself. I can't imagine not caring about unfortunate people like that poor girl in there."

I followed her gaze into the room, but I couldn't see anything except part of a white curtain around a bed and the electric glow of machines. I wished they'd stop talking and leave so I could sneak inside the room. It was hell to be so close, yet unable to even see my own body.

"It's tragic," the intern went on. "She'd just won a scholarship and had her whole life ahead of her. After I finish my rounds, I can tell you more if you're interested."

"Oh. I am."

He glanced at his watch. "My break's in a half an hour. Want to meet in the cafeteria?"

"Would I! But my break isn't for an hour."

"I'll wait for you."

Ms. Candy Striper moved toward the elevators and I bent my knees, ready to make a run for Room 311. But she only took a few steps and then stopped, turning back, her expression curious. "I was just wondering…?"

"Yeah?" he asked.

"You said it was just a matter of time for that girl." She pointed to my room. "How much time?"

"Until the heart transplant recipient is ready." He frowned. "Two days."

I sagged against the wall.

Two days—only two freakin' days!

I had to get back into my body—ASAP!

But the intern seemed in no hurry to leave. He spent like twenty minutes talking with a nurse. They consulted a medical chart, speaking in the foreign language of medical jargon. Finally he left, but wouldn't you know? The nurse didn't. She walked into Room 311, shutting the door so I could no longer see the white curtain surrounding my real body. I threw my hands up, wanting to *scream.*

Instead, I sucked in deep breaths (like my book *Chill Out, Charge Forward* advised for staying calm in frustrating situations), and counted the ticking seconds.

I had reached 137 seconds when I heard a strange sound. A dark and furry creature streaked past me so fast the breeze swirled my hair into my eyes. When I pushed back my hair, the black blur was disappearing down the hall. A dog? What was a dog doing running loose in a hospital? And what was the weird glow around its neck?

A Comforter!

"Cola!" I shouted, jumping up. "*Cola!*"

This was the best news I'd had since dying. Grammy Greta must have sent him to help me. So why was he running? Was I supposed to follow him? He must be leading me somewhere important. So I shot down the hall after my dead dog.

Racing around a corner, I dodged past a surprised-looking man. Murmuring an apology, I caught a glimpse of a shaggy tail and raced past a busy pharmacy, up a flight of stairs, and through a set of doors marked "No Admittance." A guy in scrubs shouted for me to slow down, but otherwise no one paid much attention. Emergencies happen all the time in a hospital.

Still, it was weird that people noticed me but not Cola. How could anyone miss a medium-sized shaggy black dog? It was like he was invisible.

Invisible?

That made sense because Cola's job as Comforter would be difficult if everyone could see him. But if this was true, why could I see him?

Was it because of our bond when he was alive? Or maybe because of my whole freaky out-of-body experience? But why didn't he just come up to me? If he was here to rescue me, running *away* didn't make sense. Still, his showing up when I was in trouble was too big a coincidence for it to be random. Cola must be leading me somewhere—hopefully to Grammy.

Running was agony; my throat burned and I ached everywhere. Still, I kept going, determined. Walls and people blurred as I ran, gasping for breath, heart pumping so fast I was afraid it would burst. Couldn't keep … keep going … going much longer. I didn't have the breath to shout for Cola to slow down, so I screamed it in my head.

Cola! Stop already!

And he did.

At the junction of a T-shaped hall, Cola whipped his tail around and crouched low as he faced me. With narrowed black eyes, he bared sharp angry teeth and growled.

"Cola!" I jumped back. "What's wrong?"

In my head I heard an angry snarl: *Leave!*

If he'd bit me, I couldn't have been more surprised. "Cola, you don't mean that!" I cried. "What's wrong?"

He growled again.

"Why are you acting like this?"

His fur bristled like sharp blades and he moved a step forward, glaring.

I couldn't figure out why he had turned vicious. It was like he didn't even know me.

Well, duh! I hit my palm to my head. Of course he didn't recognize me.

"Cola!" I cried softly. "I know I look different, but I'm still your best friend. Cola, I'm Amber."

He snarled, curling his lips in a dangerous, threatening warning.

I know who you are. He didn't actually speak out loud but I could hear him in my mind.

"Then why are you acting like this?"

You do not belong here, he mental-messaged.

"Don't you think I know that?" I pointed at myself. "Only no one will believe that I'm Amber, not Leah. I don't want to be in this body, but I don't know how to get back in my own. Can't you help me?"

It isn't my job.

"But my real body is going to ... to die ..." I wiped my eyes. "In two days."

His dark eyes softened as he shook his shaggy black head. *I must work. Do not follow.* Then he zoomed down the left hallway.

Of course, I followed. I kept going, determined not to lose Cola and probably my last chance to fix my body problem.

By the time I caught up with Cola, he was streaking through another set of "No Admittance" doors. Damn, what was it with him and forbidden areas? This time I didn't slip by without notice. An elderly nurse looked up from a desk in furious surprise. She appeared frail enough to be one of her own patients, but the spunky little lady bellowed, *"Stop!"* Then she gave chase.

The nurse slowed at a steep flight of stairs. I hurried up them, then made a sharp right behind Cola down a narrow hall. He passed through a closed door as if he and the door had no more substance than clouds.

You're not losing me so easily! I thought.

I touched the door: impenetrable, solid wood. Through a small square window at eye level I glimpsed a wisp of a white curtain around a bed. I bent over to catch my breath, and as I stood again I noticed a medical chart tucked in a plastic wall container. I lifted the paper and tried to make sense of the medical scribbles. All I could decipher was the patient's name: *Timothy Alfred Cook.*

Lacking Cola's ability to pass through solid objects, I twisted the knob and cautiously opened the door. The scent of antiseptics and hopelessness swallowed me. It was like falling into a coffin; sensing, without actually seeing the solitary figure in the hospital bed, that his closest companion was death.

Still, there was no going back for me. "Never give up" was a repeated theme in all of my books, advice I tucked tight in my heart.

The door fell silently shut behind me and I tiptoed forward. A TV droned on, but the wrinkled, pale man in the bed wasn't watching. He stared up at the empty white ceiling with faded eyes and sadness. There were no flowers or cards on his table, as if he'd been abandoned by life and was just waiting for his body to give up, too.

But then he noticed the dog beside his bed.

I opened my mouth to call Cola but found that I couldn't speak. I grabbed my throat, struggling to make any sound, but it was like someone had turned my volume to "off." Not even a whisper escaped. A message flashed in my mind: *Leave!*

"I can't," I whispered.

Do not interfere with my job. Leave now!

Cola sounded even angrier than before. Well, I was angry, too, at being stuck in the wrong body and no one believing me except Cola, who ordered me to leave instead of offering help. So I shook my head defiantly.

"I know your job is important," I whispered. "But so is my life … what's left of it anyway. I'm staying."

Then be quiet.

Cola's halo collar burst with golden light. The light was so bright I had to squint as I watched a change come over my dog. His dark fur shimmered, stretching into a silvery silk coat. His tail shortened, fluffed into silvery fur, and curled. The biggest change was his body, which shrunk smaller and smaller—until the animal springing onto the old man's bed wasn't a dog.

Cola had become a Siamese cat.

The old man's withered face brightened with a huge toothy smile. He sat up in bed and reached out with a joyous cry: "Shadow!"

Cola-now-Shadow mewed and cuddled into the man's bony tube-connected arms. The man's face shone with golden happiness. "I never thought I'd see you again," he whispered. "You're such a pretty girl."

And then I finally got it. This wasn't about me at all. No one was supposed to witness Cola in this mission except the old man. No wonder Cola had been so angry at me. I was intruding on something sacred and beautiful. Cola's being at the hospital the same time as me was only a random coincidence.

But I needed help, too. Cola was just the dog (cat?) to get

a message back to Grammy. Although why didn't Grammy already know? She'd assured me she was always nearby, watching out. But where was she now when I needed her most?

I didn't have the answers, but this was the wrong time for questions. Despite the glow of joy on this man's face, he was dying and Cola was here to comfort him.

Sitting quietly in a plastic chair, I watched the old man stroke Cola's fur. Purring filled the room like an angelic choir: sweet, pure, and loving. As Cola lapped the man's wrinkled skin with kisses, his age lines faded and he glowed with youthful energy. Joyous music was sprinkled in the air, the soft melody of a flute and a ripple of harp strings.

Goose bumps rose up my arms. The air in the room sizzled with electricity. The old man lifted his gaze to stare at the ceiling, beyond anything my ordinary eyes could see. I blinked and thought I saw tiny orbs glowing like floating stars, bobbing and swirling toward the bed. When I blinked again, there was nothing. The old man grinned so wide I could see gaps in his yellowed teeth. Despite his appearance, he seemed younger and radiant. He lifted his tube-connected hand and waved, as if welcoming old friends.

I saw only a "cat" and the old man, yet suddenly the room felt crowded.

With emotions tangling heavy in my heart, and clouds of tears blurring my eyes, I turned away from the joyous, terrible, wonderful miracle.

Cola was right—I didn't belong here. So I stood quietly and slipped out of the room.

In the hall, everything seemed ordinary again. Exhaustion washed over me as I sagged against the wall. I closed my eyes, grateful and humbled.

Cola's job was truly important, and I didn't blame him for growling. He must have been as surprised to see me as I was to see him. When he finished "comforting" the old man, I hoped he'd forgive me. I'd wait here for him, no matter how long it took.

With my eyes shut, I felt so relaxed that I could almost go to sleep. My anxiety faded, breaking apart and floating away. I thought of those glowing orbs and wondered if they were spirits greeting the old man—friends, family, and even pets. When I'd been with Grammy, I'd seen figures on the far side of the lake, waving. Were they my otherside family and friends, waiting for me?

This thought made me smile—until I heard the footsteps. My eyes shot open, and I found myself nose-to-badge with the same security guard I'd seen by the elevators.

"You aren't allowed here," he said.

"I'm waiting for someone."

"Waiting in an unauthorized area," the security guard (Karl, according to his badge) replied. "Nice girl like you should know better than to break rules."

There was nothing "nice" about the way he was staring at me. Creepy was more like it. And there was a strange, prickly energy in the air, raising the hair on my skin. But before I could call Cola, the guard was reaching for me— with hands that blurred like mist, with gray fingernails.

Oh my god … Dark Lifer hands!

Gasping, I jumped away before he could touch me and took off running. I didn't stop until I was through the lobby and outside. Then I sagged on a cement bench, hugging myself to calm down.

I couldn't stop thinking about the guard. What was a Dark Lifer doing here? Had I attracted him? And he almost touched me! I had to tell Grammy. But I couldn't perform my lucky chant without my rainbow bracelet. And it wasn't safe to go back inside to get it from my real body. I ached with disappointment. Would Cola look for me when he finished his assignment? Or would he leave for his next assignment without letting Grammy know I was in trouble? I needed to get a message to him before he left the hospital. But I'd never get past that creepy Dark Lifer.

I might as well give up.

Yet I could imagine Alyce saying, "Ditch the self-pitying dramatics and just do what you have to." She always cut to the reality of a situation, as if she viewed everything through a camera with a BS filter. Oh, how I missed her ... and Dustin, and Mom and Dad and the triplets and even bitchy Aunt Suzanne. I'd lose them all forever if I just gave up.

I needed to either find Cola, or return to Room 311 and try to switch back into my real body. Who knew getting inside a hospital room would be so difficult? Chad hadn't had any major problems sneaking into my bedroom. "Locks can't keep me out," he'd boasted. Did the same go for security guards and nurses?

Chad! Why hadn't I thought of him sooner? He was my solution! All I had to do was to go back to the car and convince him to help. I wouldn't give up until he came with me.

So I went back to Leah's car—only Chad wasn't waiting.
Unfortunately, a police officer was.

13

On the humiliating trip in the back seat of a police car, with doors that couldn't be opened from inside, I found out I was being "returned" to Leah's father.

I couldn't stop thinking about Chad. Why hadn't he waited for me? What happened to him? The Dark Lifer would have no reason to go after Chad. But Leah's father would. If Mr. Montgomery reported the car as stolen, Chad could have been arrested. He was too good looking to survive long in prison with hardened criminals.

Stop thinking like Amber, I reminded myself. Leah and Chad lived in a world of privilege. Chadwick Huntington Junior would be bailed out before his pedicured feet touched down in a cell.

But I wasn't so sure what would happen to me. From the officer's hostile attitude, I knew I was in a world of trouble. Escaping from the locked bedroom and driving off with "my" boyfriend were offenses that even the most easygoing father wouldn't take lightly. And Mr. Montgomery had a reputation of being the *opposite* of easygoing.

It was ironic, really, because as Amber I'd been eager to meet this music industry mogul. He was infamous for his wheelings and dealings at Stardust Studios, catapulting garage-band nobodies to overnight mega-stars. Sure, there were rumors that some of his deals were shady, like when Tay Renault didn't show up for a concert and Allejandro, a rising Stardust client, took the spot and soared to stardom. Tay was later found wandering in the desert, confused and battered. Another rumor had to do with the hot metal band, Eco-Dead, dumping their studio and signing with Stardust. I knew better to believe gossip … still, I had an uneasy sense of foreboding.

I should probably call Mr. Montgomery "Dad" or "Father," but this commanding man could be nothing but "Mister Montgomery" to me. How was his daughter expected to behave? Should I greet him with a hug or outrage? What would Leah do in this situation? Shout, beg forgiveness, or give her father the cold shoulder treatment? I had no idea.

When we reached the Montgomery house, I said nothing as he led me to his office. I withered under his penetrating gaze as he told Leah to sit down in a hard wood chair.

Clasping my hands in my lap, I looked everywhere except directly at him. I heard only my thudding heartbeat and tick-tick-ticking from a compass-shaped clock on a wall-length bookcase. Staring past my white knuckles, I noticed every tiny bird design woven into the Oriental rug. And I wished for wings to fly away.

Mr. Montgomery cleared his throat, and stood up abruptly from his desk. He wasn't a tall man, although with his sturdy, broad shoulders and his silvery head held high, he seemed like a giant as he stood over me.

"I hope you're feeling better," he said, as if speaking to a business associate rather than his only daughter. I'd expected him to shout, to chew me out for disobeying orders. But he smiled, his thin lips not quite meeting his cold gray eyes. His expression was devoid of emotion.

My throat went dry.

"It's been a while since we talked," he went on, relaxing back with his hands tucked under his desk. "I'm glad you decided to join me."

Did I have a choice? I didn't actually say this, although I would have if I hadn't been sick-to-my-gut nervous.

"I'll admit to being curious about your little adventure," he said with a tilt of his head, as if pondering deep questions of life. "Whatever possessed you to drive to Community Central? I would think you'd had enough of hospitals."

My gaze remained downcast, hiding any flicker of emotion. But my brain was buzzing. He hadn't mentioned Chad, so he must think I drove there alone. Did that mean he had nothing to do with Chad's disappearance? Chad must have left on his own. I was relieved—yet pissed off, too. I'd been worrying that something awful happened to him, when he probably took off to avoid the cops. Real loyal boyfriend—not! How could he say he loved Leah and then ditch her—me!—at the first sign of trouble?

I lifted my gaze to find Leah's father studying me.

"How did you find me?" I asked, curiosity overcoming my fear. "This isn't a big city, but it's not small either, and finding one car so quickly is mathematically improbable."

"Unless you have a GPS system," he said proudly. "I had one installed when I bought your car. Only state-of-the-art systems for my vehicles."

"I thought it was *my* car."

"You are *my* daughter."

"It's not the same thing."

"Oh … isn't it?" He paused, peering deep into my face with a wry smile that gave me chills. "Tell me why you drove to Community Central Hospital. Who'd you see there?"

"No one."

"Come, now," he said with a click of his tongue. "Gathering information is a specialty of mine, and quite an asset in my business dealings. Knowing the personal details of a celebrity's assistant or manager can mean the difference between making or losing millions. There are always ways to find out what you need to know."

I sighed, seeing no reason to lie. "I went to see this girl from school who's really sick, but visitors weren't allowed."

His forehead creased as if he was mulling this over, then he nodded. "I assumed it was something of the sort."

"You did?"

"Why does that surprise you? I've always supported your causes. What's the girl's name? I'll arrange to have some flowers sent in your name."

"I—I already sent her flowers."

"Admirable." He narrowed his gaze at me. "But I trust there will be no further impromptu trips. You're weak and need your rest. Doctor's orders are for you to focus on healing. You will stay home until you're well enough to return to school."

I nodded, because that's what he expected me to do—and something warned me not to make him mad.

"Excellent. Now we can move on to other business. Go ahead, stand up."

"W—Why?"

"Let's not play that game."

"Game?" I frowned, puzzled by his almost playful expression.

"You will do as I ask." He gave an impatient humph and tugged on my hand, jerking me to my feet. His touch startled me—it hurt because he was so rough. He stared at me, analyzing. "You're too pale, and there are dark circles under your eyes."

This was more of an accusation than an observation, and I had the ridiculous impulse to apologize.

"Stretch out your arms," he ordered.

"Why?"

"Don't be dense. You know the routine."

No, I didn't. And I was increasingly uncomfortable under his accessing gaze, as if I were a piece of livestock up for auction and he was gauging my value. Of course, that was absurd. I was his daughter (at least that's what he thought). But a normal parent concerned about a suicide attempt would be either angry or comforting, not calculating cold. I was beginning to realize that things were far from normal in the Montgomery household.

Self-consciously, I lifted my arms and stretched them out.

"That's more like it," he said, nodding. "Now turn around slowly."

"Turn around? You can't be serious."

"Am I ever anything else? Please turn around."

Face flaming, heart quickening, I turned.

Halfway around, I felt a slap on my butt.

"What the hell!" I whirled to face him. "Why'd you do that? Are you some kind of—"

"Flabby ass," he said critically.

"What?"

"You heard me. You've gotten soft and lost muscle tone."

"You're joking, right?" My cheeks burned and my butt still stung.

"I never joke about appearances, and yours is out of shape. Too much lying about in the hospital without any physical activity."

"I know flabby, and this is not it." I pointed effectively. "What do you care about how I look, anyway?"

But he wasn't listening, his gaze sweeping over me like a cleaning inspector searching for a smudge. "Overall, the damage is minor, and easily repaired by a high-protein diet and daily workout. But those eye circles may require another Botox injection."

"Botox? But that's for old people. I'm only seventeen."

"You were fifteen when you got your first injection."

"No way!"

"You're behaving oddly," he said with a steely gaze. "But I think I know why."

I gulped. "You do?"

"You need some incentive." He reached out to run his hand over Leah's long hair, the way someone would stroke a cat's fur, and I shuddered. Somehow this was creepier than his butt slap.

"Could you *not* touch me?" I asked.

"Beauty is to be savored, appreciated . . . and rewarded." He crossed over to his desk, opened the top drawer and drew out a navy blue velvet case. He flipped open the lid. Displayed on gold silk was a dazzling diamond and sapphire bracelet. "Like it?" he asked.

It was gorgeous. The sort of dazzling jewelry I one day imagined my fabulous husband giving me as a wedding gift. But the luster faded with intent. This was a bribe. What did he expect in exchange?

I pushed the velvet case away. "I don't want it."

"Of course you do." He paused, arching one silver brow. "And you'll wear it to Congressman Donatello's reception next Saturday. I've already selected an appropriate evening gown."

My head started to throb. Didn't he even care that his daughter just got out of the hospital for attempted suicide? "I don't want to go to a dumb party. You and Mrs. . . . Mom can go without me."

"Don't be absurd. Why would your mother go?" He scowled, as if I'd insulted him. "Of course you'll accompany me. Congressman Donatello is looking forward to seeing you again."

"Why would a congressman care about me?"

"Really, Leah. Fishing for compliments is so juvenile." Mr. Montgomery's laugh held irony and amusement. "Besides, it's not as if anyone expects me to appear with your mother. Her condition is a badly kept secret, and everyone is quite sympathetic. You know she hasn't gone to a social event in years. You, however, are welcomed with open arms."

"Even though I attempted suicide?" I blurted out.

His expression darkened, and for a moment I thought he would hit me. I moved backwards until my back pressed up against a bookcase.

"Do not use that word," he snapped. "You were very ill, and can't be blamed for your behavior. It's in the past, where it will remain. You're much better now."

"Are you sure?"

"Absolutely." He stepped toward me. "Because if you weren't better, you wouldn't be living in my home. Sadly, I'd have no recourse except to follow Dr. Hodges' recommendation and commit you to a mental institution."

"You wouldn't!"

"By now you should know *never* to underestimate me."

I frowned, afraid. I thought longingly of my own father, who laughed easily and loved me no matter what I looked like or how many mistakes I made. He would never threaten me or slap my butt.

"Here." Mr. Montgomery pushed the velvet box into my hand. "You'll look lovely in this bracelet. Be a good girl and I'll buy you the matching necklace and earrings. I'll have Angie bring you an exercise schedule and set up a Botox appointment."

I cringed, tightening my fingers around the jewelry box. I wasn't sure which was worse—being injected with poison that would freeze my facial muscles, or exercising. Probably exercise. At least the Botox injection would be quick and not involve sweat.

"The suicide attempt, the game playing, sneaking out and lying," he said coolly. "All of it will end now, and you will behave as my daughter should. Do you understand?"

"No, I don't," I said stubbornly.

"DeHaven Psychiatric Resort has an immediate opening," he said in an ominous tone. "They have cutting-edge treatments for the mentally disturbed. They believe in controversial methods of electric shock and isolation in padded cells. All I need to do is make a phone call. Or would you rather agree to behave properly?"

I hesitated, fear tightening a noose around my soul. Slowly, I nodded.

"That's my girl." His satisfied smile made me want to barf. "By the way, to insure you get plenty of rest, I've had a few things removed from your room and the lock reinforced. You may leave now."

I was dismissed.

As I started to go, he called after me, "Take care of yourself, Leah."

I shuddered. Not because of his threats or inappropriate behavior—but because he'd emphasized "Leah" in a tone that echoed with ownership.

And for the first time since my death, I felt sorry for Leah.

14

Computer. Desk phone. Cell phone. Car keys.

All gone from Leah's room. And the formidable dead-bolt lock on the door required two keys, which Angie, a thirty-something housekeeper with an impressive double chin and long black snake-braid, withdrew from her skirt pocket. She didn't seem friendly, and I was too emotionally numb to care. She asked if I was hungry and I nodded, although I'd lost track of time and appetite.

"I'll be back with your lunch," she said coolly. The lock double-clicked behind her.

Something clicked inside me, too—outrage, panic, fear—and I rushed to the door, rattling the knob and pounding on the wood.

"Let me out!" I shouted. Then I kicked the door and ranted about unfairness, threatening to report everyone in this household to child-protective services. They were all cruel and awful and hateful.

My rampage only lasted about five minutes, until my voice cracked and my throat burned. I sagged against the door in defeat. Leah's father had completely shut me off from the outside world. I might as well be in the crazy bin wrapped in a straitjacket—I'd have more freedom than in this princess prison. I sank to the plush carpet and huddled against the door. Tears warmed some of the numbness. I hugged my knees, rocking to ease my shivers.

Everything was so wrong and all I wanted to do was go home. I had to let my family know I was alive. Aunt Suzanne said they were suffering, and knowing that made me feel worse. Why had I given up so quickly? Aunt Suzanne didn't know me that well—she didn't even like me. If I'd reached my parents or friends, I could have convinced at least one of them. But now I was totally cut off. Alone behind a locked door, everything seemed hopeless.

I have no idea how long it was before I heard a key in the lock and smelled delicious aromas. Wiping my face and pushing back my tangled hair, I jumped to my feet so the door wouldn't smack me as it opened.

"Here's your lunch." Angie avoided looking directly at me, double-locking the door behind her as if she expected me to bolt for freedom.

She carried a covered silver dish on an oval tray. Wonderful lemon and buttery smells revived me a little. My stomach rumbled.

"Thank you," I said quietly. "It smells good."

Angie ignored me, turning to leave.

"Wait," I called out. "Stay a minute. I'd like to talk."

"About what?" she asked, flipping her braid over her shoulder in a defiant gesture. With her hands on her hips, she eyed me with suspicion. She was younger than I'd originally thought, maybe in her late twenties. Yet her plodding manner and sour expression made her seem much older, as if her inner bitch had matured fast.

"I need help," I told her sincerely. "I have to get away."

"As if!" She snorted like I'd said something funny.

"This is life-or-death important," I added, desperate enough to beg. It was awful being at a stranger's mercy, especially when there was no hint of compassion in her narrowed eyes. "Please, will you help?"

"You're saying 'please' to me?" She folded her arms around her curvy chest. "Hell must have frozen over."

"So you'll help?" I asked eagerly.

"Absolutely, positively never gonna happen."

"I have to get out of here! If you don't help me something terrible will happen."

"You can't threaten me anymore—your father already knows about Luis' past, and he doesn't care. You're a real tool and I'm not dumb enough to get screwed again."

"Huh? Whatever I did … I'm sorry."

"Sure, sorry you can't push me around anymore," she said with thick sarcasm. "I work for your father. Not you."

"He isn't my father." I sighed as her expression closed. "I mean, he doesn't act normal. It's cruel to lock me in."

"Consider yourself lucky. He should have sent you to

the loony bin. I hear you flipped out, have a dozen different personalities."

"I'm not crazy. I'm in trouble...and running out of time. At least take a message to someone for me."

"If you mean Chad, forget it. The way you jerk guys around like dogs on a chain makes me want to puke. I don't know why a sweet guy like Chad puts up with you. I was out of my mind earlier, sneaking him in and risking my job."

"You can always get another job."

"Says who?" Her dangling braid snapped like a whip as she shook her head. "My man and I got it good here. We don't want any problems. Jobs like this might not seem much to you, but Luis and I like it. So I'm doing exactly what Mr. Montgomery says. No more breaking the rules."

"But I don't belong here..." My word trailed off. Anything I said would only sound more crazy. Angie's narrowed dark eyes confirmed that she wasn't going to help. Leah may have popularity-plus at school, but not at home.

There had to be someone in this house who would help. What about Leah's mother? When she'd visited the hospital, she'd seemed to genuinely love her daughter.

"Could you at least tell Mrs...my mother...that I'd like to see her?"

Angie shook her head. "She's not here."

I didn't believe her. "Where is she?"

"At one of *those* meetings."

"Meetings?" I questioned.

Angie answered by cupping her hand and bringing it to her mouth. As she turned to leave, she gave me a scathing look, like I was the most pathetic person in the world.

Before she reached the door, keys jangling in her hand, Angie touched her palm to her head and swore under her breath. "I almost forgot. Here." She withdrew a folded paper from a pocket and thrust it at me.

My fingers closed around the paper. The door banged shut accompanied by the sound of locks clicking. I didn't make any move to read the paper, Angie's words sinking in. Just like that, I knew what she'd meant by "meetings" and her hand-mouth gesture.

Drinking.

Leah's mother was an alcoholic. And the meetings were Alcoholics Anonymous. So that was the "badly kept secret" Mr. Montgomery referred to, and the reason his wife didn't accompany him to social events. Taking his daughter instead might be normal in ultra-rich society but, combined with that butt slap, reeked of inappropriate behavior to me. Way too much dysfunction going on around here.

The paper Angie had given me rustled in my hand. I bit my lip, hoping it had nothing to do with doctors, medication, or Botox. It was worse, I realized with a groan. I found a daily exercise schedule that included swimming laps, lifting weights, and working out for an hour on gym equipment. I mentally tallied the time: two hours of exercise a day. One hour would be torture. Two hours was insane! I'd never survive.

And if I stayed here, my real body had zero chance of survival.

But there wasn't any way for me to leave, and it was hard to ignore the appetizing smells wafting from the silver tray. I had this motto that helped me deal with life's disappointments: *When all else fails: Eat.* So I lifted the shiny lid, my mouth watering at the sight of grilled lemon chicken, steamed carrots and broccoli, and a potato. Kind of low-cal for my taste, but I was too beyond starving to act picky.

As I chewed, I thought longingly of noisy dinners at home surrounded by triple high chairs and my sisters flinging food. Or all the times Dustin, Alyce and I pigged out on cheeseburgers at Grumpy's Grill and I'd laugh when Dustin pretended to get mad because I'd swiped some of his French fries. Also there was that chocolicious meeting with that boy, Eli, over the dessert buffet. Food was a primal connection that linked me to life—my real life. And I'd do anything to get it all back (my life, that is, not more food ... although food was always good).

Unfortunately, I was out of options. Being trapped in this room was as frustrating as being trapped in this body.

There was no way out.

Or was there?

I thought about how I'd gotten into this mess. I'd heard the screech of tires but I never felt the crash. Bright warm light had rescued me, welcomed me, and I had been somewhere else, far from anything physical, floating toward the outstretched arms of my beloved grandmother. Locks and doors didn't matter where Grammy was. I was sure she didn't know I was in trouble now, or she would come to help. Cola might tell her ... or he might not. I'd have to do it myself.

Maybe there *was* another way out.

All I had to do was die.

Again.

15

There's this quote about living being hard and dying being easy.

Ha! Not for me. Sure, living had its problems, but dying was damned hard. My princess prison lacked any obvious means of self-destruction. No knife, gun, pills or poisonous gas. Not that I'd have the nerve to stab, shoot or gas myself. Way too violent. Besides, I only wanted to die a little. Long enough for an out-of-body trip to Grandma and Cola, then back again—but into the right body.

Desperation short-circuited my thoughts, numbing my emotions and logic so that anything seemed possible. I couldn't sit around doing nothing until it was too late to save my real body. A temporary death wouldn't be suicide—

more like a quickie visit with Grammy. I was confident she would make sure I landed in my real body this time.

So I spent the rest of the day planning my death.

Method was my first challenge.

After searching Leah's drawers and closet, the most dangerous thing I could find was a silk belt. Death by fashion accessory ... hmm, would it work? A belt could make a nifty noose—but was silk sturdy enough? I twisted it into a loop and fitted it around my neck, but I was never good with knots and it kept slipping over my head. I tried a few other belts, but gave up on this idea because I couldn't find anything solid in the ceiling to hang a belt over, anyway.

How about asphyxiation? Mom was always bugging me to toss plastic bags away so the triplets wouldn't suffocate. This wasn't a bad method, because it wouldn't scar and I'd black out before it hurt too badly. But I couldn't find a plastic bag—only some trendy cloth bags with name-brand logos. I guess rich folks didn't have to choose "paper" or "plastic," just opted for designer carry bags.

Running out of ideas fast, I went into the adjoining bathroom and opened the medicine cabinet. The glass shelves were empty except for toothpaste and vitamins.

Then I noticed a razor.

Carefully, I plucked the silver-sharp blade from the razor, squatted on the cool tile floor, and aimed the blade over my wrist.

My fingers trembled. I hesitated ... would it hurt a lot?

A lot. And I really, really, *really* hated pain.

Besides, wrist-slashing wasn't easy. I'd seen this news report and they said how slashing your wrists was a bad cliché and usually done wrong. It only worked if you cut horizontally ... or was it vertically? Which one was right? Frankly, I just wanted to forget the whole horrible idea.

Don't wimp out, I told myself. *Think of family, friends, and going home.*

Besides, with Grammy on my side (and the Other Side), what could go wrong?

I ran through a mental checklist of my plan:

Cut, bleed, and as I felt myself losing consciousness, I'd scream bloody murder (was that a pun?) to insure that someone found me ASAP. Okay, so this wasn't a great plan. There was too much room for error. But I couldn't let myself dwell on the list of *Things That Could Go Wrong.* I had to be strong for everyone I loved.

Still, it was hard to hold the razor, my hand was shaking so much. Forget horizontal or vertical—any slash I made now would veer off into a wild zigzag.

What was I doing, anyway? Taking a sharp blade and slicing myself? Maybe I really was crazy. Spurting blood was an all-around terrible idea. And way too messy. There had to be a gentler way of achieving white light.

With enormous relief, I tossed aside the razor and looked around for a better idea.

My gaze drifted across the room. How about jumping from a window? I imagined myself crashing to the ground. Extreme ouch. Not a gentle way to go, and it would be a crime to smash Leah's body. I'd rather temporarily die in a completely painless, non-bloody way. That's why I nixed the blow dryer in the bathtub method. (Plus, I might still end up in the wrong body, but with a serious case of bad hair.)

What about drowning?

Hmmm...now this idea had potential. I should have thought of it first. Minimal pain, and maximum opportunity for survival (as long as someone found me in time). So I had to "drown" in a public place, not alone in the bathroom. There was also the nudity factor to consider. I'd rather be rescued wearing a swimsuit, not a birthday suit.

"The swimming pool!" When I'd gone outside with Chad, I'd glimpsed turquoise blue water glittering in an oval-shaped pool. I may be locked in my room, but swimming laps was part of Leah's ordered exercise regiment.

One problem decided.

Next problem—what swimsuit would I wear?

Leah owned fourteen bathing suits. I found them hanging in her walk-in closet, arranged by size and color. It was a new experience to model swimsuits, one that I confess I enjoyed far more than I should have given the morbid circumstances. I narrowed my choice to a black strapless bikini, a red tankini, and a neon-yellow string bikini. They all looked amazing. As Amber, I never could have fit my chubby thighs into suits this sexy. But Leah could wear a ragged towel and look like a runway model.

I finally settled on the tomato-bright tankini, because it would be an easy-to-spot target on the floor of the pool.

Walking back to the bed, I picked up the printed exercise schedule and ran my index finger down the list. I stopped at the notation, "Swim Laps: 9–10 A.M."

I'd always groaned that exercise would kill me.

Now I was counting on it.

16

The next morning, I shut out any fear of pain and all the things that could wrong. If my plan went right, that was even scarier. I pretended nothing was real, my movements robot-like as I slipped into the red tankini and focused on the one thing I could control. I longed to shout at Mr. Montgomery, "You don't own me!" Then I'd raised my hand, tuck in four fingers, and flip him off to my death.

With a towel tied around my waist, my hips moved in a natural sway. Very unnatural to me. Nothing really seemed real, anyway, which in an odd way made things easier. Like I was an actress playing a role. Starring Amber Borden as Leah Montgomery.

Angie arrived promptly at five minutes to nine. She

told me to follow her down the hall, her attitude surly as ever. She didn't even talk to me. That was fine, since casual chitchat was not in my plans. Only moving forward and doing what I had to. Wordlessly, I followed Angie downstairs and through a back door that opened into an enclosed yard—with a swimming pool as its centerpiece.

"One hundred laps," Angie ordered.

I nodded.

"Don't cheat and quit early."

I nodded.

"Stay in the pool until you finish your laps."

"I'll stay," I replied obediently, shutting off my mind so I wouldn't think too far ahead. One step at a time, that's all I had to take.

Draping my towel on a wicker chair, I scanned the pool. Sparkling clear blue water with a strong odor of chlorine. Dustin loved to swim … no, don't think of Dustin or anything connected to my real life. Just get through this with no mistakes. Should I jump into the deep water, or wade in from the shallow end?

While I was deciding, I heard the squeak of a door and glanced over to see Angie leaving. But that would ruin everything! Angie didn't know it, but she had a key role in my plan. Despite her thoroughly disagreeable personality, she wouldn't let the boss' daughter drown. She'd jump in to save me—although I hoped it would be Leah she'd pulled out of the pool.

"Where are you going?" I called out to Angie.

She glanced over, annoyed. "None of your business."

"But aren't you supposed to watch me?"

"I got better things to do."

"I might try to escape."

"As if anyone could do that!" She made a humph sound. "You'd need wings to get over that twelve-foot wall. Then you'd have to get past your daddy's trained dogs."

"I love dogs."

"Since when? Those dogs are so mean they don't even like themselves. Vicious beasts, but they do their job. Now I have my own job, and it doesn't include wasting time with you. Get busy with those laps."

"You can't force me to swim."

"Maybe I can't but your daddy can, and he's got security cams all over this place." She pointed up to a black camera fixed high over a doorway, its lens aimed at the pool like a weapon. "Now get busy exercising. I'll be back in an hour."

"An hour! But that's too long."

"Not unless you're a speed swimmer," she said, misunderstanding. Then she went inside, shutting the door behind her. Locking it, too, I was sure.

Frustrated, I sank in the lounge chair. I was still operating on "numb" and knew that if I stopped to think, the odds were high I'd chicken out.

Focus on the plan, I ordered myself.

I wasn't a strong swimmer, but I could doggie paddle and float on my back. I'd already realized that a flaw in my plan was my inability to stay underwater until I started to black out. Instinct to survive would kick in, and I might not be able to resist coming up for air. Unless I weighed myself down.

The swimming pool was enclosed by a cement-block

wall circling around perfectly pruned shade trees and artificial grass that looked real enough to fool hungry cows. Rushing water echoed in a lyrical rhythm from a faux waterfall that cascaded onto rocks. Hmmm... rocks.

Unfortunately, most of the rocks were too heavy, and I couldn't pick them up. My arms may have looked muscular, but they were pathetic at lifting. I stepped over the larger rocks and searched for smaller ones. As I bent over to pick up a fist-sized rock, I had the odd sense of being watched. The shade trees rustled slightly from the spring breeze, and a few birds swooped through the branches. I didn't see anyone, but did spot another security camera fixed over the pool house. Normally I'd hate the idea of cameras spying on me, but now I was glad to have them. They were extra insurance for a rescue.

Slipping into a mindless numb zone, I sorted through the rocks until I found five that were heavy, yet also slim enough to fit into my tankini. I squeezed in two up top and three below. My suit sagged, lopsided, and I balanced the rocks so my tankini bottom didn't fall off. I barely felt the rocks up top under Leah's surgically enhanced boobs.

A clock affixed on the pool-house wall pointed out the time. I calculated how long it would take to jump into the water, lose consciousness, see the light, chat with Grandma, pet Cola if he was around, then presto-chango, body switcheroo. Factoring an estimate return for Angie, I concluded that if I entered the water in exactly forty-seven minutes, Leah's body had a 74 percent chance of survival. Not great odds, but better than my chances of returning to my body once it was pronounced dead.

This is not suicide, I reminded myself. It's survival.

One minute passed. Then three minutes. Only another forty-four to go—too much time to think, to stress, to dissect every little detail. Did the rocks weigh enough? What if I floated to the top? I had to make sure I was heavy enough to stay on the pool bottom until I saw the light.

That's when I noticed a discarded brick leaning against a brick flower planter on the far side of the pool. Five rocks *and* a brick would add plenty of weight. Walking with rocks scraping my skin beneath my swimming suit was uncomfortable. So I moved slowly, with my arms stretched out for balance, as I maneuvered around wicker patio furniture. A lounge chair blocked the way, and as I bent down to push it aside, something shifted in my swim top. A rock popped out and plopped down.

I yelped as the rock smashed onto my foot.

Crying in pain, I jumped and grabbed my sore foot. The hopping jarred the other rock out of my top. I grabbed for it, but couldn't get a grip. The rock slipped through my fingers toward my other foot. Instinctively I lunged backwards, my arms flailing as I teetered on the edge of the pool. And then I fell...

Something hard smacked my head.

I never heard the splash.

17

When I opened my eyes, a cloudy face hovered over me. "Grammy?" A sharp pain throbbed in my head.

I didn't remember hurting so much and feeling so cold last time I visited Grammy Greta. And it was so dark. Had I landed in the wrong place? I'd heard that people who commit suicide never made it to heaven and were trapped in an eternal black hole of nothingness. Had I taken a horribly wrong turn and been sucked into the darkness?

"You're okay." The voice speaking was male—definitely *not* Grammy.

Blinking, I watched as the face swam over me. Brown hair curled in a familiar way, and there were hazel eyes. Not a devil or angel. And as my vision cleared I realized I wasn't in the dark pits of hell—just under a shady tree. My bathing suit was soaking wet and I had a horrible headache, but like the guy said, I was okay.

Unfortunately, I was also still Leah.

When I tried to sit up, pain exploded in my head and everything went fuzzy. "Ooh ... my head ... ouch ... hurts."

"It should. You got smacked in the head with a rock and nearly drowned."

His voice ... so familiar ... I had a feeling I knew and liked him. Yet something in his tone suggested he wasn't too crazy about me.

Weakly, I rubbed my eyes. When I opened them again I gasped. No way! Impossible! How could he be here? It just didn't make any sense. Maybe I wasn't so okay after all ...

I was sure I was hallucinating, until I saw a soggy chocolate bar poking up from his wet shirt pocket. That's when I knew it was real—that he was real.

"Ohmygod!" I gasped. "Eli?"

"Shhsh!" He pushed back his dripping hair and glanced around uneasily. "Keep your voice down."

"You? Here? I can't believe it!"

"Don't throw anything." He crossed his hands over his chest protectively. "I'm only the messenger."

"You're a miracle!" With an excited squeal, I jumped up and wrapped arms around him. His clothes were dripping wet, but then so were mine.

"'Thanks' is enough. More than I'd expect from you."

"Thank you! Thank you for being here. I'm so glad to see you!"

"Glad, like getting poison oak or food poisoning." He pried off my hands. "Don't pretend with me."

"Who's pretending? Eli, you have no idea what I've been through and what I almost did because there was no one to help me. But now you're here. And you jumped in the pool to pull me out like a real hero!"

"I'll probably regret it. What were you thinking, anyway?" He sounded angry, not at all like the shy and sweet Eli I met at Jessica's party. "Putting rocks in your suit was beyond dumb. You almost drowned!"

"I tried, but I screwed that up. Ooh … my head."

"It's just a bump. You're not bleeding."

"It still hurts." I reached up and winced as my fingers touched the bump and exploded into pain. Lights flashed, circling around and around. I swayed, my legs buckling.

"Steady there." Quickly, Eli reached out and wrapped his arm around my waist. He eased me into a wicker chair. "Sit down."

"Thanks," I murmured.

"You're thanking me? You're obviously not yourself."

"You can tell? That's amazing!" I felt overwhelming relief. Finally, someone was on my side. "You have no idea how good it is to see a friendly face. Everyone here hates me or hates her—it's hard to keep it all straight. I just want to go home. No one else knows, and I've been so scared. They keep me locked in my room most of the time and my body is going to die tomorrow if I can't get out of here."

Instead of showing sympathy, he stepped back with a wary look. "Uh … maybe you should take a pill."

"No more pills or doctors or hospitals! I've been out of

it for too long. Just get me away from here and I'll explain everything."

"You don't owe me any explanation. Save it for Chad."

"Chad?" I repeated, confused. "You know him?"

"How hard did you hit your head? Of course I know Chad—he's the reason I'm here. And for the record, I didn't want to, but you know how persuasive my brother can be. He conned me into playing messenger." Eli scowled as he reached into his pocket and handed me a damp red envelope. "Here's your love letter."

I felt my face go hot, wondering if he had guessed I liked him. But wait . . . the letter wasn't from Eli. "Your *brother?* Chad is your brother!"

"Not exactly a news flash." He wrung out a corner of his damp shirt and glanced down mournfully at his soggy chocolate bar. "Why do I get myself in these situations? Next time Chad asks for a favor, the answer is never again."

I still couldn't believe that Chad and Eli were brothers, although now that I thought about it, I'd welcomed them both to school a few years ago with a "Hello Halsey" basket. Chad may be a good kisser, but it was Eli who had made my mouth water when we bonded over oh-so-sweet chocolate.

Just my luck. I finally find a nice guy who really gets me, on the day that I'm run over by a mail truck.

I'd hoped to see Eli again, to find out why he'd left so abruptly and if there was potential for anything real between us. Now here he was . . . only he clearly did *not* want to be with me. The "mmm" factor was missing. And I realized why when I glanced down at the red envelope. Leah's name.

My first love letter—and it was for the wrong girl, from the wrong guy. I bit my lip, struggling not to cry.

Eli was here by coincidence. Chad's brother! And Chad was Leah's boyfriend. Unfortunately, the way Eli was looking at me was seriously hostile.

"It's been ... uh ... wet." He wrung out a corner of his shirt so pool water dribbled onto the cement. "I only came to give you the letter. I'm out of here."

"NO! Don't go!" I tossed aside Chad's envelope and grabbed Eli's arm.

"What's your problem?" He gave me an "are you nuts" look.

"You wouldn't believe me. Just take me with you. Don't leave me in this prison!"

"A prison?" He snorted. "Relaxing by a heated pool surrounded by wealth and luxury? Yeah ... poor you. I can really sympathize."

"You don't understand!"

"No argument there. How hard did you hit your head, anyway?"

"My head's okay, but I'm not. I have to get out of here before it's too late. They'll force me to have Botox injections. And exercise! It's barbaric!"

"Excuse me for not giving a shit."

"How did you get in here, anyway?" I kept a tight grip on his arm so he couldn't bolt. "It would take wings to get over that fence."

"Or a ladder," he said with a shrug. "Now if you—"

"What about the dogs?"

"Not a problem if you come prepared." He nonchalantly

pulled a small packet labeled "Canine Candy" from his pocket. "Besides, they're big puppies and not really vicious."

He moved to go, shaking off my arm. But I recovered quickly and grabbed hold of his wet shirt. "Please don't go. Help me get away."

"Leah, you are the last person to need my help. I can't believe you're even talking to me, instead of telling me to get lost and calling me stuff like 'dork' and 'geek.'"

"I've changed. I'm a different person." I moved directly in front of him and stared into his eyes. "Eli, look at me."

"Why?"

"Really look at me—deep into my eyes. I'm not who you think I am."

"Oh, really?" he said sarcastically. "So, who are you?"

"Amber Borden."

"Shut up!" He jumped back angrily.

"It's true!"

"You're—you're sick!" he sputtered.

"No, I'm not. I'm scared and I just want to go home. I'm Amber."

"Don't you ever say her name again!" He glared then abruptly turned to leave. "You think you're all that, but you're just a big fake. Amber is real."

"But I'm the real Amber!' I cried, flinging myself forward to block him. "Would Leah even talk to you? Would she care what you thought? Can't you see that this body isn't really me?"

"You're crazy."

"I'm not! Honest!" I was close to tears. "Let me explain … *Please!*"

"I don't know what kind of sick game you're playing, but save it for Chad."

"I don't want Chad. I want you."

"Hitting your head must have scrambled your brain."

"My head is okay, but my real body is in danger. I only look like Leah. Inside, I'm Amber."

"You have no right to talk about her—you didn't even know her." His face reddened. "But I was starting to and … well … just show some respect."

"You *are* talking to her. A squared plus B squared equals C squared. Would Leah know that?"

"No, but—"

"See, that proves I'm not Leah."

"Anyone can spout off math. Even you."

"I'm not the *me* you think I am." I pushed back long blonde hair and shivered as a cool wind brushed my skin. "We first met when I gave you and Chad a 'Hello Halsey' gift basket. I didn't get to know you then, not until Saturday at Jessica's party when you recognized me. Remember the dessert table and how you calculated how many candies were there?"

His eyes narrowed. "How did you know about that?"

"I was there!"

"No, you weren't. Jessica asked me where you were and I didn't know. No one knew you were sick until later."

"That was Leah—not me. I'm Amber. Really, I am."

"Stop talking crazy!"

"When we talked at Jessica's party, I was wearing my friend Dustin's baggy shirt." Before he could call me crazy again, I started talking fast, explaining about the car accident and seeing my grandmother but making a wrong turn at the Milky Way and suddenly becoming Leah.

"I know it sounds insane. Finding myself in this body—not me anymore—has been a horrible nightmare." I glanced down at my perky breasts, slim waist, and long, golden-tanned legs. "Please believe me."

"This is beyond weird," he murmured, but his tone was different now, almost compassionate. Sympathy for the crazy girl, I guessed.

"It's all true. My explanation is the only way it adds up."

"Oh?" he asked skeptically.

"Think back to Amber's accident and Leah's illness. Both happened the same day, but Leah was already in the hospital before you met me … I mean, Amber. Amber went directly home from the party where I—she—was hit by the mail truck. There's no way Amber could have told Leah—who was already in the hospital—about our candy sampling and conversation. The only one who knew that is Amber. Me."

"Interesting timeline," he admitted. "Too bizarre for belief and I should get the hell away from you."

"So why aren't you running?"

He squeezed more water from his shirt. "On the night my grandfather died, I dreamed he visited me. The next morning I found a penny on my desk dating 1929—the year Grandpa was born. Let me think for a minute."

"Hurry." I glanced at the house. "Angie will be back soon."

He nodded, but his gaze was distant as if calculating a complex equation. Finally he nodded, was quiet for a moment as if deep in thought, then turned to me with a solemn look. "Answer one question. Something that only Amber would know."

"Anything."

"What did Amber call Domino candy?"

"Zebra candy," I said without hesitating. "The black-and-white stripes reminded me of zebras—and they tasted sooo good. I kept eating them even after you left. Why did you leave so abruptly anyway? Did I say something wrong?"

"It wasn't you—it was me. I'm such a klutz, bumping and dropping stuff like always. Chad says I'm a walking disaster area. I figured you'd be glad I left."

"Actually I was disappointed ... I mean ... I was really liking you."

"You were?" He sounded surprised.

"Well ... yeah."

"Really? You didn't think I was a klutz?"

"I thought you were nice and I was hoping you'd ask for my email or phone number."

"Serious?"

"As serious as quantum physics. You have great taste in desserts."

"So do you ... you really are ..."

He stopped abruptly, the color draining from his face. Then he went still as stone. I wasn't sure he was even breathing. It was as if I'd shocked the life out of him. Then his expression changed. His frown curved up into a smile, and light sparked in his eyes. He took a step forward, reaching out with his right hand. All he said was, "Amber."

Then he offered his chocolate bar to me.

Crisp silver foil fell away as I tore into the candy bar. The scent of rich milky chocolate was an intoxicating high that only a true chocoholic could appreciate. I divided the candy into eight perfect cubes, and slipped a pure, one-eighth fraction of joy into my mouth.

"Ooooh," I moaned in bliss.

I'd died and was reborn with milk chocolate: melting sweet hope. The taste evoked memories of happier times, a connection to my real self. I gazed into Eli's face, over-whelmed by passion, love and desire. For chocolate.

When I finished off the remaining seven-eighths, I licked my lips. "Do you have more?" I eyed his pockets.

"Greedy girl," Eli said teasingly. "You didn't even offer to share."

"Don't judge me. I've had a bad week."

"That's an understatement."

"But chocolate makes everything seem better. I could eat a dozen of these and still want more."

He laughed. "You are so not Leah."

"Well, duh? What have I been trying to tell you?"

"It's uncanny and impossible."

"Yet it happened, and I have only one day to get to my real body. It's at Community Central Hospital. Will you help me get there?"

"On one condition," he told me seriously.

"What?"

He wagged a finger and gave me a stern look. "Repeat after me: I will not try to kill myself."

"Oh... that." I shrugged. "I only wanted to die a little so I could have an out-of-body visit with my grandmother. It wouldn't have been suicide, but more like a visit to see my grandmother. I knew she would guide me back to my real body if I could just talk with her. I never meant to kill myself."

"For a smart girl, you have some dumb ideas. You can't control life and death."

"Well... it might have worked."

"You're nuts."

"That's what Leah's family and her shrink think," I said with a sigh, gesturing back toward the house. "If I stay much longer, they'll lock me away in a mental institution. They've been keeping me a prisoner in my room, only letting me come out to exercise—which is the same as torture. The whole Montgomery family is messed up. Leah's mother drinks, her dictator-like father is beyond scary, and her little brother thinks he's a tough street kid. If I don't escape, I'm doomed. Let's get out of here."

"Uh..." Eli hesitated, looking at me with reddening cheeks. "You're not exactly dressed for the public."

"I'm slipping on my sandals now."

"Uh, that's good but not enough. I mean..." He cleared his throat and pointed. "Do you have something to cover up... uh... those."

I glanced down at my perky cleavage. They were kind of obvious and ripe for drawing attention. So I draped a towel around my shoulders and hurried after Eli as he went to the sprawling oak tree that towered up against the formidable concrete wall.

Jumping up, he grabbed a sturdy branch with both hands. Swinging out with the flexibility of a gymnast, he flipped up and over to straddle the branch. His grass-stained white sneakers dangled over my head as he called down, "Your turn."

"Yeah, right," I said with a dubious look at the branch, which seemed miles above my head. Gym was so not my favorite subject. Whenever I tried to climb a rope or rock wall, I usually stumbled and earned snorts of laughter from my classmates.

"You can do it," Eli encouraged. "I'll give you a hand up."

"You can't lift me. I'm too heavy."

"Heavy? At what—110 pounds?"

"I weigh more than ... oh yeah ... I guess not anymore."

"So stop stalling and give me your hand. I may not have muscles like Chad, but I'm stronger than I look." To prove this, he reached down and hoisted me up to the branch beside him.

Unfortunately we still had a long way to go.

The next step was even harder—climbing up to a higher branch. I didn't see any footholds and had to hug the tree, digging my fingers into the rough bark and pushing myself up with my rubber-soled sandals. Somehow I made it without losing my towel. Then I balanced precariously on a shockingly narrow branch, arms straight out like an acrobat, my knees slightly bent.

"Don't look down," Eli whispered.

"Uh ... too late." Damn, it was a long way down.

"Come on, Amber," he urged. "You can do this."

"I'm trying."

I focused ahead to the top of the wall, where I wanted to go. I crossed slowly over the arched branch that connected the tree to the wall. My legs shook, leaves rustled, and I was afraid the branch was going to snap in two or I'd slip and fall. But that didn't happen. Even more surprising, despite all the strenuous climbing, I wasn't even out of breath.

Lucky for exercise-hater me, Leah loved working out.

"Follow me down the ladder," Eli said as he scrambled down like he was part monkey.

I was about to climb down, too, until I heard frantic barking. Two dark creatures burst from around a corner. Guard dogs. German Shepherds with bristling gray-brown fur and large sharp teeth—aiming toward Eli.

"Watch out!" I shouted, but it was too late.

The dogs sprang at Eli and attacked—with doggy kisses. They slurped his face and wagged their tails.

"Hey, girls! Is this what you want?" Eli reached into his pocket and tossed them doggy treats. The treats must have tasted as good as chocolate because I would swear the dogs smiled as they chomped.

"Wow," I said from my perch high on the cement wall.

"What can I say?" Eli shrugged. "Dogs love me. If your father was kind to them, they'd love him too."

"Mr. Montgomery is not my father," I snapped. "And I happen to love dogs."

"Sorry, Amber. Momentary Leah lapse—won't happen again. Climb onto the ladder."

I hesitated on top of the wall, looking down at the far-away ground. The dogs didn't scare me but this body shivered at the sight of them, as if the cells retained some memory of Leah. I remembered Angie saying Leah didn't like dogs.

"Don't just stand there, Amber. Climb!" Eli called. "Grab the next rung and lower your foot. Yeah, that's right."

As I took another step down, there was the sharp slam of a door and a shout.

Angie had returned!

She waved her fist and shouted Leah's name. Her dark hair flew around her furious face as she ran after me. I didn't think she'd actually try to climb the tree to get over the wall, but I wasn't taking any chances and reached out for the ladder.

My legs wobbled. As I grabbed a metal rung to steady myself, the towel slipped off my shoulders. I wanted to grab for it but couldn't risk letting go of the ladder. Instead, I watched the towel sail down to the pool side of the fence, snagging on a branch and dangling like a pale ghost.

Holding tight to the ladder, I didn't want to let go. I flashed back to the cemetery, when I'd landed in the nettles. The ground here seemed so far away. My vision blurred. I imagined myself falling through the air like the towel…

Then Eli was climbing back up, offering me his hand.

"Thanks," I said, leaning close to Eli and liking it.

"You okay?" he asked.

"Very." And I meant this is many ways.

Eli may not have his brother's athletic physique, but his arms were strong and secure. My skin tingled and warmed where his fingers touched. He smiled at me. I smiled back. I could get used to this, I thought. His face flamed as he caught my gaze and he pulled away. I held onto his hand and squeezed to let him know I liked what was going on with us. We did some more smiling at each other. *More of this later*, I silently messaged with a small nod. He nodded back.

For the first time in days I soared with hope. Everything was going to work out. Soon I'd reunite with my real body, save Leah, and discover if I was just feeling gratitude for Eli or something real. And if it was real, Eli and I would be spending a lot more quality time together.

I had so much to live for.

19

Walking down the street in a skimpy, every-curve-revealed swimsuit was an attention grabber. Despite misconceptions about sunny California, bikinis before summer are not common. And a busty figure like Leah's was hard to ignore. When I passed a woman watering her garden, her hose trailed off and sprayed a car tire while her mouth puckered with disapproval.

On the next street, a paunchy, balding man backing his sports car out of a driveway smiled appreciatively. This was such a nice change from the puckered woman that I smiled back. But the smile died fast when we passed a house with a basketball hoop and some college-aged guys, shooting hoops, made obscene hoots and wolf whistles.

"Assholes. Ignore it," Eli said, glowering at them.

"This is all so weird," I admitted. "Should I be flattered or insulted?"

"There's nothing flattering about those guys disrespecting you. I don't know how Chad puts up with it. Guys are always that way with Leah."

"It's okay." But I wasn't sure. I walked faster, wrapping my arms around myself. I used to envy the pretty girls who attracted this kind of attention. But being reduced to a body, not a person, was embarrassing. Still, the analytical part of me flared with curiosity, so I asked, "When guys call out to Leah, how does she usually respond?"

"Different ways," Eli answered. "I've seen her flirt back and blow kisses. Once she lifted her top for a quick flash. But another time she freaked out and chased after the guys, swearing she was going to kill them. Chad and I had to pull her back, and a few minutes later she was smiling like nothing had happened."

So Leah had a dark side? Not a big surprise, considering her suicide attempt. Everything I'd learned about her so far proved she'd been troubled. I wanted to know more, to understand her motivations. It was like I watched from outside this body, studying and learning. For my own survival, I needed to discover Leah's secrets.

"Only one more block," Eli said apologetically. "Sorry I don't have a car to drive you around. Chad would never make you walk anywhere. He's had some kind of vehicle ever since he got his permit—several cars, and now a motorcycle. He thinks I'm nuts to refuse Dad's offer of a new car from his dealership."

"So why did you refuse?"

"I wanted to save up and earn my first car on my own. Not a handout my father chose for me. Besides, I knew the offer was a bribe to join the family business and work for him selling cars—which I'd hate. Still, a car would sure come in handy now."

"That's okay. I don't have my own car, either."

"Sure you do … oh, that's Leah's car."

"I would have borrowed it if Mr. Montgomery hadn't taken the keys."

"Well, I know where Dad keeps his keys, so we can borrow one of his cars. He always has a few extra in our garage. We're almost to my house."

"What if Chad's there?" I asked uneasily.

"Not today. The real Leah complained about his obsession with golf because he wouldn't miss a lesson even to go out with her."

"Oh, yeah. He's into golf."

Eli tensed. "I thought you didn't know Chad."

"I've met him, but I don't really know him," I said cautiously. Would Eli change his mind about me if he knew it was Chad who'd taken me to the hospital yesterday?

Being with Eli when I was supposed to be Chad's girlfriend could get seriously awkward. If I was with both of them together, I'd trip over my own lies. Besides, what if Chad wanted to kiss me again? I couldn't do that, not in front of Eli.

So I had to avoid Chad. Kissing him once had been nice in an experimental kind of way—something to file under the category of New Experiences. In the book *Grab*

Life with Both Hands, there was a list of a hundred things you should try at least once, and kissing someone you didn't love was in the top twenty—along with climbing a snowy mountain, bungee jumping off a bridge and spending a day at a nudist colony.

But now it was Eli I wanted to grab with both hands. And the idea of kissing someone as randomly as sampling free food at Costco seemed sleazy. When Eli and I kissed— if it ever happened—it would be for all the right reasons.

I glanced up and caught Eli gazing at me with an unfathomable expression. Was he thinking about me like I was thinking about him? Before I worked up the courage to ask, we arrived at his house.

It wasn't as huge as Leah's, but it was still about three times the size of my home.

Eli retrieved a small electronic remote, and the garage door lifted up. "This way," he said, glancing around furtively. We moved past two shadowy cars, but Eli told me that his parents' cars were gone. "All clear," he murmured

He led me through a side garage door into the kitchen, then down a hallway. We passed a family room with a huge, flat screen TV, an L-shaped leather sectional, and several recliners arranged around a fireplace. Eli gestured for me to follow him down another hallway.

"I'll find something you can wear," he said. "You can't go to a hospital like that."

"Thanks, it would be good to get out of this wet suit. But if the same security guard is on duty, I won't be able to get into the hospital no matter what I'm wearing. "

"If my sister still lived here, you could borrow something

of hers. But Sharayah moved into a dorm and doesn't even bother to visit anymore."

"Why not?" I asked, noticing his bitterness.

"She says she's too busy. But I think she's just being selfish. Oh well ... she's the one missing out."

And you miss her, I thought, with sad understanding. Missing the people you loved hurt even more than physical pain. I tried not to think of my own parents and family.

"Wait in my room," Eli said as he opened a black door painted with glittery stars. "I'll check Mom's closet."

His room had dark green walls, which were the background for movie posters, and a ceiling covered with glazed puzzles of fantasy scenes. Walking underneath the dragons, turreted castles, and flying wizards was like entering a fantasy world.

"Uh ... you're probably wondering about the puzzles," Eli added self-consciously. "Chad says they're childish. I guess I should take them down."

"Don't. I like them."

"Really? Thanks. I started putting them together with Sharayah when I was little. She lost interest, but I didn't." He gestured for me to sit down. "I'll be right back."

Except for the colorful puzzles, Eli's room was bland: a computer desk, a four-drawer bureau, shelves, an end table. There were no piles of dirty clothes or discarded shoes. His closet was partially open, and I saw shoes stacked in a metal rack. His shirts and pants hung in an orderly way, but cords and a karaoke microphone were tangled in a corner. Math, puzzles, and karaoke—Eli continued to surprise me.

I paced his room, pausing to study photographs arranged

on a wall. There was one of a bald baby (Eli?), another of Eli in a soccer uniform posing with a ball, and a formal framed portrait of his family. His father looked exactly like Chad, while Eli had his mother's kind eyes and lopsided smile. Sharayah was posed in the middle, with dark hair curling above her shoulders, intelligent blue eyes, and a shy smile. She didn't look wild or irresponsible, but the picture was from a few years ago. I wondered if I'd ever get the chance to meet her.

Lifting my gaze to the ceiling, I played a game of guessing the movies and books that matched the puzzles. Some were super easy, like the hobbit wearing a gold ring, the sword-wielding rider astride a sapphire blue dragon, and the Quidditch players flying on brooms. But I was still trying to guess the dark-haired girl riding an armored polar bear when Eli returned.

"Here." He tossed me a tie-dyed T-shirt, like something from the seventies, and a pair of flared jeans.

I started to say, "No way are these skinny jeans gonna fit," but then I remembered who I looked like. No surprise—the jeans not only fit, they were baggy.

"You can turn around now," I told Eli. "I'm decent."

"Words I never expected to hear from Leah's lips," he teased, then grew serious. "It's still so freaky how you look like her. We hate each other, so I avoid her."

"No avoiding allowed," I teased. "This may be Leah's body, but she's not home."

"Got it ... but what's the deal with Leah?" His forehead puckered. "Where is she?"

"I honestly don't know. But I'm hoping she's in my

body waiting for me to show up so we can switch back. That why I'm desperate to get to the hospital."

"I'll drive you there."

"Thanks, but it won't be easy." I explained to him about Dark Lifers. "The glowing-energy thing should have almost worn off me, but I don't want to get near that creepy security guard again. He's probably still guarding the elevators."

"I'll distract him." Eli sat in his computer chair and swiveled to face me. "And if you can't use the elevators, try the stairs."

"Good idea—but I'll still have to get past the nurses and into the room." I flipped Leah's long hair over my shoulder as I sighed. "It'll never work. I always have such high expectations, but then things never turn out like they should. I can't screw up again or it's all over."

"What do you mean?"

"My body will die. It's so hopeless, like I'm doomed to fail."

Instead of sympathy, Eli frowned at me. "Are you always this dramatic?"

"Well ... not *always*," I admitted. "I just get overly emotional sometimes. Sorry. One of Alyce's nicknames for me is a mix of drama and Amber: Dramber."

"That's too drab and very depressing. How about 'Amberama'?"

"I like that—and I know Alyce would, too." I sighed. "I miss her so much. And Dustin, too. They could come up with an amazing plan to get me into the hospital."

"Dustin Cole?"

"You know him?"

Eli nodded. "He's in my science class. Cool dude but terminally opinionated. He can't just listen in class, he gets in arguments with the teacher."

"That's Dustin all right." I smiled sadly. "When he has a strong opinion, you're gonna hear about it or read it online. He goes after anyone abusing power. When he puts his mind to a project, nothing can stop him."

"Sounds like the guy to help us. Should we visit him?"

"I can't... not looking like this."

"Yeah, you're so ugly," he joked.

"That's not what I mean. I know what Leah looks like. But this isn't me, and Dustin would never understand."

"Give the guy a chance. I believed you, didn't I? Show him who you really are and he'll believe you, too."

I bit my lip, considering this. As much as I longed to see Dustin, I was terrified about him seeing *me*. How could I face Dustin with *this* face? Alyce's nickname for him was "Dustspicious," because he distrusted everything until he had documented proof, video, or fingerprints. And it would take more proof than I could offer to convince him I was now residing in Leah Montgomery's body.

Miserably, I shook my head. "There isn't time to ask him or anyone else for help. Let's just figure out how to get into the hospital room. I have no idea how."

"I do."

"What?" I gave him a curious look.

"It's an extreme, risky idea." Eli tilted his head with a sudden change of expression. "But if you're up to the challenge, it might just work."

Then he told me to take off my clothes.

20

I weighed the percentages for and against Eli being crazy while I waited in his room. I deduced 32 to 68 percent odds that he had a good plan and a reasonable amount of sanity. He was an honor student, after all, not a pervert. So why did he loan me clothes, then tell me to take them off?

"Sorry I took so long," Eli said the moment he returned. "But I finally found this."

I eyed the bulging plastic bag in his hand. "And it is … what?"

"Your uniform."

"You've got to be kidding."

"I'm serious." He handed me the plastic bag. "A uniform is like an invisibility cloak."

I bit back a retort about him reading too many fantasy novels and instead opened the bag. Inside I found khaki slacks, a matching cap, and a button short-sleeved top. "This is a guy's uniform."

"That shouldn't matter. Try it on."

"Way too big," I said dubiously. "Like something a janitor would wear."

"Bingo. Only the official term is Maintenance Engineer. My Uncle Trey wore this uniform when he stayed with us after going bankrupt and losing his house. He's a lazy jerk, but still he's family, so Dad gave him a job. Uncle Trey complained he was allergic to dirt, and quit after one week. Last I heard he was living with his second ex-wife and still allergic to work. He left the uniform in the guest room."

"Once I put on the uniform, then what?"

"I drive you to the hospital and you breeze inside wearing your 'Get Into Hospital Free' uniform. People only see the uniform, not the person."

"Security Guard Karl won't be fooled."

"Leave him to me. You just get to the stairs."

"Okay," I nodded, hope rising again.

Leah, hold on a little longer, I thought, willing my thoughts to reach her wherever she was. *I'm on my way.*

What would have been a very long walk to the hospital took less than fifteen minutes in Eli's father's mint-green deluxe Camry.

When we stepped out of the car, I was so nervous I

didn't even notice I'd fastened the buttons on the uniform crooked. Fortunately, Eli did. Blushing, he pointed at my chest. I quickly redid the buttons.

"Thanks," I said, letting the simple word mean many things. Thanks for his friendship. Thanks for the help. But mostly thanks for believing me.

We agreed it was safest for Eli to go in first. I'd wait five minutes, then follow.

Before Eli left, he gave me a pep talk, describing his favorite box of chocolate, a very eclectic blend of nuts, creams and caramels, and how we'd share them once I was me again. With this image firmly fixed in my brain, I found a bench outside the hospital to sit on and waited.

Shifting uncomfortably on the bench, I worried that everyone who passed stared at my ugly, oversized uniform. The cap covered my hair and my forehead. The short sleeves hung like long sleeves and the pants legs had been folded short and stuck in place with duct tape. I ran my fingers idly over raised letters of the "Maintenance" insignia below my right shoulder. Eli said uniforms made people invisible. Please let no one notice me!

After it felt like five minutes had passed, I sucked in a breath and visualized myself as an ordinary janitor coming to work.

The automatic doors swished open at my approach. A woman and two men on their way out of the hospital passed without even glancing my way. Letting out my breath, I entered the crowded lobby, afraid to look for Security Guard Karl at the elevators. When I risked a peek,

I saw him deep in conversation with Eli. I couldn't hear what they were saying, but Karl seemed annoyed.

Walking swiftly, I bypassed the elevators and slipped into the stairwell.

Yes! I punched my fist into the air. I'd made it this far, now just up to Room 311. At least this time I knew where to go.

Almost there, I thought when I reached the third floor.

Peeking out the door, I checked until the hall was clear. Then I casually strolled out in the janitor's uniform. I sailed through the "Restricted Area" doors, holding my breath, afraid someone would shout "Imposter!"

But no one even noticed me. A nurse, sitting at a desk and absorbed in paperwork, barely glanced up. And a guy in green scrubs breezed by as if I were invisible. Eli was so right about the uniform; people just didn't notice janitors.

Until someone called out, "Hey, you!"

Heart stopped. Mouth dry. Oh, no! Not her!

It was the elderly nurse I'd run from yesterday.

"Janitor Gal, I'm talking to you," she snapped in a raspy tone.

I crouched, ready to run again.

"The garbage in Room 303 stinks. Would you take care of it?"

"Uh … garbage?" I repeated like a total idiot. I kept expecting her to recognize me and shout an alarm.

"Geez, don't they hire people with half a brain around here?" She threw up her age-spotted arms in disgust. "Just dump the garbage. What's your name, anyway?"

"Uh … Jessica Bradley," I lied. "I'll get the garbage right now."

With the nurse watching me, I had no choice but to go into Room 303.

Phew! The garbage did stink. One look inside the plastic-lined container and I nearly vomited—but obviously someone beat me to it. I offered kudos and sympathy to all the janitors in the world. I looked around the room, noting the two neatly made beds, one empty and the other occupied by someone with a snoring problem. Tiptoeing over to the door, I checked in the corridor. The bossy nurse was gone, and only a cheerful, chubby blonde nurse sat at a desk, engrossed in a phone conversation.

It was almost too easy to sneak out of the room.

I counted down room numbers: 371, 357, 332 …

My heart revved up as I neared Room 311.

I was almost there when I came to the waiting room I'd noticed yesterday. The door was propped open. The chairs were empty but two figures sat dejectedly on the couch—Alyce and Dustin!

My friends—here! I could hardly contain my emotions—thrilled, terrified, anxious, joyful. Shaking, I wrapped my arms around my shoulders to hold myself together.

They were only a few feet away.

Yet miles apart.

Dustin held his computer-phone in his hands, tapping out an email. I was so used to that sound of soft clicking and how his eyes glazed over, as if he were transporting on the sound waves with his messages. Was he creating another faux political website, revealing embarrassing facts about corrupt politicians? Or emailing mutual friends, telling them about my condition?

Alyce stared down at the sketch pad propped in her lap, her pencil stilled. With her long legs folded into her chair, only a glimpse of her sheer black tights visible under her baggy, midnight-black skirt, she seemed swallowed whole by misery. Her face paled with sadness—a stark contrast to her usual silver eye-glitter, kohl shadows, and shimmering ruby red lipstick. A trail of dried tears glistened down her hallowed cheeks.

More than anything, I wanted to rush over and smother them with hugs. I had so much to tell them—all of it totally unbelievable, which is why I just stood there, disappearing like a ghost of myself as the janitor cap slid low over my forehead.

There was a footstep behind me. A hand touched my shoulder.

I whirled around to find Eli. "Amber?" he whispered. "What is it?"

I pointed, my arm shaking. "They're here."

"Your friends," he guessed in a sympathetic tone that nearly broke down my resolve not to cry.

"We better go," I managed to say.

But as I spoke, Dustin looked up from the couch. His eyes widened. He set down his cell phone and stood, rubbing his chin thoughtfully.

"Hey, I know you," he said.

Was I imagining the recognition on his face? But how could he possibly recognize me in this body? Unless he had psychic powers or our friendship was even stronger than I thought. This was like a miracle! Would Alyce recognize me, too? I'd known her longer than Dustin, since first grade. Yet she just sat on the couch, staring with a look as blank as the sketchbook on her lap.

But Dustin moved forward a few steps, until we were a touch away.

Then he turned away from me.

Toward Eli.

"Eli Rockingham?" Dustin nodded in greeting. "From Halsey High?"

"Yeah. Hey, Dustin," Eli said, with a sideways glance at me.

"I thought I recognized you from science class."

"With Mr. Walberg."

"Yeah. You sit in the back and never say much."

"Who needs to with you in the class?" Eli joked. "You say enough for everyone else."

"True. Mr. Walberg needs someone like me to keep things interesting." Dustin paused, frowning. "So what brought you here?"

Me! I wanted to answer. But Dustin didn't glance my way, as if the uniform really did make me invisible. With my blonde hair pulled back and no makeup, Leah's best friends probably wouldn't recognize her.

I bent over a garbage can as if I really were a janitor and covertly watched Dustin. He was a mess. His hair was uncombed, his shirt was wrinkled as if he'd slept in it, and his socks were two different colors. Without me around to double-check his colors, he probably didn't even realize his mistake.

"I'm here to visit someone," Eli told Dustin.

"Hope it's not serious. A family member?" Dustin asked.

"Well … uh … not my family … a friend." Eli hesitated. I guessed he was composing a convincing lie. So I almost fell over when he admitted, "I came to see Amber Borden."

"Amber?" Dustin tilted his head, startled. "You know her?"

"I was just getting to," Eli said.

"Amber never mentioned you." Alyce came to stand supportively beside Dustin. Her narrowed black eyes challenged Eli to "prove it."

"We'd met years ago, when she welcomed my brother and me to school with a great basket. We got to talking at Jessica's party and found out we had a lot in common."

Alyce folded her arms across her chest. "Like what?"

"Chocolate and math."

"Her favorite things." Alyce's face crumpled and she leaned against Dustin. "She used to help me with my math homework. I'm horrible in math. And I don't care much for chocolate. But Amber and I were still closer than sisters. I–I miss her so much."

Dustin smoothed Alyce's black hair. "It's okay."

"No it's not!" Alyce sobbed. "You heard what the doctor said … what he's going to do to her body. Cut her up like some science experiment—I can't take it! Amber and I had all these plans, like getting into the same college, sharing a dorm room. Her little sisters will never get to know her now, and she won't be there for me when things at home make me crazy and I need to talk to her."

"I'm here for you," Dustin offered.

"It's not the same."

"It's hard for me, too." A tear trickled down Dustin's unshaven cheek. He glanced up at Eli. "I'll tell Amber's family you stopped by."

Eli frowned. "I really hoped to see her."

"Sorry, man. Only family and close friends are allowed in her room. But she's beyond knowing, anyway... and it'll be over—" His voice cracked. "I-It's hard to talk about. We're waiting for the doctor to come for us... to let us know..."

"Isn't she going to make it?"

Dustin gritted his teeth, still holding onto Alyce as he shook his head. "It doesn't look good."

Shocked by the finality in his voice, I stumbled and knocked over the garbage can. Trash spilled around my ankles and a soda can rolled toward the door.

Dustin moved quickly, coming over to pick up the can. "Here," he said.

"Thanks," I murmured. "This should go into recycling, though, not the trash."

Dustin started to turn, but then stared into my face. There was a flicker of curiosity—or maybe puzzlement—in his gaze. "Do I know you?" he asked.

I nodded, slipping the aluminum can into a pocket of the uniform.

His eyes widened, then knitted together. "You're... you're—"

"Yes, Dust?" I asked hopefully.

"Leah Montgomery!"

Wrong answer, I thought, disheartened.

"You can't possible work here," he said incredulously. "As a janitor?"

"I'm here because of Amber. Please, Dustin...Can't you see who I really am?"

"Everyone at Halsey knows who you are. I've seen you at lunch in that center table. It's cool you're...um...working here. Not what I'd expect...I mean...any job is great...even when your family is, like, rich." Put him in front of a crowd at a rally and he was confident, but in front of a pretty girl, he forgot how to talk.

"Relax, Dust," I told him. "There's no reason to be nervous with me."

"Who's nervous? I'm not."

"And I'm not Leah."

"We don't care if you're a janitor or queen of the universe." Alyce pushed between us, her sorrow shifted to anger. "This isn't about you—it's about my friend Amber. I don't believe you even know her."

"I know more about her than you think."

Alyce rolled her eyes. "I doubt you even know her favorite color."

"Jade green."

"What does she collect?"

"Self-help books. Piled all over the room and you make dumb jokes about how Amber needs a self-help book on how to organize self-help books."

Dustin looked impressed, but Alyce sneered. "Anyone could know. You're pathetic. Amber would have told me if you two were friends—she told me everything. Being here won't impress anyone, so why don't you leave? If you hadn't noticed, our best friend is ... is—" Her voice cracked.

Eli quickly moved beside me. "Leah cares. She's wearing that uniform because she's a hospital volunteer. I ran into her on my way to see Amber and found out she had the same idea."

Dustin tilted his head toward me. "Did you send flowers?"

"Flowers?" I blinked.

"The card said they were from Leah Montgomery, but I didn't believe it. The bouquet was so big the crystal vase didn't even fit on the tray, so it had to go on the floor."

The flowers I'd bought with Leah's credit card. "Yeah, I sent them. Her accident was so tragic. I couldn't feel worse if it had happened to me."

"I know she'd appreciate it if she could ..." Dustin looked away, wiping his eyes.

"Tell Mo ... um ... Amber's family that I send my condolences."

"Sure," Dustin said.

"And, Dust?" I added, a lump in my throat.

"Yeah, Leah?"

"I have to tell you something."

"What?"

I whispered into his ear, "Your socks are mixed shades of black."

Then I left the waiting room.

Eli and I moved silently down the hall. I didn't want to talk; I couldn't without crying. I kept thinking of Dustin and Alyce, wanting to turn around and explain everything to them. But getting to my body was more important.

We didn't encounter any nurses, doctors or security guards on the way to Room 311. It was like someone (Grammy Greta?) was guiding me back to myself.

"Go ahead," Eli urged. "I'll stay outside on watch."

"Are you sure you don't want to come with me?"

"No. This is your moment."

"And Leah's," I said solemnly.

When I pushed open Room 311's door, sterile whiteness enveloped me: white walls, ceiling, linoleum, window shades, and a plastic white curtain draped around a bed. The only vibrant colors came from a tray crowded with cards, potted plants, and bouquets. I recognized the largest bouquet—fragrant pink, yellow, and red roses blooming from a crystal vase. There was no sound except the drone and beeps from machine. I moved quietly toward the white curtain and drew it back. I could see the outline of a shape underneath white covers.

Alone with myself.

If there was oxygen in the room, I must have used it all up with the huge breath I sucked in as I stared at the motionless girl in the bed.

Me.

She was *me.*

Un-freaking-believable!

I'd never looked at myself full-on before, of course. A reflection or photo isn't even close to the same thing. Twins must know what it's like to look at your own face, but until now I'd never had that experience—and it was uber-weird.

My eyes were closed, and tubes crisscrossed over my pale face. My chest rose and fell rhythmically in tune with a beeping machine on the opposite wall. The real me looked so frail and vulnerable. I wanted to reach down and pat my hand, then tell my unconscious body things were going to be all right now that I was here.

And that's what I did.

Sitting on the edge of the bed, I touched my own hand, confused for a moment as to which hand was my own. Of course, it was obvious, since the girl in the bed wore a taped

IV on one wrist and a plastic identification bracelet. Also, there were faint red bumps like a rash on her arms. Nettles.

But where was Grammy's lucky rainbow bracelet? Had it been destroyed in the accident? Without it I couldn't send a message to Grammy about the Dark Lifer I'd met. Once I was myself again I'd find a way to contact her.

"We'll be okay," I said, giving my body's hand a squeeze.

And I meant Leah, too. I was beginning to understand that she wasn't a goddess to be worshipped from afar for her beauty and popularity, but a complex human with flaws and problems like everyone else. Maybe she needed so many friends at school because she had no real support at home. Her brother was a pint-sized brute, her mother had drinking issues, and her father was the worst. I still couldn't believe he'd slapped my butt. There was something weird about his relationship with his trophy daughter.

Fortunately, I wouldn't have to deal with creepy Mr. Montgomery much longer. With some heavenly luck, I should be myself again soon. I wasn't sure what would happen to Leah and prayed she'd be okay.

Glancing up at a wall clock, I realized I'd already been here for nearly ten minutes. Why hadn't the magic worked yet? I squeezed my hand and closed my eyes. Visualize changing bodies, I told myself.

Time for the big switcheroo.

If I could just be myself again, I vowed never to complain about all the things that used to annoy me: homework, washing dishes, taking out the garbage, babysitting instead of hanging with my friends, and inheriting Mom's potato thighs. I felt like Dorothy, clicking her heels together and wishing, "There's no place like home." Amen.

Dizzy sensations swept over me; I could visualize myself slipping into my real body. The tingly feeling grew stronger and a dull roar echoed in my head. Focus and concentrate. Bring on the magic.

Only when I looked at myself, nothing had changed.

"Switch back. Now!" I held Leah's and my hands tightly, squeezing hard, closing my eyes, and wanting this more than I'd wanted anything in my whole life.

I opened one eye. Then the other and...

Damn! Still in the wrong body.

Strangling cords of doubt and fear tangled around my heart. Why wasn't this working? It had to! Grandma? Cola? Where are you? Please make this happen!

A rustle of footsteps. I whirled to find the door swinging open.

"Oh! It's you." I sank back with relief. "Eli, don't scare me like that."

"Leah?" Eli eyed me uncertainly.

"No." I shook Leah's head sadly. "Still Amber."

"Well, change back already!"

"Don't you think I'm trying?"

"Try harder. I just spotted your parents and a doctor at the elevators."

"Mom! Dad! Are they headed here?"

"I think so. Do the switcheroo fast!"

"But the magic hasn't happened yet."

"We can't wait around or we'll get kicked out of the hospital. We have to go. We'll come back once they're gone.

Hurry!" Before I could object, he yanked me away from the hospital bed. I glanced longingly at my Amber body, then hurried after Eli.

We made it to the stairwell just in time.

Peeking out, I saw my parents' ashen faces, which nearly broke my heart.

Mom, Dad! I wanted to call out. *Everything is okay. I'm not in a coma—I'm right here! I'm still alive, just horribly misdirected!!*

I turned away so I wouldn't fling myself into their arms.

Instead, I huddled with Eli in the stairwell, lost in a baggy janitor's suit and misery.

Why hadn't I been able to switch back? I'd squeezed my own hand and felt nothing. No zap of magic. I must have needed more time with my body to trigger the magic. Next time I'd wait longer and call out to Grandma for help. She said she watched over me, so she could pull some heavenly strings.

"I have to get back to my body," I told Eli.

"Not yet," he said with a glance through the crack in the door. "Wait until the doctor and your parents leave."

I knew he was right—damn it. A janitor's uniform could only get me so far—especially one designed for a car dealership, not a hospital. But I assured myself this was just a delay. Soon I'd get another chance with my real body.

Until then, Eli and I waited in the cafeteria. I hadn't brought any money (obviously!), but Eli bought us both sandwiches and hot fudge sundaes. He ordered a super jumbo sundae for me. It was so sweet—Eli's thoughtfulness, not the ice cream—well, actually, the hot fudge was sinfully hot and rich and ooh-so-yummy.

For a while I forgot about all the scary stuff and just enjoyed being with Eli. While we ate, I studied him: his changing green-hazel eyes, his wavy hair that needed a trim, and his hesitant smile that was slightly crooked on one side. Not the model-handsome looks of his brother yet much nicer in so many ways. I bet he kissed nice, too.

We waited a long half hour before returning.

The door to Room 311 was closed. We watched a while, alert for any hint that medical staff or my family were still in the room. But it seemed quiet. Mom and Dad must have gone. This might be my last chance to get to my body.

I prayed the magic worked this time—and fast.

"You go in," Eli told me. "I'll wait out here."

"Thanks," I said softly, wanting to say so much more. Eli had believed the impossible, and gone out of his way to help a girl he hardly knew. Looking at him, I felt a rush of emotion—and without planning to, I leaned over and kissed him on the cheek.

He reddened and flashed a goofy smile. "Let's try that again when you're you."

"It's a date." I had a feeling my smile was goofy, too.

As I crossed the hall, I felt his gaze on me, watching my back like a real friend and making me feel like nothing could go wrong.

But when I reached the room, the door swung open from the inside and I nearly bumped into a grayed-haired doctor. Oops! I guess the room wasn't empty, after all.

"Excuse me." Dr. Lewin (according to his badge) frowned. "What are you doing here?"

"Uh…it's just some…" I glanced down at my janitor uniform. "Uh, routine maintenance."

"It'll have to wait," he told me disapprovingly.

"Why?"

"Because that poor girl's parents are sitting by her bedside…and they deserve their privacy." He glanced over his shoulder then back to me. "We're getting ready to take her to the operating room for organ harvesting."

"Harvesting?" My hand flew to my mouth. "But I heard she had one more day."

"Plans changed." The doctor sighed. "It's all over for Amber Borden."

22

Shock cast a numbing effect over me. I was hardly aware of Eli leading me downstairs to the main lobby. He sat me in a chair and said something about getting me water. I nodded, dazed and not caring.

It's all over for Amber Borden.

Over and over I heard these words.

An echo of finality; an epitaph of my life.

So lost in my misery, I didn't notice Security Guard Karl until he grabbed me. His fingers pressed hard, making me dizzy. I wanted to scream, but his touch drained my energy so I couldn't struggle or say anything. It was as if my energy was blood, and he was a vampire sucking my life away. But then he suddenly stopped at the sound of footsteps, and from a dim place far away I heard him call, "Here she is! I found Leah Montgomery!"

I looked up to see who he was talking to—and groaned.

Mr. Montgomery's hired police.

Caught again.

I said nothing on the drive back, sinking deep into depression. I'd failed at everything. I was a soul without a home; and the only identity left to claim was the one I'd inadvertently stolen. And to make things worse, I'd been grabbed before Eli returned with my glass of water. He probably thought I'd ditched him.

When I was escorted into the Montgomery house, Leah's father was waiting, rabid with threats. Blah, blah, blah. I tuned him out and didn't comprehend a word he said. All I could hear was the doctor announcing my death.

Angie smirked, a triumphant gleam in her black eyes, as she locked me back in my room. She pulled an envelope from her pocket and handed it to me. "Don't forget your love letter," she said in a snippy tone.

I stared blankly at the red envelope. From Chad, I remembered, but he seemed like someone from a distant past. Someone else's lifetime—not mine.

Then I tossed the letter in the garbage.

When Angie left after sealing me inside my luxurious tomb, I crawled under the silk covers and thought of my parents. Poor Mom and Dad. Grieving by my bedside, holding a lifeless hand, making funeral plans. Dustin and Alyce would be sad, too. And I thought of my body, far from perfect, yet more precious than I'd ever known, and doctors slicing it open on a treasure hunt for life-giving organs... until there was nothing left of Amber Borden.

Tears fell, and sobs racked my body. I didn't want to be here, trapped in this cage of skin. Now it was too late to save everything that mattered. Too late. No hope... no hope... Never again. Huddling under the covers while despair sucked me into a black void of nothingness, I let go what was left of my identity... releasing... escaping...

Time must have passed although I had no concept of it, only an awareness of noise. A door knob rattling, and footsteps. I could tell it was Angie by the thudding steps and the smell of food. I stayed huddled under the covers.

"Get up and eat," Angie ordered.

I shut out everything, hiding my face in the pillow.

"I set your dinner on the dresser." She sounded bored.

I said nothing.

"You should eat soon or the food will get cold."

Food was something to enjoy, to share with friends, a joyous noisy affair at the Borden household. My stomach ached with an emptiness impossible to fill. I burrowed deeper under the covers.

Angie snorted. "Starve, for all I care."

The door slammed. The lock clicked.

I ignored the tray, hating food because Amber loved it so much. I stared at the ceiling, imagining the faces of the people I loved in the swirls of paint. There seemed to be no end of my tears. Sleep was the only escape, so I drifted off somewhere so far away that no one could find me.

I was snatched from that peaceful place when Angie returned later.

"Get up so I can take you to the exercise room," she ordered.

I feigned sleep, ignoring her like a lump of nothing.

"You know the routine. Your father insists that you exercise." She tugged on my limp arm. "Get up this minute and come with me."

I sagged, limp and resistant.

"Leah Montgomery, get your lazy ass out of bed!"

Her fingers dug into my skin, and while I was aware of the pressure, I felt nothing.

Angie couldn't physically force me, so after shouting threats that were no more than a faint buzz in my ears, she left. I was aware of her fading footsteps and the door's sharp slam, but I didn't care. Not about anything or any-one, including me. What was the point anymore? I was gone, didn't exist, and was only alive by default. My real family was mourning me... so I was in mourning, too.

Through rivers of tears, I saw everything I'd lost. My parents, sisters, Dustin, Alyce... I should have told them all how much they meant to me when I had the chance. Instead of thanking my parents for the million things they did for me, I'd griped about not having nice enough clothes and complained about babysitting the triplets. I shouldn't have lost my temper whenever Cherry, Melonee, or Olive tore up my homework or played with their dirty diapers. I should have just hugged and kissed them. And I should have supported Dustin more in his campaigns and helped Alyce out whenever she went to photograph gravestones.

All that mattered were the people I loved.

Now they were lost to me.

Maybe forever.

Time must have passed, because the next time I awoke there was no light outside my window. Only darkness, mirroring what I felt inside. Memory and sadness came crashing back, and I started to sink back into an oblivious sleep. Except there was a noise, and a crack of light at the door.

"Leah, honey," a voice called out softly.

I peeked out from my covers to find Leah's mother entering my posh prison.

"Are you awake, Leah?"

Dumb question. I didn't answer. I wasn't Leah.

Mrs. Montgomery flipped on the overhead light, startling me with its aching brightness. I groaned and covered my eyes. Through my fingers, I watched her pull up a chair beside my bed and plop a large bag from Nordstrom on her lap. "Honey, I brought you a gift. Wait till you see it."

I turned over and pressed my face against the pillow. *I don't want to talk to anyone*, I thought. *I want my real mother, not a fake one. Just leave me alone.*

"Come on, baby girl. You'll love this."

The real Leah might have been tempted by the bribe of an expensive gift. But Amber-Leah didn't care.

"Please, Leah?" she persisted. "You're going to go wild when you see my gift. Open the bag and try them on.

They're the suede laced-ankle heels you admired. They'll look gorgeous on you."

Her voice droned on with the importance of a fly's buzz. I was aware that she was talking, but couldn't fathom the words. Why was Leah's mother offering me a gift? She didn't even know me. I didn't belong here. I thought of my real mother, as I'd seen her with Dad at the hospital, who was probably choosing caskets and contacting relatives.

I pulled the covers over me, inviting darkness.

A hand touched my face, forcing me into the light. "Don't cry, baby," Mrs. Montgomery soothed. "I'm here for you."

Shutting my eyes tight, shunning the light—and Leah's mother.

"Everyone is worried about you." She kept a firm hold on me so that I couldn't hide. "Your friends care about you, too. You've received many get-well cards and flowers. Jessica, Kat, Moniqua, Tristan, Chad and even Chad's brother have been calling for you. They all want to see you, but your father is too angry. Why do you set him off, Leah? That only makes things worse. He's furious that you disobeyed him. Why did you go back to that hospital?"

There was silence as she waited for the reply I refused to give. *Just leave me alone!* I wanted to shout. I tried to jerk away from her, but she kept a firm hold on me.

"It's all right if you don't talk," she continued in a patiently weary tone. "I'll do the talking and you can listen. I went to my second meeting. You'd be proud at how I spoke up. We don't use last names there, so I just introduced myself by my first name and admitted that drinking is a problem. I thought it would be so hard to say those words, yet I did it. And you know why? For you. So I can be strong enough to help you."

She paused, as if waiting for me to reply.

"I can't help you if you won't talk to me. Please, say something."

"Go away!" Flinging her off, I pressed my face against the pillow.

Then I slipped away into the silky darkness under the blankets, not knowing or caring when the room stilled with silence. I escaped into the sweet oblivion where no one could call me Leah.

I dreamed of my little sisters.

Cherry, Melonee, and Olive were playing hide and seek. They ran through the house, hiding from me. I looked under beds, behind furniture, and inside cabinets. I could hear them giggling, but I couldn't find them. I shouted their names, panicking. I tore apart cushions and ripped into walls. If I could find them, everything would be okay...

Fear gripped me so tight that I woke up. Breathing fast, clutching a blanket to my chest, I gazed into murky darkness, startled to be in a stranger's room.

Until I remembered.

Leah. Not Amber.

Hugging the tear-damp pillow, I rocked back and forth, too exhausted to even cry. I heard a rumbling and winced at the cramping in my stomach. Hunger pangs. Outside it was dark night. A glance at an illuminated clock showed it was not quite three in the morning.

My stomach growled louder, demanding food. But I

preferred to sleep and dream about my family. The concept of eating repulsed me. Yet the gnawing hunger was too severe to ignore. So I flipped on a bedside lamp and half-rolled, half-stumbled out of bed. Pushing back tangled blonde hair, I checked the room for a food tray. But there was nothing. Angie must have removed it when I was sleeping.

I prowled the room like a wild animal foraging for food, digging in drawers, the closet, and even under the bed. The only interesting thing I found was a journal with just a few pages of writing. I put it aside to read later—after I found something to eat. If this had been my room, I would have found my hidden stash of candy, granola bars, and red licorice. But Leah didn't even have a stick of gum.

Frustrated, I stomped my feet and kicked at the door.

The door flew open. Unlocked?

Stunned, I just stood there. Who had forgotten to shut and lock the door? Angie? Leah's mother?

Unexpected freedom should have thrilled me. Yet what did it matter? Being freed from Leah's room didn't free me from her body.

Still, I should take advantage of my freedom and do something like…

a) Find a phone and call someone for help (Who? I had no idea.)
b) Find Leah's car keys so I could escape. (But where?)
c) Find the kitchen and eat.

Since I had no idea who to call or where to escape to, I gave into my growling stomach and chose "c."

Twinkling night-lights guided me downstairs and into the spacious kitchen that I'd passed on my first escape attempt.

The kitchen was dark except for a soft glow from the far corner. As I drew closer, I saw that the glow came from the refrigerator door—which hung wide open.

On the floor squatted a small boy wearing only pajama bottoms.

"Hunter?" I exclaimed.

"Shssh!" He set down a bowl of cereal and glared up at me. "Do you want to wake up the whole house?"

"No." I lowered my voice. "What are you doing?"

"What does it look like?" He gestured toward his cereal. "Get lost."

"Forget it. I'm starving."

"I got here first. I was sent to my room after Dad's lawyer bailed me out. I didn't steal that much, just some dumb CDs, so I don't know what the big deal is."

I gave him a shocked look. "You were arrested?"

"Just a misdemeanor." He shoveled in a spoonful of Captain Crunch cereal. "Why is everyone freaking out?"

"Why steal, when you can afford anything you want?"

"I said it was no big deal. Just messing around with the guys." He shrugged. "Dad was laying into me, but then you showed up in even worse trouble. I was punished with no dinner, but he never said anything about breakfast."

I pointed to his bowl. "Any cereal left?"

Crunching noisily, he gestured toward a box on the counter beside a gallon of milk.

"Where are the bowls?"

"Where they always are." He shook his head like he thought I was nuts as he pointed to a cupboard above the microwave.

Stainless steel appliances, granite countertops and hanging brass pots gleamed throughout the kitchen. I tried three drawers before finding a spoon. Then I couldn't find any chairs. Those must be in the dining room, which could be miles away in such a humongous house.

My stomach growled approvingly as I poured cereal. I scooted down to the floor across from Hunter. Without his gangsta clothes and knife he seemed like a normal kid. We sat like that, chewing and swallowing. I started to talk, but then caught his hostile look and remembered that he hated me . . . well, Leah. I wasn't that crazy about him, either.

I downed two bowls of cereal and still felt hungry. So I opened the fridge and rummaged around for something else to eat. There were unrecognizable leftovers in plastic containers. I eyed them suspiciously. Ultimately I settled on an apple and packaged string cheese.

Sitting back down on the floor, I started to unwrap the string cheese when Hunter lunged for me. "No! Leah!" he shouted.

He snatched the cheese stick out of my hand, his bowl clattering to the floor and splashing milk and cereal every-where.

"What the hell?" I plucked cereal from my hair. "Are you insane?"

"Not me. You are!" He waved the cheese stick at me.

"You're the one stealing my food like a crazy person," I said with a tight hold on my apple, afraid he'd grab it next. "Why'd you do that? If you'd wanted cheese, you could have gotten your own."

"I didn't want the stupid cheese. I just didn't want to watch you die."

"Die? You're delusional."

"And you're allergic to cheese."

"I am?" I sank against a cabinet, shaking.

Cradling the apple in my lap, I stared at Leah's hands. I'd almost killed myself, again. Amber was already gone. I couldn't change that, and I had to take better care of the only body I had left. Despite everything, I wanted to live.

"I'm sorry, Hunter," I finally said. "Thank you."

"Whatever," he said roughly. "Clean up the mess."

Then he left the room.

I should probably have left, too. But I was still hungry.

After finishing the apple, then finding a bag of Oreos in the pantry and scarfing down half the bag, I cleaned up Hunter's spilled cereal and washed our dishes. Doing ordinary chores made me feel almost normal. If I blocked out the luxurious surroundings, I could even pretend I was back home.

My stomach was full but I still felt empty; there was a hole inside that only my family and friends could fill. So why didn't I just call them? I had the house to myself; no one except Hunter knew I was awake.

So what was stopping me?

Fear and love, I realized, as I glanced up at a wall phone

with illuminated buttons. My family and friends had suffered enough. Eventually I'd talk to them, but now was just too soon. It would only confuse and upset everyone more. I considered calling Eli—only I didn't know his number.

I had no one to turn to and no place to go.

So I returned to Leah's room.

And crawled back into the dark oblivion of sleep.

Sunlight stuck me in the face like a brutal assault.

"Rise and shine!" Angie said with cheerful venom as she opened blinds on each window. "I didn't bother bringing your breakfast because you won't bother eating it. I'm only here to pass on a message."

I hid my face in my pillow.

"Your father is waiting for you in the dining room."

I shut my eyes tight.

"You can't hide in here forever." Angie clicked her tongue. "But that's your problem. I've done my job."

Footsteps, and the door slammed. I listened for the sound of the lock, but there was none. Tugging my covers over my head, I disappeared into a dreamy void.

But my peace didn't last long.

Heavy footsteps thudded. Then the door burst open with such force that I jumped up in bed, clutching the covers to my chest.

Mr. Montgomery loomed in the doorway, his expression furious.

"Your tantrum ends now." He spoke with icy control. "Leah, we are going to talk. Privately."

Angie smirked behind him in the hall before he shut the door and stepped inside the room. I wanted to hide, but that wasn't an option. Trembling, I met Mr. Montgomery's narrowed gaze.

"Leah, was there any reason why you ignored my breakfast invitation?"

I tried to look away, but his compelling voice snared me.

"You missed a delicious breakfast. No one makes omelets like Luis." He actually smiled—way creepy. There was no hint of emotion or anger in his tone. He pulled a chair uncomfortably close to my bed. "So, what do you have to say for your childish behavior?"

I shook my head, not daring to utter a word.

"Leah, Leah," he said with a shake of his head. "You disappoint me."

Get used to it, I wanted to say. I avoided looking directly into his eyes. He was angry, so why didn't he act like it? His faux-friendly smile scared me.

For good reason, I soon discovered.

"Now you're going to tell me the truth." He leaned closer. "Don't lie. I want to know how you escaped from the pool yard. Did someone help you?"

I reached for my pillow to hide my face, but his steel-like arm snaked out and grabbed the pillow. He tossed it to the floor. "No more hiding in bed," he said firmly. "I want to know exactly what happened yesterday."

"It's not important," I murmured, relieved that he didn't seem to know about Eli. We must have been out of range of the surveillance cameras.

"You will tell me—or else." Mr. Montgomery glared at me with a controlled rage.

"There's nothing to tell."

His head tilted, as if confused by my behavior. I doubted many people dared to stand up to him, especially his own daughter. But threats meant nothing to me. Drained of hope or emotion, I just didn't care. I'd already lost everything that mattered. I only wanted to numb myself back to sleep.

"If that's how you want to play, that's your choice. A very unwise choice," he added ominously. "I've brought some light reading for you."

I lifted my brows, only a little curious when he withdrew a paper from his pocket and shoved it into my hand.

The pamphlet showed a sprawling, rustic collection of buildings on spacious green grounds ringed with majestic oaks. A caption read:

DeHaven Resort: A restful place for healing body, mind and spirit.

A description of mental health treatments, in poetic language, masked the harsh reality of the "resort." There were medical terms like "somatic therapies," "electric shock," and "psychosurgery." I understood too well what this was all about, and why Mr. Montgomery was showing me the brochure. DeHaven was the punishment place for misbehaving teens, with prison walls more formidable than those surrounding the Montgomery estate.

"They have a room available for your immediate occupancy," Mr. Montgomery added as I read the brochure.

"But I'm not sick."

"Mental illness manifests in subtle forms. I've spoken with the director, and she's quite sympathetic to our situation—especially when I described your depression."

"I am not depressed!"

"How else can you explain your despondent behavior? Relentless crying, sleeping all day, not eating, inability to function normally." He pressed his fingers together: smooth, pale fingers with shiny nails as if he regularly had manicures. "An extreme case of clinical depression."

I tossed the pamphlet at him. "I won't go."

"That is not your decision to make. You're a minor until your eighteenth birthday and as your concerned father, I decide whether you go back to school or are committed to the DeHaven Resort. It will be a difficult decision, but I'll do what is necessary." He smiled. "But I'm willing to discuss alternatives."

I dug my fingers into the covers, struggling not to break down. The threat of being locked in a place for crazies was terrifying. I had no doubt Mr. Montgomery would do it.

"What do you want?" I asked, defeated.

His smile widened, chilling me. "First of all, you will eat your meals."

I hesitated, then nodded.

"You will resume your exercise regime."

Exercise? Every day? Horrors! But exercise was better than a straitjacket and electric shock treatment.

Reluctantly, I nodded.

"Also, you will accompany me to the banquet on Saturday evening."

Another nod.

"Then, on Monday morning, you will return to school."

"School? But I can't!" Not when I looked like Leah. It would never work. Her friends would have expectations of me that I wouldn't live up to. My friends would ignore me. And Chad would want to kiss me when I'd rather kiss his brother. Awkward!

"You will attend school," Mr. Montgomery insisted. "I'm sure you miss your friends and, to show you what a nice guy I am, I'll bend my rules and allow you to see one of your friends today. Jessica Bradley is a delightful girl and you know how much I respect her father. I've spoken to Jessica and she's been collecting your homework assignments. She'll be here with them, soon."

He glanced down at the DeHaven pamphlet, waiting for me to respond.

I gulped, eyes glued to the pamphlet, weighing my options:

a) Refuse, and risk shock therapy at DeHaven
b) Agree, and live a privileged life as Leah

This should be an easy decision, yet it wasn't. Giving up my real identity and hiding the truth was like selling my soul to the devil.

But the devil in front of me held all the power.

One day I will have power, I thought.

But not today.

"Leah!" Jessica squealed as she entered the room and dumped a backpack on the floor. Her shiny black hair shone with silver-blonde weaves, and she wore a mid-length silky skirt and a sheer, plunging V-necked blouse.

She hugged me. Prompted by thoughts of DeHaven, I hugged her back.

"You're so pale!" Jessica stood back to survey me. "Oh my poor Leah, have you been miserable?"

"It hasn't exactly been a night at a prom," I said wryly.

"Of course not—the prom isn't for another month." Her tone was all serious. Didn't she have a sense of humor? "But by then you'll be back to your usual self."

"I'm not my usual self."

"I know what you mean—just look at your hair." She grimaced. "But I'm here now, and you know how fabulous I am at giving makeovers. I'm considering a major in cosmetology and opening my own day spa. Sit back and relax while I work my magic. I remember where you keep your makeup case."

Before I could reply, she rushed into the bathroom and came out carrying a blow dryer, brushes, and a black leather case.

"I really don't need any—" I started to say.

"Leah, let me do my thing, okay? You can thank me

afterwards when you see how gorgeous you look. Now sit up straight and lift up your face."

Who had the energy to argue? Not me.

I used to think getting a makeover would be an insightful "new experience" for an aspiring entertainment agent … not that those ambitions mattered anymore.

Did Leah have any ambitions? I wondered about this as Jessica smeared goop on my face. Leah could go to any college she wanted or even start her own business. But what sort of business would interest her? There weren't any clues in her room. No knickknacks, bookshelves, or a hobby like Eli's puzzles. There weren't personal photos displayed, either. It was as if her room came ready-made from a home magazine.

Jessica rubbed lotions into my skin with circular movements, plucked hairs, swept on blush and eye shadow, and painted my lips with cherry-flavored gloss.

"Now, for your hair," Jessica said with a mad-scientist's delight as she tugged and yanked and raked a brush through Leah's long hair. I'd always longed for straight hair, but when Jessica twirled a curling brush and blasted my hair with the blow dryer, I missed my untamable brown curls.

I swallowed my complaints. This was supposed to be fun, after all.

"Now, don't you look beautiful?" Jessica shoved a mirror into my hands.

Holding the mirror, I looked into Leah's face: soft blush highlights, curved cheekbones, creamy unblemished skin, bow-shaped lips, and wide blue eyes with only a shadow of the hidden person inside. Blonde hair spiked up in a crown, then cascaded down in flowing waves—a wicked blend of beauty and attitude.

"Uh ... thanks," I said, since it was expected.

"You're welcome." She grabbed some makeup-smeared tissues and bent over to toss them in the garbage, then gave a little gasp. "Hey, I recognize Chad's writing—what's his letter doing in the garbage?"

"Um ... I guess I dropped it there by accident."

"Lucky I noticed!" She scooped out the letter.

I grimaced at the red envelope. "It's nothing."

"'Nothing' looks an awful lot like a love letter—and you didn't even open it," she said with reproach. "If it were mine, I would have read it a zillion times. Then I'd frame it and put it on my wall. You're so lucky to have such a cool boyfriend."

I didn't feel lucky. I didn't feel much of anything.

"Mind if I read it?" Jessica asked.

"Whatever."

She took this as a "yes" and slit the letter open with her long purple fingernail. Her lips pursed as she read a single sheet of white paper. She murmured, "Oooh." Then she folded the letter back up and plopped down beside me on the bed.

"I repeat," she said with a dreamy sigh, "you are so lucky to have Chad. I wish I had such a hot romantic guy. Are you sure you don't want to read his letter?"

"Maybe later."

Jessica reached out to touch my hand sympathetically.

"What's wrong, Leah? You sound kind of down. How are you feeling?"

"I'm better ... I guess ... just tired."

"So lean back and rest. Can I get you anything?"

I shook my head, wishing she'd leave so I could go back to sleep.

"I've been freaking since I heard you were in the hospital. I begged to visit you, but they said you might be contagious. Your father said it was some kind of brain flu. I never even heard of anything like that. Did your doctor explain about how you got it?"

My head hurt trying to keep up with her conversation. "The doctor didn't tell me anything." Except that I was delusional. "I'm definitely *not* contagious. But I don't remember much about being ... uh ... sick. I've been sleeping a lot."

"Your father said you're going to school on Monday."

"Yeah." Against my will.

"Cool! School has been dull without you—except for the tragedy about poor Amber."

"Amber Borden?"

"You know her?" Jessica wrinkled her forehead.

"Um ... I heard about her accident."

"Who hasn't? It's been all over the news—'Mail Truck Goes Postal, Runs Down Local Girl.' Did you know Amber came to my party? Oh ... I guess you wouldn't, since that's when you got sick. Anyway, I was sure you'd think I was a dope for inviting her, but she begged to help with the food-drive fundraiser and I couldn't refuse. Big mistake! She didn't fit in and it was all kinds of awful. If I'd just asked her to stay longer, not let her go off so angry, she wouldn't have gotten into that accident. I feel so guilty."

You should! I thought. For all the vicious things you and your friends said about me at the party.

"Oh, well." Jessica let out a deep breath, then brightened. "Here's your homework. I went around to all your classes and got everything." Opening the backpack she'd brought, she handed me a folder with "Leah Montgomery" printed on a small label.

I groaned, dreading the prospect of returning to school. I wouldn't even be able to attend my own classes, and had no clue about Leah's schedule.

"Here. It's all taken care of." Jessica winked as she handed me the papers.

"What is?" I flipped open the folder and saw typed pages with Leah's name printed across the top. Essays written and math problems calculated. "You did all my work?"

"Not me." She giggled. "You know the arrangement."

"I do?"

"Rebecka did a great job. Check out the history essay— she got your handwriting down so well it would fool me."

"Rebecka Zefron? That short girl with the—" I stopped myself. Rebecka had a slight problem with facial hair. "The girl who sits at your table?"

"Sits at *our* table," Jessica corrected. "A small price to pay for good grades. And I've given her the name of a good electrologist to get rid of her mustache."

It started adding up. Leah might sweat while exercising,

but not over ordinary responsibilities like homework. Why do the hard work if you could pay someone else to do it for you? I was disgusted—and impressed. Leah was taking advantage of her opportunities, and delegating duties just like my book *Leaders on Board* advised. Still, cheating was dishonest, and didn't feel right.

The math homework wasn't right, either.

"Look." I pointed. "Problems two and five are wrong."

She squinted as if she needed glasses. "They look fine to me."

"The results are completely off. Doesn't Rebecka know anything about math?"

"As if you do?" she scoffed.

"The errors are so obvious."

"Not to me." She tilted her head, studying me. "Leah, you're acting ... odd."

"What's wrong with caring about my homework?"

"It's more than that. Something is off with you, I don't know what exactly. When you talk, it's like you're acting in a play and not being natural. And then there's my hair." Her mouth puckered into a pout. "I've been waiting and waiting and still you haven't said one thing about my new extensions."

"Uh ... your hair looks nice."

"Nice? Is that all you can say? And since when do you call anything nice?"

"It's really pretty."

She snorted with disgust. "I have the weirdest feeling

I'm talking with a stranger. Chad warned me you were different, but I didn't believe him—until now."

What a tempting chance to explain my real identity. But I knew she wouldn't go for it. And what if she told Mr. Montgomery I was crazy? He'd ship me off to DeHaven faster than I could calculate the square root of pi.

I carefully considered what I knew about Jessica: how it was important to her to be liked and have others admire and respect her. She tried to be a good person, but she was easily influenced by her friends. She possessed a soft heart—and soft hearts could be manipulated.

All I had to do was think of my parents, sisters, and friends to bring on my tears. I wasn't faking, just drawing on my very real pain. Immediately Jessica was by my side, wrapping her arms around me.

"Everything is so confusing," I sobbed.

"Oh Leah, I'm sorry. You've had a rough time and I haven't made it any better. Yell or throw something at me—I deserve it for being a horrid friend. If your homework is wrong, I'll ask Rebecka to do it over."

"No, it's okay." I'll fix it myself later, I thought.

"Well, you let me know if you need anything."

She really meant it, and I was glad that Leah had such a good friend.

Except that Leah was gone and all that was left was ... me.

Realization slammed like a fist into my gut.

I was Leah Montgomery—for the rest of my life. At school Jessica was *my* best friend. She'd hang out with me and we'd sit with Moniqua, Kat, Tristan and other popularity-plus friends. Classmates would admire and envy us. Some—like Rebecka—would even pay for the privilege of being with us.

This was my reality. It was time I accepted my fate.

Amber Borden was dead and gone forever.

Leah Montgomery lived.

24

Jessica rambled on about school and friends and shared memories I didn't share. Her presence filled my room, overwhelmingly, giving me too much to think about. I craved to be alone but sweet, sincere, determined Jessica showed no interest in leaving.

When Jessica found the gift bag Mrs. Montgomery had left, she squealed in ecstasy over the suede laced-ankle heels. She said I had to go out to show off my new shoes. Then she swept through my closet like a fashion cyclone, searching for a matching outfit and accessories. Her clashing opinions about styles made me dizzy. Short was in but mini was out; white was the new black yet black never went out of style; and low-waist jeans were tacky unless accompanied by a sexy, low-back tattoo.

Finally, I told her bluntly that I needed to sleep.

"I'll go—if you promise to come to my house tonight for a fundraising meeting."

"You can't be serious. I only got out of the hospital a few days ago."

"So it's time you had some fun—and show off your fabulous new shoes. It'll just be our group and afterwards Mom's serving a yummy Hawaiian barbeque dinner. It'll be so much fun—and even more with you there. Come on, Leah, please, please, please say you'll go!"

"Tonight?" I laughed bitterly. "My father will never let me out of here."

"If your father agrees, you'll go?"

I nodded, positive his answer would be a stern "no."

"Great." She lifted her head confidently. "I'll handle your father."

Jessica hurried out of the room and returned less than ten minutes later—*smiling.* Her powers of persuasion were phenomenal. If she wrote a book on the topic, it would be an immediate bestseller—and I'd probably read it.

Once she'd left, I slapped my forehead. "Stupid! Stupid! What have I done?"

I wasn't ready to hang out with Jessica and her backstabbing friends. They knew more about Leah than I did—which could be humiliating. And considering how badly my first Jessica party had turned out, I was in no hurry to repeat the mistake.

Still, I couldn't hide in this room forever. Eventually, I'd have to face Leah's crowd. I'd be a jumble of nerves, expecting to be called out as a fraud. But how would they know? I certainly wasn't about to tell them.

Since I looked like Leah, for my own survival I'd have to learn to act like her.

Beginning with the daily schedule Angie had given me.

Leah liked exercise.

I could learn to like it, too.

With this resolve, I didn't complain as Angie led me down to the pool to swim laps. She must have worried I'd escape again, because she kept a sharp eye on me. Not being a skilled swimmer, I doggie paddled and floated on my back. The heated water cocooned me against chilly breezes. My mind wandered and my body slipped into auto-pilot, until to my surprise I found myself slicing through the water with powerful strokes. Hey, I was really swimming. Cool.

Next on the schedule: one-hour workout in the gym.

I'd heard the wealthy people had complete gym facilities in their homes, but I'd had never been in one until now. There were two treadmills, a computerized stationary bike, a stepper, weights, and elliptical equipment. I spent an hour trying out the different machines. It wasn't pretty. I groaned, sobbed, and sweat. But instead of the expected aching muscles, I had this incredible mental rush, like I'd climbed a mountain or soared into air from a bungee. This body thrived on exercise.

All that thriving made me hungry.

Lunch was served in the dining room. I was the only one at the table since Mrs. Montgomery had taken Hunter to consult with his lawyer, Mr. Montgomery was at his office, and Warden Angie was who-knew-where-and-who-cared off running errands. Only Angie's husband Luis remained to serve me.

A chubby and fuzzy-bearded teddy-bear, Luis moved and spoke in a relaxed, hippie-like way. He dished up food so fabulous he could have been a chef in a five-star restaurant. I could tell he didn't like me, but that didn't stop him from gossiping about his passion—soap operas. I knew a fair amount about this topic myself, thanks to my neighbor Dilly, who considered it her duty to fill me in on all the drama of *All My Children*, *General Hospital*, and *The Young and the Restless*.

I didn't interrupt Luis as he talked—except to ask for more food. He gasped (I guessed Leah didn't eat much), then he rushed into the kitchen and returned with more creamy homemade clam chowder, honeyed corn bread, and fresh salmon fried in a spicy batter. It was the best meal I'd had since landing in the wrong body.

But then Angie returned and spoiled everything. She snapped at Luis to get back to work. He smiled at me conspiratorially, then collected the dirty dishes and hustled to the kitchen.

I had no other place to go except my room. Sinking onto the bed, I stared up at the ceiling. I couldn't sleep, or even cry anymore. How was I going to pass empty minutes without a computer, TV, or anything to read except some fashion magazines? I considered searching Mr. Montgomery's office library for something to read, but didn't want to go into that formidable room again.

Boredom swallowed me whole and gnawed...until I remembered the journal.

I dug it out from under the bed (dumb hiding place!) and settled myself in a chair by the window. I hoped for intimate diary passages as juicy as Luis' soap operas. But a quick flip of the book showed mostly empty pages, and only some brief writing on the first few pages—not typical entries, either.

Page One: A scribbled red heart with Chad's name written inside—like something a ten-year-old with her first crush would draw.

Page Two: Jagged pieces of a heart, ripped apart. Instead of Chad's name there were ugly slashes of black Xs.

Trouble in Love City?

There was only one more page, and it contained just six scrawled lines:

They called me a slut
So I slept around.
She called me a bitch
So I became one.
He said he owned me
So I lost my soul.

I reread the lines, quaking inside with the certainty that Leah was writing about herself. Had these been her last thoughts before taking the pills? She seemed so unlike the confident leader I'd admired at school, breezing through the halls with her entourage, smiling and waving at friends. Was that all an act? What was really going on with her? The line about her sleeping around bothered me the most.

What had this body I now inhabited experienced?

If only I could have saved her, somehow. Now I was afraid she was gone. Not trapped in my real body, as I'd first thought, but banished to a dark place for suicide victims. I'd survived because of her loss—it didn't seem fair. But what Leah had written in her journal wasn't fair, either. Instead of accepting responsibility for her actions, she blamed the unknown "They," She," and "He."

I couldn't help getting hit by a truck, but Leah sure could have stopped herself from swallowing pills. Maybe I still would have gotten lost on the way to my own body. Maybe I would have ended up in a completely different body or no body at all. I had no way of knowing what might have happened to me. But if Leah had held on longer, if she'd believed in herself, I know what would have happened to her.

She'd still be alive.

Aside from being cook, gardener and handyman, Luis also acted as chauffeur.

When he dropped me off at Jessica's mini-mansion, I clutched my beaded handbag tightly, swallowed hard, and shoved everything "Amber" from my mind.

"Leah, it's so lovely to see you!" Mrs. Bradley, Jessica's elegant, dark-haired mother, enveloped me in a hug. Her hands sparkled with ornate gold, diamond, and sapphire rings—middle-aged versions of Jessica's ring-covered hands.

I murmured "Hello" in my most polite tone, then followed her into a vast room of windows showcasing a gleaming piano. In another corner, leather chairs and a couch were arranged around a glass-topped coffee table. A familiar trio sat on the couch.

"Leah!" Kat and Moniqua squealed.

"Leah," Chad said in completely different tone: husky, with intimate undertones. He crossed the room, pulling me into an embrace. "I know it's only been a few days but it's like I haven't seen you for months. I've been crazy trying to get in touch with you. Your damn father gave orders not to accept my calls. You know what I miss most?"

When his hands wandered up from my waist I stiffened. "Not now, Chad."

"Come on, Leah." He brushed his fingers across my hair. "Don't be mad. I never would have left you at the hospital if I didn't have to."

"Oh, you had to?" I asked sarcastically. "I go back to the car and instead of finding you in it, there's a police officer."

"Sorry, but I have some unpaid traffic tickets and I'd have been screwed if that officer ran my license. Still, I felt bad about leaving you." He didn't sound very sorry.

"Of course, you had to ditch me," I said with heavy irony.

"I knew you'd understand."

"More than you realize."

The young, dark-haired maid I remembered from my last visit came in carrying iced tea. Although I didn't know her, I felt a kinship; both of us were forced into roles that masked our real personalities. Her dark eyes shone like someone who laughed easily when she wasn't working. I would have liked to follow her out of the room and hang out. Instead, I sat in a leather chair, avoiding Chad.

Jessica propped a laptop on her knees, clicking her keyboard with one hand while sipping tea with the other. "Meeting starts now. Thanks for coming, everyone." She gave me a warm smile. "Especially Leah. Welcome back."

"Yay, Leah." Kat applauded. "I wouldn't even know you'd been sick if I, well, didn't know you'd been sick. You look fabulous."

"Ain't that the truth?" Moniqua added with a rattle of her beaded braids. "Kat actually thought brain fever would make your hair fall out. We downloaded some sites for wigs. But she was wrong as usual."

"I didn't say for sure, just that I heard it could happen," Kat explained.

"She read it off the internet. Probably one of those fake medical sites."

"Whatever." Kat jabbed Moniqua with her pointed black shoe. "All that matters is having Leah back with us, looking as gorgeous as ever."

When they talked around me, I felt more like furniture than part of this conversation.

"Can we get on with this meeting?" Chad complained, moving possessively closer to me. "Leah and I want to have time to go someplace alone ... if you know what I mean."

"Maybe none of us care what you mean." Jessica scowled at Chad. "Can you at least pretend to take this meeting seriously? You're only here because of Leah, but the rest of us care about starving people who depend on our fundraisers."

"I care." He flashed a cocky smile.

"Then show it," she snapped. "We only have one day to come up with a fundraiser. The principal has offered us a wonderful opportunity to use the auditorium this Friday, after school."

"In three days?" Moniqua exclaimed. "You've got to be joking. No way can we plan anything that soon."

"Did I say it would be easy? No, I did not. That's why it was so urgent we meet tonight. We need to come up with something amazing enough to get the whole school excited. Any suggestions?"

"Leah could ask her father to bring in one of his bands," Moniqua suggested.

"Cool!" Kat clapped. "A concert for the poor."

I cringed, because I couldn't imagine asking Mr. Montgomery for anything. Fortunately, Jessica was more realistic. She pointed out that with spring break coming up there wasn't time for a big music event. "What we need is something like a spontaneous rally, where everyone shows up to donate money."

"Or bags of food," Chad said.

"Exactly!" Jessica flashed him a wide smile. "But if we want to inspire kids to join in, we need to keep it simple. How about a canned-food drive?"

Everyone was nodding, so I did, too. At Thanksgiving last year, Alyce and I had volunteered at a homeless shelter. I'd gotten this emotional rush, and realized that I liked helping people. Jessica seemed genuine about her project, too. But what about Leah? Was she motivated by a big heart or a big ego?

I'd probably never know.

The canned-food drive got a unanimous vote. But no one could think of a fun event to bring in a crowd. "Hardly anyone will stay after school just to donate food," Jessica added. "What should we do?"

Moniqua wanted a have a dance-a-thon; Kat thought a game like Bingo might be fun; and Chad offered to invite a famous pro-golfer pal to sign autographs. No one asked me for any suggestions, so I sat quietly, listening.

After a while, Mrs. Bradley came in wearing a flowing flowered skirt and a lei. "The Hawaiian barbeque is ready," she announced. Tangy and sweet aromas swirled deliciously in from the kitchen. "But go ahead and finish your meeting. Everything is being kept warm in heated dishes, so no rush. When you're ready, join me in the sun room."

"Smells great," Chad said, smacking his lips appreciatively.

"Nothing fancy tonight, simply casual buffet." Mrs. Bradley reached up to tuck a white blossom behind her ears. "I hope you don't mind serving yourselves. The little boys can be so noisy, so I'm letting them eat in the playroom with their nanny."

"Thanks, Mom," Jessica said.

"How old are your brothers now?" Moniqua asked. "I just love little kids."

"Three and five, and they're adorable little monsters," Jessica said fondly. "But I'm glad they won't eat with us—they love having food fights and I don't think any of us wants to wear more food than we eat."

I was the only one who didn't laugh. My little sisters

loved food fights, too. Cherry, Melonee, and Olive always giggled hysterically from their high chairs when they tossed food at each other. I used to get mad, but now I'd give anything to hug them—even if it meant getting splattered with spaghetti and green beans.

"Returning to our agenda." Jessica tapped the end of her pen against the coffee table. "Any more ideas?"

The others shook their heads while I continued to be silent, wondering if this was usual for Leah. I'd expected her to be the take-charge type, but instead that role seemed to fall to Jessica. Still, I did have some ideas. I thought of the list I'd prepared before the car accident, which was full of charity-event ideas, the names of local businesses that frequently donated to good causes, and raffle items that parents, teachers, and students couldn't resist.

Should I stay quiet, as everyone seemed to expect? The more I talked, the more chance there was of making a mistake and saying something totally un-Leah. Still, good ideas were a shame to waste. Biting my lower lip, I slowly raised my hand.

"Yes, Leah?" Jessica said. "What's on your mind?"

"I think we should ... um ... have a raffle."

"We don't have enough time to come up with fantabulous prizes." Jessica flipped a page of her notebook and scratched something out. "I just don't see it as possible."

"But it is possible," I continued in a louder voice. "I know what to do."

"You do? Really?" Jessica sat the notebook down, staring with clear surprise.

She wasn't the only one staring at me. The others

watched curiously, puzzled even, as if this was a new behavior for Leah. My heart jumped. Oops. If only I could swallow my words. I'd never felt so out of my element—not even that other time at Jessica's. At least for a while, there, I'd had Eli and all that chocolate. But this was like acting on stage—without knowing any of my lines—in front of a tough audience. I was sure I was saying everything wrong.

Then I was saved from answering—by the maid.

The dark-haired girl appeared in the doorway. "Excuse me," she told Jessica.

"Yes, Violet? What is it?"

"You have another guest." She moved aside, gesturing for someone behind her to step forward.

No way! I thought. My hand flew to my mouth, cutting off my gasp.

Chad stood and demanded, "Who the hell invited you?"

It was Eli.

A marathon of emotions raced through my head as I stared at Eli—none of them having to do with fundraisers. Thrill, shock, disbelief, and a wicked amount of desire. I wanted to rush up and throw my arms around him. My sweaty palms, pounding heart and chills added up to trouble. Eli was just a friend, yet seeing him so close and unexpectedly made me crazy happy.

"What a surprise, Eli." Jessica's lips puckered with irritation. "Is there something I can do for you?"

"You better have a good reason for butting into our meeting," Chad warned.

"I do." His gaze sought mine, sending a message I didn't understand.

"Well, what is it?" Chad demanded. "Does Dad want me at the dealership?"

"No, Dad's cool. I came to … to offer help with your fundraiser. I'm all for helping starving kids."

"This is a private meeting."

"It's all for a good cause and I'm here, so why not let me help?"

"Just how did you get here?" Chad scowled at his brother. "Dad said you weren't to borrow any of his cars without asking again."

"I asked Mom." Eli sniffed the air. "Hmmm, what smells so good?"

"Hawaiian barbeque. Mrs. B always makes plenty; maybe you could stay." Kat grinned at him, a bit too flirtatiously in my opinion. "I've seen you around school but we've never been introduced. You must be Chad's younger brother."

"Only a year younger. But I'm in honors classes, and I'm already taking some college-level classes."

"You are such a pathetic geek." Chad rolled his eyes. "I've told you not to bug my friends, so get out of here."

"Oh, let him stay." Kat came over and ran her fingers up Eli's arm. "On reality shows, geeks are full of surprises. I'll bet Eli has some great ideas."

Not the kind of ideas you have in mind, I almost spat at her. What an obvious flirt. It took supreme control not to yank her hand away from Eli's arm. But I didn't have any rights to Eli. Leah belonged to his brother.

"Speaking of ideas," I said, "I was about to tell Jessica my idea for the fundraiser."

"Can't it wait?" Eli gave me another one of those looks. "I need to talk to you. Now."

"You need to talk to *my* girlfriend?" Chad demanded. "You crack your head on something? You know Leah can't stand you."

"People change." Eli stepped toward me. "Leah, you can make your own decisions. Do you want to talk with me or would you rather stay here?"

"Of course she'd rather stay here." Chad planted a firm arm around my waist. "Leah's got better things to do than talk to you."

"Excuse me, but this is my meeting." Jessica gestured to her notebook. "Can we get back to the fundraising discussion? I want to hear what Leah has to say."

Eli leaned around his brother to look into my face. "You know I wouldn't be here if it wasn't important. I heard you were going to be here and knew it might be my last chance—maybe yours, too. Who do you really want to be?"

The others stared at him like he was talking crazy, but I knew exactly what he meant—and it ripped at my heart. Of course I wanted my real life back. But I couldn't be Amber, even though I desperately wished it were possible. Couldn't Eli see that I didn't have a choice? I was trapped in Leah's body, and subsequently her life. The Montgomerys would never believe I wasn't really their daughter, any more than my real family would believe I belonged with them.

"Eli, are you on something?" Chad jerked Eli's arm so they faced each other. "I didn't think you did that shit, but you're acting messed up. Don't embarrass yourself, just go on home."

"Not until I talk to Leah." Eli shook his brother off.

"Leah doesn't even like you."

"Can you let her make her own decisions?" Eli stared hard at me. "Come on, let's go outside where we can talk privately."

"Privately? With my girl?" Chad exploded. "Forget it. Leah, tell him to get lost."

But I shook my head, saying nothing.

"Damn it, Eli, do I have to kick your sorry ass out of here?"

"No kicking," I begged. Turning to Eli, I whispered, "Can't this wait?"

"No. You have to trust me on this."

I did trust him, but I didn't trust people who held power over me—like Mr. Montgomery. If I didn't play the role of daughter, friend, and sister convincing enough, I'd be committed to DeHaven. With drugs blurring my mind and locks confining me, I'd be more of a prisoner than I was already. I might even start believing that being Amber was only a dream.

I shook my head. "Not now, Eli. You don't understand."

"I understand more than you think." His gaze challenged me to choose him, to leave everything and become Amber again.

"Enough, okay?" Jessica came forward to stand between us. "I don't get what this is about, but we can sort it all out later. If Eli wants to stay for dinner, he's welcome. But first I want to hear Leah's raffle ideas so I can complete our meeting."

"Well..." I was totally aware that all eyes were on me. "I think a raffle is the best way to get people to show up at the fundraiser. But we have to raffle off really cool prizes."

"I already thought of that, but I can't see how it can be done quickly." Jessica sounded discouraged. "Three days doesn't give us much time to get donations from local businesses."

"So we create our own prizes," I told her.

"Like what?"

"Designer gift baskets," I explained. "With candles, candy, flowers, bath accessories, and gift certificates."

"Like the baskets from the Halsey Hospitality Club?" Eli said with a challenging edge to his voice. "The club created by Amber Borden?"

"Poor Amber," Jessica said sadly. "Baskets would be great, but I doubt that club will continue without Amber. So who would make the baskets?"

"I can do it," I admitted.

"You?" Jessica laughed. "You can't even wrap your Christmas presents. You always hire someone else to do it."

"I can make baskets," I insisted.

"Tell them how you learned," Eli said pointedly.

I frowned at him. I couldn't be who he wanted me to be.

Chad grabbed Eli by the shoulder. "You're leaving."

"Let go!" Eli couldn't get loose from his brother's muscled grip. "Leah, talk to me now. Do it for Amber."

"Amber is gone," I said softly.

"She doesn't have to be! Not when you're still here—
Hey, Chad! Not so rough!"

Chad dragged Eli toward the door. I wanted to claw at
Chad's arms and pull him off Eli ... but I just stood there.
Helping Eli would raise suspicions about my sanity and
lead to all kinds of trouble with my friends and family.

Not your *friends and family,* I thought. *None of this is
the real Amber. You're more than a physical body—the real
person is still there.*

What if Eli was right? Was there a way I could reclaim
my life? Was that the important thing he had to tell me?
He'd risked a lot to come here. For me. Amber.

"Chad, let him loose!" I shouted and pulled on Chad's
arm.

"Leah, lay off. Are you freaking crazy?"

"Maybe," I admitted. "I've changed my mind—I want
to talk with him."

"You do?" Eli said eagerly.

"You do?" Chad demanded in the complete opposite
tone.

I sucked in my breath, courage gathering like powerful
rain clouds. I'd gone along calmly for too long—it was time
to let loose my inner storm. "Yes, I want to talk with Eli."

"No way." Chad growled.

"You wouldn't understand about loyalty, Chad, but
your brother does. Eli was Amber's friend, and talking to
him is the least I can do in her memory."

Chad loosened his grip on Eli, tossing his brother aside
like brushing off lint, and turned to me. "Babe, you don't

mean it. Why waste your time with my geek brother? You don't even like him."

"I'll make my own decisions about who I like." I pushed away from him.

"You're talking strange, Leah," he said, frowning.

"Yeah, I notice that, too." Kat came forward, shaking her head. "Leah, you're not acting like yourself. Sure, Eli is kind of hot in a skinny geek way, but you always go for jocks. And since when do you care about Amber Boring-Borden?"

"Don't call her boring. We're closer than you know—I even sent flowers to her hospital room."

Kat shared an incredulous look with Moniqua. "See what I mean? Leah, you're so different since your sickness—like someone I don't even know."

"Well, I think she's great," Jessica said, smiling at me. "Sending flowers was such a classy thing to do. Leah, I'm proud to be your friend."

"You are?" I asked.

"Seriously proud. Since Amber had her accident right after leaving my party, I've felt sick about it and wanted to do something for her. Now I find out you sent her flowers while I did nothing. I should be more like you. Now it's too late for Amber ... but not to show support for her family." A thoughtful gaze crossed her face, then she snapped her fingers. "That's it! A super idea for a fundraiser that will draw a huge crowd."

"What?" Kat, Moniqua, and Chad asked.

"We'll combine our fundraiser with a farewell memorial

for Amber." Jessica jumped excitedly. "A canned-food-drive memorial service!"

While everyone had their eyes on Jessica as she discussed her ridiculous idea (a canned-food memorial?), I slipped my hand into Eli's. We shared a look, then escaped, hurrying through the foyer and out the door. Fresh air and hope buoyed my footsteps. Free, free, free! I wanted to run, keep running—far from Leah's Montgomery's messed-up life.

"Where are we going?" I asked.

"To my car." Eli pointed down a ways to a parked silver BMW. "Or to be exact, to my mother's car."

"Are you kidnapping me?" I said, only half-hoping.

"I was considering it before you agreed to come."

"What's so important that you had to tell me?"

"I'm taking you to my car to show you."

"Now you're confusing me."

"Not as much as you're confusing me, looking and sounding like my arch-enemy Leah," he teased. "For a second there I wasn't sure it was you. When you sided with Chad you had me afraid you'd gone over to the dark side."

"It'll never happen. If Chad has good qualities, they're hidden. No offense, but I think your brother is a jerk."

"Join the club. For an initiation prize, you get to ditch my brother and have a kiss." He blushed at my startled look, then dug in his pocket. "A chocolate kiss," he amended, giving me a foil-wrapped candy.

"Yumm." I ripped off the foil faster than you could say "Amber Borden is a chocoholic" and popped it into my mouth. Funny, though, as much as I craved chocolate, I was a little disappointed the kiss offer was only chocolate.

As we neared the car, I caught a glimpse of a figure in the back seat. I slowed, uneasy about meeting Eli's friends.

"You brought someone with you?" I asked accusingly.

"Relax." He put a calming hand on my arm. "He's a friend."

"This isn't a good time to meet your friend."

"I didn't say he was my friend. I hardly know him. But you do." Eli cleared his throat, stopping on the sidewalk. "Go on ahead without me. You should talk alone."

Before I could ask anything else, the car door opened. A lanky leg wearing brown pants with a yellow sock poked out—and that was all I needed to know.

"Dustin!" I shouted, rushing forward until I realized he couldn't possibly recognize me. I stopped. What was I thinking? He wouldn't know me now any more than he had when we'd talked at the hospital.

So I was totally shocked when Dustin moved toward me, grinning in that familiar goofy way. "Eli's been telling me an impossible story."

"He has?" I asked cautiously.

"About body-snatchers." He stopped a foot from me, studying. "Lose any cell phones lately?"

"Not since I fell into the cemetery."

"And ruined your clothes."

"But you rescued me and loaned me—"

Eli drove us to Dustin's house; a single-story wood-paneled home in one of those cookie-cutter neighborhoods.

Dustin's father, an electrician, was off early and did a double take when I walked through the living room hand-in-hand with Dustin. It was so amazing to be with Dustin again that I didn't want to let him go. Dustin rarely invited girls to his home, and never one that looked like Leah. No wonder his dad was surprised, impressed even.

I smiled and played it up, leaning against Dustin and giggling like I had hair gel for brains. Dustin whispered, "Cut that out!" while turning an interesting shade of red.

"Are you sure you want me to?" I vamped.

"Amber, can't you control yourself?"

I just grinned. He'd called me *Amber*.

We headed for Dustin's self-proclaimed "Headquarters." Not a bedroom, like a normal person would have, but a room crowded with desks and electronic equipment, including three computers linking networks around the world for radical anti-government reasons. There was no bed. Dustin liked to sleep on the saggy leather couch in a sleeping bag. His mother had given up years ago trying to convince him to sleep on a mattress.

Once I teased her: "It could be worse—he could sleep in a coffin like Alyce."

Not true; Alyce wasn't that Goth-centric. But Dustin and I cracked up over his mother's shocked expression. When Alyce heard about my joke, she smacked my arm hard. Even after Dustin told his mother the truth, she still acted nervous around Alyce.

Eli's gaze rose to Dustin's ceiling, where the myriad of keys he'd collected as a locksmith circled the top of the walls. Eli seemed awed, spinning slowly in place to look at the hundred-zillion keys. Dizzily, he caught himself before he tripped over some cables twined like black snakes on the floor.

"Cool," was all he said as he sat in a swivel computer chair.

Then we sat down and got to talking.

I hardly knew which of my zillion questions to ask first. I stared at these two guys, one a very new friend and the other closer than a brother. At first glance someone might shrug them off as geeks, since they were both smart and went their own way rather than following popular trends. But that's where their similarities ended. Dustin was a born activist, intense and idealistic. Eli seemed easygoing, considerate and a little shy.

"I never expected you two to hang out," I told them.

"It was all Eli's doing," Dustin explained. "Your pal here wouldn't leave me alone until I heard him out. He cornered me at school today and told me that you needed him. I thought he was nuts and blew him off—but he kept after me. The more he talked, the more things added up. I knew there was something odd when I met Leah...you...at the hospital. The way you moved and talked made me think of Amber—which made no sense. Then, when you told me about my socks, using the exact words Amber always said...well, I didn't know what to think."

"Socks?" Eli interrupted.

Dustin glanced away like he always did when reminded of his color-blindness.

"It's nothing," I said quickly to save his pride. "A joke between Dustin and me."

"Which is what freaked me out." Dustin shook his head. "I couldn't stop thinking about you...well, the girl I thought was Leah...and it didn't make any sense. So when Eli told his impossible story, I listened. I mean *really listened*."

"And believed," I said gratefully.

"Not at first. But I was hooked with curiosity and figured why not check it out. Then the weirdest thing happened—as you walked toward me, looking exactly like another girl, I knew it was you. And when you talked about nettles I was positive, 'cause you did that funny crinkly thing with your nose and stuck out the tip of your tongue like you always do when you're grossed out."

"I do not!"

"Yes, you do. Even when you're not you anymore." He stared at me solemnly. "Geez, Amber! How did this happen?"

I blew out a sigh, sinking into the cushioned chair. "I wish I knew."

"You're so ... so different. I don't think I can get used to it."

Eli leaned in with a serious expression. "You won't have to—if we figure out a way to switch her back."

"I've tried and tried, but even when I was in the hospital room nothing happened." I swallowed the lump in my throat. "And by now ... my real body is ... gone."

No one spoke for a few minutes, and except for the soft hum from the computer monitors, the room was still as death.

Then Dustin tapped his desk top, swiveling in his chair and clicking commands onto a keyboard. "Never say never," he declared in the tone he used to use when on the debate team. "Even when obstacles seem insurmountable—like when I'm pitted against some mega corporation—there are battle strategies. I can't stop big money from funding dirty politicians, but I can still fight back." He waved, as if his hand were a magic wand, toward the monitor where a handsome silver-haired man smiled. "Meet Councilman Beaumont, a great family man, friend to the environment, and all-around good guy. At least that's what he wants his voters to believe."

"I've seen his commercials," Eli said. "But what does this have to do with Amber?"

"I'm getting to that. First, look at the councilman's official website, where he makes nice with the public. His people invested tons of money and energy into their website to win over voters. But voters don't know that his influence is for sale to the highest bidder, and since my sources won't go public, I have to attack the councilman in a more subtle way." He clicked a few more keys and a different website popped up. At first glance this looked exactly like the official Beaumont website, except the picture of Councilman Beaumont showed him with a sly expression as he stood with a sleazy-looking guy, his hands on a large envelope. The caption below the picture read: Councilman for Sale!

"Anyone searching for the dishonorable Councilman will find my alternate website," Dustin explained proudly.

"Score one for the good guys," I said, applauding. "Alyce would call Beaumont a corruptician."

"Actually, she did." Dustin hit a button and the screen blacked out. "I hope this website and others can even out the justice scales—at least until they're shut down. I didn't solve the problem, but I found another way to fight back. And you can, too, Amber."

"How? I'm stuck in this body."

"You can still get your life back. You do want to go home, don't you?"

"More than anything," I admitted softly. "But my family won't even recognize me."

"I did," Dustin pointed out.

"Only because you have a very strange mind."

"A logical mind has to accept the impossible when there is no other explanation. Unfortunately most people aren't logical." Dustin twisted his lips in a way that told me who he was thinking about.

"Like Alyce," I said sadly.

"When I talk to her about you, she shuts me down. Today she skipped school. Afterwards I went by her house, and her mother wouldn't let me in—said that Alyce didn't want to see me."

I nodded, understanding too well. Alyce moved on emotion. I'd known her long enough to sense when one of her dark moods was coming on, and could tease her back into smiles. But I couldn't make her smile if she wouldn't let me prove who I was.

I wanted to go to her house right now and make her listen. But when I glanced over at the clock, panic struck. An hour had passed since I'd left Jessica's party—soon Luis would arrive to pick me up. All hell would break loose if I wasn't there. Each time I'd run away, Leah's father had had someone bring me back. He'd warned that there wouldn't be a third time—that he'd send me to DeHaven, where I'd never be able to escape.

Unless he couldn't find me.

I'd hide out with my friends, change my appearance, and start over with a new identity. But what would it change?

I'd still be living a lie, pretending to be someone I wasn't, unable to live with my family.

And what about school? My career? My future?

Running would solve nothing. Besides, no matter how far I traveled or how much I changed my appearance, Mr. Montgomery would find me.

Dustin patted my trembling hand. "You okay?"

"Not really. I want to stay, but I better leave."

"What are you talking about?" Eli furrowed his brow. "You don't have to go anywhere. We'll protect you."

"That's for damn sure," Dustin agreed. "I have a network of friends who can help."

"So does Mr. Montgomery," I pointed out. "Rich and powerful friends."

"So what?" Dustin shrugged. "You don't have to pretend you're Leah. We'll help you explain to your parents that you're alive. Last time I saw them, they were talking about funeral arrangements. It's not fair to let them go on thinking the body in the hospital is all that's left of you."

"It's not fair that I look like this." Tears blurred my eyes. "I don't want to hurt anyone...all I know is that if I don't go back, things could get worse."

"She's right." Eli folded his arms across his chest and turned to Dustin. "Mr. Montgomery is bad news. Our families hang in the same social circles, so I've seen him con people. He comes off as sympathetic because he puts up with an alcoholic wife. But I've heard rumors that he bullies his employees and even his family."

He's worse than that, I thought uneasily, remembering

his creepy obsession with Leah's appearance and the sting of his slap.

"I don't want Amber to go back anymore than you do," Eli told Dustin in a grim tone. "But if she doesn't, Mr. Montgomery will probably send the FBI looking for her."

"Let them look," Dustin argued. "They'll never find her."

"What kind of life would that be? But if she goes back, it'll give us time to come up with a plan so she can get away for good."

"No!" Dustin smacked his fist on his desk, rattling pens in a container. "I've searched Mr. M online and he's deep into shady dealings, even if no one can prove it. Amber isn't safe around that creep. If you won't protect her, then I will."

"I never said I wouldn't. I-I care, too." Eli bumped his elbow on the desk and caught the container of pens before it fell over.

"Then work with me to hide her."

"Excuse me! I'm right here." I threw up my hands, shoving between them. "I can make my own decisions."

"I just want to help," Dustin said.

"Me, too," Eli added.

"Arguing isn't solving anything," I pointed out.

"Okay." Dustin studied my face. "Tell us what you want."

"Yeah," Eli said. "Where do you want to go?"

They both watched me, waiting. But I didn't know ...

I had no idea what to do. It was like being trapped in a pitch-dark room with no windows or doors. No way out.

Eli couldn't hide me in his house—not with Chad living there. And Dustin couldn't exactly offer to share his couch. Where did that leave me?

Homeless in a borrowed body.

So I said, take me back.

To Leah's life.

Dustin vowed to keep searching online for dirt on Mr. Montgomery. Eli said he'd fish around for information from his parents. And I said, "Good-bye."

I made it back to Jessica's house just as Luis was driving up in the Montgomery's black Lexus. Relieved by this small piece of good luck, I slipped behind bushes and parked cars, came over to the car, and slid into the passenger seat.

Luis didn't ask why I was so quiet on the drive back.

But when we reached the Montgomery house, things were far from quiet. The house was ablaze with lights. As I walked up to the front door, I heard shouting.

"Um ... maybe you should take me back," I told Luis. "I don't want to go in there."

"I don't blame you. They argue a lot but never so loud. Want to wait it out in my apartment?" he offered.

"Thanks," I said, genuinely touched. "But Angie would kill us both if I showed up."

"Nah, don't mind her. She's just hot tempered and hangs tight to a grudge."

"I probably deserve it." I gave him a weak smile. "Get out of here—save yourself. I better go in and find out what I did this time."

Only the shouting wasn't about me.

I crept through the foyer but stopped before going into the living room, pressing against a wall and peeking out with caution.

"—don't care what you think I should do!" Mr. Montgomery raged at his wife. They stood close to the couch, facing each other with tight expressions, separated only by a glass coffee table which I half expected to shatter from the high pitch of their anger.

"But he's just a little boy," she argued.

"Big enough to commit a crime."

"I'll talk to him, and he'll promise not to cause any more problems."

"He's already caused too many. He was warned this would happen."

"I won't let you send him away!"

"I wasn't asking for your permission. The decision has been made."

Mrs. Montgomery clutched her husband's arm. "Please,

don't do this. If you care at all for me, don't send him there."

"Would you let go of my arm?" he asked coolly.

The hostility in his tone shocked me—my own father would never be so cruel to Mom. Of course, my soft-hearted father was nothing like ruthless, dominating Mr. Montgomery. Kudos to Leah's Mom for standing up to him.

"He's your son, dammit!" She glared at her husband. "You can't fire him like he's one of your employees."

"But I can ensure he gets the education he's missed ditching school and running with hoodlums. Camp Challenge will teach him respect and the value of hard work. He'll never amount to anything if he keeps screwing up."

"You put unreasonable expectations on him."

"I'm through coddling the boy—it's time he acted like a man. At his age I was doing odd jobs to earn money. I didn't have any family to give me hand-outs. Why shouldn't he learn the same work ethic?"

"Hunter isn't like you."

"Damned right he isn't. I blame it all on you." He wagged his finger in her face. "You're too soft on him."

"I have my faults. But at least I've tried to be a good parent."

"You're saying I haven't?" he accused.

"Maybe with Leah, but not with Hunter. You don't even try to understand him. All you do is criticize. You're a terrible father."

It happened so fast—his hand whipping out, striking her face. Her cry, and stumble backwards. I blinked, horrified. I wanted to rush over to Leah's mother—but she was already running out of the room, sobbing.

An echo of the slap seemed to linger in the room. Mr. Montgomery stood there as if stunned, frowning at his hand. For a moment I thought he was remorseful. But then I noticed a shadowy hue coming from his palm. He swore under his breath and reached into his pocket. Withdrawing a small beige bottle, he opened it and then rubbed something on his palm. The unearthly aura coming from his hand disappeared—hidden by makeup.

He strode into his office and slammed the door.

I hugged myself to calm the shaking. The shadowy aura! The makeup on his hand! Mr. Montgomery—a Dark Lifer? I shook my head, disbelieving. The grayness must have been a trick of the shadows.

Confused, I stood there, uncertain what to do. Go after Mrs. Montgomery to make sure she was all right? Or hide out in my room?

Hiding seemed safest.

But when I got upstairs, I heard sobbing. I thought it was Leah's mother until I realized the sounds weren't coming from her room. They were coming from Hunter's.

Without knocking, I tried the knob. The door opened easily.

The sobbing figure on the bed didn't notice me. I wasn't sure whether to leave or go over to him. My gaze swept around his pirate décor. The walls were a rusty shade of brown, with a mural of a pirate ship sailing on blue waves. There was an unnatural orderliness to the room, as if every drop of paint and decoration had been selected with expertise, not for living in but for showing off. Leah's princess-pretty room was like that, too. It was as if this house sucked the personality out of people.

Hunter continued to sob, although more quietly now. Should I go to him? Or turn around and slip away without getting involved?

Not that I cared about him ... well, maybe a little.

We did share great taste in cereal.

"Hunter," I said softly, placing my hand on his quaking shoulder. "Are you okay?"

"Go away," was his muffled reply.

"I heard them arguing," I continued. "Mister ... I mean, Dad said something about a camp. Is he threatening to send you away, too?"

"Too?" Hunter sat up, wiping his face with the back of his hand. "What do you mean? Is Dad going to send you to Camp Challenge?"

"Not there—a worse place."

"Nothing's worse," he said, sounding scared. "They call it a camp but it's not really. It's jail with guards beating on you if you don't do what they say. My friend Jake went there and came back all bruised and afraid to even talk."

"That's awful. But so is DeHaven Resort." I sat down on the edge of his bed. "It's not a real resort, but a last resort for crazy people. I either do what Dad wants or get locked up in an insanity ward."

"He won't do it to you—you're his favorite. He's always bragging on you and taking you to cool parties. But he can't wait to get rid of me." Hunter scowled. "I hate him!"

"I hate him, too."

He raised his brow. "But he gives you presents and everything."

"Bribes," I said.

"Better than being yelled at."

"So why do we put up with it?" I asked sadly. "And Mrs...Mom, too."

Hunter rolled his eyes. "Mom's just as bad."

I shook my head. "I just heard her standing up to him, telling him not to send you to camp. She really loves you."

"Not as much as she loves booze."

"That's not fair."

"Since when do you care about being fair?" He narrowed his eyes at me. "Why are you even talking to me? You hate me."

"No, I don't." I spoke sincerely, sorry for the little boy who was trying so hard to be tough. His tear-stained face tugged at my heart. He needed someone to love and support him no matter how badly he behaved. "I care what happens to you. And I'll do whatever I can to help."

"Can you stop him from sending me to camp?"

"I don't know..." I hesitated. "But I'll try."

"You mean it?" he asked. "Promise?"

I looked him squarely in the eyes.

And promised.

"Oh, shit," I murmured over and over as I stood outside Mr. Montgomery's office door. What was I doing here? I really must be crazy.

I lifted my hand and rapped on the door.

"I'm through talking with you tonight," Mr. Montgomery called out sharply. "We'll discuss this in the morning."

"Uh ... Dad?" I managed to say despite my thudding heart.

The door opened right away.

"Leah," her father said with a weary smile. "Sorry, I thought it was your mother. Do you want something, sweetheart?"

"Just to ... um ... talk."

"Well, come on in." He tried to put his arm around my waist but I moved out of his way. I didn't really believe he was a Dark Lifer, but I wasn't taking any chances. "You're looking lovely tonight, not as frail and out of shape."

"I guess it's all the exercise," I admitted.

"Well, keep it up. Also, I like how you've styled your hair."

"I didn't ... er ... I mean, Jessica fixed it."

"Clever girl. I've always said she'll go far in society. She's even more beautiful and gracious than her mother." He relaxed back in his desk chair. "Did you have a nice visit at the Bradleys'?"

I nodded. "Jessica is organizing a canned-food drive and Mrs. Bradley made a Hawaiian barbeque dinner." No reason to add that I missed dinner and the rest of the fundraising meeting. What had I heard about it as I was leaving? Something about a canned-food drive and memorial for *me*. Too weird. I must have heard wrong.

"What's on your mind?" Mr. Montgomery asked, folding his hands—ordinary, without any unusual aura—on his wooden desktop

I bit my lip, wanting to turn around and bolt. But I had come this far and might never work up the courage again. "Actually, it's about Hunter."

"Oh." He blew out a weary sigh. "What has he done this time?"

"Nothing...not to me. But I heard you and...uh... Mom talking. You aren't really going to send him to a reform camp?"

"This doesn't concern you."

"I don't want to see him get hurt. I've heard those camps are brutal."

"Drastic measures are needed to teach that boy discipline." Mr. Montgomery's jaw tightened, as if he were struggling to control his temper. "Leah, I applaud your concern for Hunter, but I'll handle this. I know what I'm doing."

"And so do I," I said in an accusing tone. "You can't handle Hunter, so you want to ship him off."

"First your mother, and now you. Is this a conspiracy against me?" Instead of sounding angry, he smiled in that creepy way that I hated. It threw me off balance. I'd expected him to shout like he'd done with his wife. But instead he just seemed amused.

"I want you to go easy on Hunter," I said.

"And why should I? The little punk was arrested for shoplifting. Should I let him go to juvenile hall? That's one of the options presented by the judge."

"No, but can't you give him a second chance? If you treat him like a criminal, he might become one." I'd read this in one of my books. "Why can't he do community service instead of being locked up?"

"Community service." Mr. Montgomery stroked his chin with his finger, a gold ring sparkling in the lamplight. "Interesting idea."

"So you'll do it?"

"That depends." The look he gave me sent chills up my skin. "On you."

I stepped back. "Me?"

"The Governor's Reception this Saturday is an extremely important event. This morning I was chatting with Congressman Donatello, and he asked about you. He said for you to save a dance for him. It would mean a lot to me if I could tell him you're eager to dance with him."

Yuck! I didn't want to dance with an old guy—especially since I wasn't even sure how to dance at a formal event. What if they did ballroom dancing? I was going to refuse—until I noticed the calculating expression in Mr. Montgomery's gaze. That's when I realized how high the stakes were. I wasn't just defending Hunter. I was fighting for myself. A trip to DeHaven was only a threat away.

Be Leah, I told myself. How would she handle this? Neither an outright refusal or an easy acceptance. Everything about her seemed to be an act. I had a feeling that the real Leah had been making wrong turns for a long time, hiding her emotions so deep inside that she lost herself along the way.

"What's in it for me?" I finally asked.

Mr. Montgomery threw back his head and laughed.

"Now that's my Leah. Out for what you can get and eager to take advantage of all opportunities."

Take advantage of all opportunities. Common advice in self-help books. Reach out and grab what you want; make your dreams come true. But Leah's father made this strategy seem shallow, as if being ambitious were wrong.

"I'm not asking you to do anything difficult," he added in a wheedling tone. "Simply dance with an old family friend."

Old was the key word here. Congressman Donatello was probably a pervert, too. But I should be safe in a public place.

"All right," I agreed. "One dance."

"Excellent. For offering the privilege of your lovely company, I'll up the limit on your credit card. Would fifty thousand be enough?"

Fifty thousand? Dollars! That was practically what my parents made a year.

"Money is always nice," I said carefully. "But what about Hunter?"

"What about him?" Mr. Montgomery scowled.

"No camp."

"Last month you begged me to move Hunter to another bedroom. You said he stole stuff and couldn't be trusted. Yet now you're defending him? Your behavior doesn't make sense." He gave me a puzzled look. "Are you feeling well?"

"I'll feel much better when I know my brother is safe."

"Stubborn and persistent—I like that." He gave me what I guessed was an affectionate smile. "You win as usual.

I'll make some calls about community service work. Are you happy now?"

I forced a smile, shrugging instead of giving a direct answer.

Then I fled his office, before he could tell me to turn in a circle or slap my butt.

28

I stopped by the kitchen and raided the fridge. Leftover chicken, tangy vegetable salad, and a big slice of blueberry pie. Yummm...

When I returned to my room—surprise! The flat-screen TV, computer, and phone were back. Was Leah forgiven for her past bad behavior, or being rewarded for future favors?

The phone blinked with the number "2," so I pushed on the "collect messages" button and crossed my fingers, hoping the calls were from Eli or Dustin. No such luck.

"Leah, you there?" came Jessica's voice. "I tried your cell phone but it's still not picking up. What happened to you? Why did you go off with Chad's brother? Chad was so pissed he hardly said a word during dinner. Call me."

The second message was also from Jessica.

"Leah, it's late and I'm worried about you. If you don't call soon I'll try your parents."

Oh, crap. Just what I didn't need tonight!

Then I panicked because I didn't know Jessica's number. And twenty-three minutes had already passed since she'd left the message. If I didn't contact her soon, she might call Leah's parents and say that I'd left her party. Fortunately, the phone had a call-back feature. With heavy relief, I dialed Jessica's number.

She answered on one ring, peppering me with questions.

Where were you? Are you in love with Chad's brother? Why didn't you come back for dinner? Are we still best friends? Is Chad's brother a good kisser?

I assured her we were still best friend and denied kissing Eli. To avoid answering the other questions, I asked her about the fundraiser—but I didn't like her answer.

She really was going to have a canned-food-drive memorial service for "that poor Amber Borden." How was I supposed to respond to that? I considered telling her the truth—that no one would attend, not even Dustin and Alyce. Alyce would be insulted about the whole canned-food thing, and Dustin shunned school events.

If I wasn't already presumed dead, I'd die of humiliation.

While I was reeling with all of this, Jessica asked me

the most outrageous question ever spoken in all of human existence. A bad situation squared by a *worse* situation:

"Will you come to Amber's memorial?" she asked.

Forget. It.

I invented an excuse about a doctor appointment on Friday. Jessica begged me to postpone it, but I refused.

Then I called Dustin and clued him in.

"You're joking," he said.

"I wish I was."

"I can just imagine Jessica announcing over the loud-speaker, 'May she rest in peace and please be sure to drop off your canned food.' That's sick."

"Jessica thinks it's brilliant. And she's sure the whole school will come to say good-bye to me. I'm sure only a few teachers will show up. You and Alyce are my best friends, and you won't be there."

"What makes you think that? I can't speak for Alyce—especially since she isn't speaking to anyone lately—but I wouldn't miss it."

"Don't you dare go!"

"How can I resist?" He chuckled. "Should I bring a can of soup, chili, or fruit cocktail?"

"Not funny. I can't even guess how my parents will react when they find out about the memorial."

"Oh. I hadn't thought of that." His tone changed instantly. "Yeah, that would be rough on them, especially when they're planning their own ... well anyway, I see your point. Sorry for being an insensitive jerk."

"You're not a jerk, and only marginally insensitive."

"It's hard to mourn you when I'm talking to you. But I

know this sucks for your family. I don't know how to stop them from finding out about the memorial. Damn, you really have to tell them the truth."

"When I'm free of Leah's family, I'll make my parents listen and prove who I am." I sighed. "But I don't know how long that will take. Leah's father may not let her go even when she turns eighteen—whenever that is. Isn't that sad? I don't even know her birthday."

"July fourteenth."

"How do you know?" I asked, surprised.

"From surfing online about the Montgomerys. I've found interesting stuff. Rumors about a shifty connection to a congressman named Donatello. Ever hear of him?"

I didn't answer right away, ashamed to admit about the dance. "I've heard a little."

"Nothing good, I bet. He acts like he's a respectable family man, but he was accused of beating up a hooker. He denies everything of course. If he shows up, stay away."

I nodded silently.

Then I changed the subject, asking Dustin about his latest campaigns. He launched into the political buzz about who-did-what, etc. I admired his zeal for justice, even if I wasn't sure about his methods—like the "fake official" website he was creating to expose the use of illegal chemicals by a supposedly organic nursery.

Even though we were talking about flowers, the word "nursery" reminded me of the weekend I helped paint the triplets' nursery canary yellow. Mom was on bed rest by then, so Dad and I tackled the walls, splattering yellow paint all over ourselves. When Mom saw us, she laughed so hard we were afraid she'd go into early labor.

That evening, as I changed into Leah's nightgown, I was still thinking of the family I missed and wondered if they were thinking of me, too. I crawled under Leah's silky sheets and drifted into a sleep … dreaming of yellow paint and laughter.

Another day, another daily schedule.

Only this time when Angie handed me the printed sheet, she didn't scowl. And when I thanked her, she even said, "You're welcome." No feet stomping or door slamming. Not exactly the road to BFF status but hey it was a start.

I stared helplessly in the mirror at my tragic case of bed head. Without Jessica's help, I didn't know how to style my hair. So I twisted the blonde tangles into a braid and flipped it out of the way. Then I tossed on the most comfortable jeans and shirt I could find and headed for breakfast.

Mrs. Montgomery sat alone in the dining room by a large picture window with the shades closed. She wore a lavender robe and stared at nothing. She was turned away from the table, with one arm leaning on the glass-top table and her fingers curling around a wine glass.

I stared down at the ruby liquid shimmering in the glass, disappointed.

She must have heard my footsteps, because she turned

her head toward me. A myriad of emotions played across her face: surprise, worry, shame.

"It's not what it looks like," she said, pushing the glass away.

"You don't owe me any explanations." I really didn't know what else to say. I hardly knew her and was likely to say something completely wrong. Retreat was the safest option. "I'll just get some cereal and go back to my room."

"Don't go." Her hand shot out to gently touch my wrist. "We should talk... about many things. We don't do enough talking."

"Because you do too much of *that*." I gestured to the wine glass. Immediately I covered my mouth, shocked at my rudeness. "I'm sorry... I shouldn't have—"

"It's okay. I appreciate your honesty, and admit I've had serious issues." She stared down at the glass with hate and longing. "After last night, I couldn't sleep and finally came down here at four in the morning."

I frowned at the faint bruise on her cheek, knowing exactly what had upset her last night.

"It's all so overwhelming," she said with a heavy sigh. "You can't know... how I feel... like everything is out of control and I can't find the right direction to turn. I've screwed up so many times, so why even bother to try? I just couldn't take it anymore and was going to quit my meetings. I poured this glass and... well, nothing."

"Nothing?"

"I never took a drink."

"You've been sitting here since four in the morning?"

"Staring at a glass." She laughed bitterly. "Hard to believe, isn't it?"

"Not really. You're stronger than you know. You can beat this—I know you can."

"You always say that."

"I do?" I asked, surprised.

"Many, many times. But I've never believed you … and somewhere along the way I know you stopped believing in me, too." She sighed. "All I can say is, I'm sorry. I'm a lousy mother."

"At least you try. Your glass is still full."

"That's right—it is." Her smile hinted at sadness and pride as she stood swiftly and picked up the glass. I tensed for a moment, afraid she'd drink it. But she marched into the kitchen and dumped the entire glass into the sink.

I followed her and applauded. "Go, Mom."

"Yeah, I'm going all right—going to call my friend in AA and talk about what almost happened." She turned toward a granite counter. "Thanks for your support, Leah. It means more than you'll ever know."

She held her head high as she crossed the room to pick up a cordless phone. I had an impulse to wrap my arms around her and hug … as if she were really my mother.

Ridiculous! I told myself as I watched her leave. There was only one "Mom" for me, and even if I had to stay in this body forever, Mom would always be the slightly over-weight, always over-worked, mother of four daughters.

Yet I seemed to care for Leah's Mom, too—confusing!

What kind of freaky phenomenon was going on here? Did Leah's body have its own memories? Would they gradually replace mine? No, I couldn't let that happen. I refused to forget who I was. Identity was deeper than skin, somewhere trapped in between.

So why did my heart ache for Mrs. Montgomery? This feeling was stronger than an intense craving for chocolate. Perhaps it was similar to Mrs. Montgomery's longing when she stared down at the ruby-red liquid.

Weird thoughts, I told myself. Get over it, Amber!

With resolve, I opened a kitchen cupboard.

And poured cereal.

By the afternoon, I'd finished my workouts and spent a few hours watching soaps with Luis. He filled me in on the plotlines while I munched on his delicious homemade cheesy popcorn. When Angie came by, she shot us a disgusted look. But all she asked was if I'd done my exercises and homework. Wow—she was acting almost friendly.

When the soaps ended, Luis went outside for gardening chores and I returned to my room. I tried to figure out Leah's password to her computer, but couldn't. If I could read through her emails it would help to know her better, save me from any embarrassing mistakes.

Once school was over, my phone started ringing—Jessica, Chad, Kat and Eli. I let the machine pick up for the first three, but when I saw Eli's name on the caller ID, I couldn't grab the phone fast enough. We talked, nothing serious, just casual stuff that seemed more interesting when shared with Eli. I had to admit, even to myself, that I was falling for him. How could Leah have preferred Chad?

After I hung up, I sat on Leah's bed and thought about my day. Strange, surreal, almost enjoyable. I was starting to feel comfortable in this skin. When I stared at myself in the mirror, I wasn't only looking at Leah or at Amber, but at a blend of the two of us.

AmberLeah.

A knock on my door startled me out of my thoughts.

"Leah, are you busy?" Mr. Montgomery asked as he opened my door.

"Uh … not really," I said, sitting up straight and clasping a small pillow on my lap. "What do you want?"

He draped his arm on my computer chair. "I just had an enlightening talk with your friend."

My heart skipped a few beats. "Who?"

"Jessica Bradley. She said that you seemed to be avoiding her calls today," he added, with a disapproving glance at the phone on my desk.

"I've been busy doing homework," I lied.

"Is it done?"

I nodded.

"Excellent," he said with a nod. "I'm pleased by how well you've recovered. So pleased that I'm returning these."

A set of keys dangled from his fingers.

"My car keys!" I rejoiced, taking the keys. I could almost smell my freedom, and couldn't wait to tell Eli and Dustin I had wheels to go wherever I wanted.

"You deserve them," he told me. "Jessica told me how you helped come up with the fundraiser plans, so I figured you'd need your car. You aren't expected back in classes till Monday, but there's no reason you can't help Jessica."

"Help Jessica do what?" The sharp end of a key stabbed my palm.

"I'll make an exception for such a worthwhile endeavor. I told Jessica you could go, and that I'd be happy to donate cases of canned food." Smiling, he gave my braid a light tug. "Have fun—at the fundraiser."

The auditorium displayed a huge blow-up of my (hideous!) junior year picture on a pedestal surrounded by boxes of canned food. What a send-off! I wasn't sure whether to laugh or cry. No one but me saw the irony in memorializing a foodaholic with a canned-food drive.

Even more ironic—the dead girl was present.

Dustin and Eli had both tried to talk me out of attending, afraid I'd break down. But Mr. Montgomery's direct order could not be ignored. So I arrived early to set up, carrying boxes and bags of canned food.

Every time I walked up near the stage, I cringed at the life-size picture of my own face. My hair was frizzed on one side, my eyes were squinting because the photographer's lights were too bright, and a pimple poked out on my chin. Could Jessica have found a worse picture of me? Doubtful.

Kat was also pitching in to help, carrying canned food with a cheerful attitude. I found nothing to be cheerful about, and kept busy to avoid talking to anyone.

The memorial was scheduled for four o'clock.

At ten to four, there were still only three of us present.

I knew it, I thought, both angry and relieved. *No one is coming*.

But then the door opened. Dustin and Eli stepped in.

Dustin held a box loaded with canned food. Eli carried just one can—but it was the largest can I'd ever seen. He'd put a bow on the top like it was a birthday gift. Then he came over to me.

"Here's my donation." He had a twinkle in his eyes.

"Couldn't you find anything bigger?" I joked.

"I'll try next time you have a memorial service," he joked. He handed me the giant can of chocolate syrup.

My arms strained to hold it. As I carried it over to one of the growing pile of canned goods (quite a few donated by Mr. Montgomery), there was a rumble of voices. I looked over my shoulder and saw dozens of my classmates, and some teachers, filing into the room. Principal Kimbrough was even there, taking a seat in the front row.

I watched in a daze as row after row was filled—everyone donating at least one can before sitting down.

They can't all be here for me, I told myself.

But then Aunt Suzanne and Cousin Zeke arrived, and spoke to Dustin. Dustin caught my gaze and winked.

This was insane. I never expected any of my family to

show up. I also didn't expect the next person who walked through the door.

Alyce.

I stared, shocked, sure I was hallucinating. But it was Alyce all right, dressed in her usual black: a pleated skirt and a sheer, long-sleeved blouse over a black shirt. Her hair was twisted in a bun with bone-like sticks holding it together, and her powdered pale face looked gaunt with smudged black eye makeup. She took a seat in a back row.

"Come on, Leah," Jessica whispered, grabbing my arm. "It's about ready to start."

I went with her, still trying to see Alyce—only the room was so crowded I couldn't see her anymore. When Jessica waved me over, I gave up looking and sat beside her in the front row, next to Principal Kimbrough.

"I've never spoken at a memorial before—wish me luck!" Jessica swept up to the podium and thanked everyone for their donations, then added that the Principal would like to say a few words.

Did Principal Kimbrough even know my name?

"Thank you all for coming," he said in a deep voice that echoed through the mike. "When I told Jessica she could have the auditorium today for a fundraiser, I expected the usual raffle or a game of bingo. But she far exceeded my expectations by using this opportunity to remember a student we all loved and respected."

Loved and respected?

He had to be talking about someone else. But then he said my name and spoke about my work on the Halsey Hospitality Club. "Amber Borden and the other members of the HHC have made this school a welcoming place for students. Some people move through life without thinking of others, but Amber wasn't like that. She shone a light of friendship and welcome to new students. And she will be sorely missed." His voice thickened with emotion. "Now, I believe Jessica Bradley has something to say."

Jessica took the podium and started off by thanking everyone for coming. "Your donation of canned goods will help feed needy people. This canned-food drive was Amber's idea."

It was? Not even close.

"I spoke with her only hours before her tragic accident, and she was excited about working on our committee to help less fortunate people. Her caring efforts brought us all here today. I only hope I can live up to her generous example." Jessica then invited anyone else who wanted to say something about Amber to come up to the podium.

In the front row, I kept shaking my head in disbelief. None of this was about me. That couldn't be happening. I mean, I'd never done anything special. I was just ordinary.

"When I transferred to this school," Betina Cortez began, "I was still recovering from a kidney operation and didn't have the energy to make friends. But on my very first day, Amber Borden welcomed me to Halsey High with the most beautiful basket I'd ever seen. I loved the gifts inside, but mostly I loved Amber for being kind to a new girl. I didn't get to know her well after that—she already had two best friends—but I never forgot her kindness ... and I'm so sorry she's gone."

Wiping her eyes, Betina left the stage.

Next at the podium was Trinidad. The tiny diamond in her nose sparkled in the bright ceiling lights. She was small, but she carried herself with style and an awareness of the audience. So much diva potential, if she only knew it.

"Amber welcomed me, too, with a great basket. Then she offered to give me a ride, just because she was so nice." Trinidad wiped her eyes. "I think what I admired most was the way she listened and really cared. She made me feel like I could do amazing things. But really, she was the one who was amazing. I didn't know her well, but I miss her and all the special things that won't happen without her around."

There was a moment of silence as Trinidad left the stage. Then my cousin Zeke came up. He still had that goofy wave of red hair falling over his eyes, and teeth so big he looked like he was smiling even when he wasn't. And he wasn't now. I could tell he'd been crying, because his eyes were almost as red as his hair.

"Amber was my cousin, and she was a lot of fun," he said, choking up as he went on to tell about how we'd ruined his sister's wedding cake.

When he was done, I glanced back a few rows to my Aunt Suzanne. Through her tears, she was laughing at Zeke's story. Laughing? When did she get a sense of humor? And her tears were real—as if she truly missed me.

More people came up to share thoughts and memories. My trig teacher praised my math skills and promptness in turning in homework. My chemistry teacher told the humiliating story about my putting a combustible chemical tube on a heated Bunsen burner. He showed the burnt corner of his eyebrow that had never grown back after that small fire. He chuckled sadly and said how much he'd missed my "fiery personality." Then my gym teacher said I was a great example—of someone with no athletic aptitude who kept trying anyway.

I listened as if disconnected from reality. All these wonderful, sweet, funny, heartbreaking stories were about me. I began to feel sad, too, about my being dead—until I remembered that this memorial should be for Leah. She was the one gone forever. What would people have said about her? She was popular. She was pretty. She had a hot boyfriend. But did anyone know what she was really like? She played different roles and drifted in her popularity. It was Jessica who seemed to be the real force behind Leah's image.

Then Kat and Moniqua went to the podium together and recited a prepared speech that rang totally false to me. They acted liked we'd been best friends. Not one word about dissing me and calling the HHC members "Basket Cases." But did it really matter?

No—and I continued to be awed by my many genuine friends.

Margrét came hesitantly to the podium, speaking softly with a lyrical Icelandic accent. She was slim and fragile and it seemed like a loud voice could knock her over. She held a small stuffed toy bird—the puffin from her welcome basket.

"Amber was so sweet to me, so friendly when I knew nothing about your school and little about America," Margrét said. "I lost this puffin for a while but Amber found it and returned it to me. So small a thing—but it was big to my heart. Amber shared her big heart and asked for nothing in return. In her honor, I'm going to join the Halsey Hospitality Club and welcome new students like she did."

Applause fluttered across the room like wings of an idea taking flight. This idea spread as more people stepped forward to talk about the gift baskets they'd received. Over a dozen students volunteered to join the HHC.

Always quick to action, Dustin stepped up with a notebook to take names of the new club members. I looked around for Alyce, to see if she was excited by all the new members. But I couldn't see her. I'd been hoping she'd come to the podium to say something—I mean, she was the closest person to me in the entire auditorium.

But she never spoke up.

Dustin said a few words—mostly about how I started HHC and worked hard to keep it going. He credited Alyce with the creative design of the baskets, but even then Alyce didn't come forward. Maybe she'd left already.

Three more classmates (all recipients of HHC baskets) came up and said nice things about me—how getting a welcome basket gave them confidence in a new school. They all said they liked how I smiled and waved whenever we passed in the hall.

I'd made people feel good simply by being friendly and smiling?

But that was so easy.

Then Jessica took the podium again, thanking everyone for coming and especially for their generous contributions of canned food. "Your donations will brighten the lives of many people—like Amber brightened yours. And

I'm sure that wherever Amber is, she's watching us right now … smiling."

Yes she is, I thought.

Chairs scraped the floor and voices rose as people filed out of the room. Some stayed to pay respects by lining up to view a "memorial box" that my Aunt Suzanne had brought from my family.

"Amber's parents couldn't come—they're at the hospital dealing with sad things," I heard her tell Jessica.

"The hospital?" Jessica asked. "I thought Amber passed … um … a few days ago."

My aunt seemed to hesitate. "At the last minute, my sister insisted that Amber moved her hand, so the doctors postponed everything. But it was only false hope. Everything should be over now." She sighed. "Amber's parents appreciate this lovely tribute, so they sent along a few mementos of Amber."

The box was the size of a shoe box and wrapped in silver foil with my name glitter-glued on the front. What had my parents sent? Curious, I joined everyone else in line. I managed to be the last one, so I could look without anyone watching over my shoulder.

When I reached the box, emotions swelled in my throat. Inside the box were pictures of me as a baby, toddler, and a few recent ones that looked much better than my awful junior year picture. In one photo I was hamming for the camera at my thirteenth birthday party, posed between Dustin and Alyce, our arms around each other. But instead of a smile, there was an uncomfortable look on my face.

My stomach had ached because I'd just eaten one-sixth of my double fudge strawberry cream birthday cake.

Now my stomach ached for sad reasons. I missed me so much.

I picked up the photo, caressing it fondly, when I noticed a bright object hidden underneath. Rainbow thread, woven by my grandmother—the bracelet I was wearing when I died.

My lucky bracelet! Staring down at it, I thought fast. No one else cared about this bracelet. It would probably be tossed out or tucked away in a forgotten corner of the attic. No one would even remember it . . . except me.

I wanted my bracelet back.

So I glanced around furtively. Jessica was talking with the principal, Dustin was deep in a conversation with Margrét, and a small group of people I vaguely recognized were talking near the door. No one was watching me. I slowly raised my hand, acting all casual like I was going to push my bangs back. I touched my hair, then slowly lowered my hand. My fingers shot out—and I snatched the bracelet.

I hurried away from the box, snaking down the aisle and passing the people still talking by the door, and left the auditorium. I ducked around a corner, leaned against the wall, and gazed at my precious bracelet. So many memories twined in colorful thread, binding me to my grandmother.

I started to slip the bracelet on my wrist when I heard a shout behind me.

"Take that off!"

Whirling around, I saw Alyce.

30

"I said to take it off!" I'd never seen her so angry.

"Alyce!" Even though she looked angry enough to hit me, I was thrilled to be with her again. "It's so good to see you!"

But she was having none of me, pointing her finger in my face like she'd take my eyes out if I didn't do what she wanted. "Take off Amber's bracelet."

"Let me explain," I said quickly as I backed away.

"Shut up and give me that bracelet."

"Alyce, please listen. I'm not who you think."

"I know who you are and you can buy anything you want, so why bother stealing my best friend's bracelet? You're pathetic."

"I wasn't stealing it—I was taking it back. Alyce, look into my eyes—don't you recognize me?"

"Everyone knows who you are."

"But Dustin knows who I *really* am. Ask him—he'll tell you about the body switch."

"Body switch?" She was the one who stepped back now. "Not only a thief, but crazy."

I held tight to the bracelet. "Alyce, I want to tell you everything, but I'm afraid you won't believe me. Dustin will tell you I'm not Leah. Why don't you get him?"

"So you can run off with Amber's property while I'm gone? No way." She held out her hand. "Give it to me or I'm going to walk back into the auditorium and announce over the loudspeaker that you're a thief."

"Don't, Alyce! Besides, my lucky bracelet isn't worth anything except to me."

"Lucky bracelet?" Her voice dropped. "How do you know about that? Did Dustin tell you?"

"How could he? Dustin doesn't know. I promised Grammy I wouldn't tell anyone except you, because I always tell you everything...like when I got my period while we were on a hike and had to use an old shirt for a pad. Or when we had that water balloon fight and you threw one so hard I got a black eye but we told everyone that Chris Bundry hit me. That bully was always hitting kids, so everyone believed me."

"And he got grounded." She started to smile, then gasped. "No...no way! You can't know those things...only Amber does."

"That's what I'm trying to tell you." I glanced around

cautiously, then whispered, "You know how I have such a bad sense of direction? You're always saying, 'Dramber, you could get lost walking out of your own bedroom.'"

"Ohmygod," she moaned. She sagged against the wall.

I could tell she was listening even though it would take more to convince her. So I went on. "When I got hit by Sheila's mail truck, I went to the light—and guess who I met there? Grammy Greta and Cola."

"But they're...dead."

"I couldn't believe it either, but Grammy and Cola convinced me it was real. We talked awhile, then Grammy told me it wasn't my time yet. She said to turn left at this Milky Way place—only I got it all mixed up and turned right. And I landed in the wrong body."

"But you're...you're Leah." Alyce rubbed her head. "Only you're talking like Amber. I must be sick."

"You're fine. I'm the one stuck in the wrong body."

With her back against the wall, she sank to the floor. "I-I don't know...it's impossible. Prove it."

"Haven't I already proven it? Who else would know everything I just told you?"

"You're talking with Leah's voice and moving in her body. I don't even know why I'm listening to you—this is impossible."

"I can prove it. Ask me something that only I would know."

She pointed to the rainbow bracelet. "You say you know that's a lucky bracelet. But do you know the ritual to make the luck work?"

I nodded. "Sure."

She narrowed her brows skeptically. "So do it."

"Here? What if someone walks by?"

"Do it now."

"Oh all right. But it's humiliating."

I looked around to make sure no one was around. Then I turned the bracelet to the right two times and to the left once. I whispered the childhood chant:

Fuzzy Wuzzy was a bear.

Fuzzy Wuzzy had no hair.

Fuzzy Wuzzy wasn't very fuzzy.

Was he?

Then I sealed the magic with a kiss. Embarrassed, I looked up to find Alyce's powder-painted face dripping black stains of tears. She sobbed out my name, then opened her arms and hugged me.

Eli, Dustin, and now Alyce knew.

You'd think that would solve everything, and I could be myself again.

But there was still the problem of Mr. Montgomery controlling my life.

When Dustin finally spotted us together in a corner of the hallway, he raised an eyebrow. Alyce and I shared an "I know what he's thinking" look and giggled.

"Oh, no!" Dustin threw up his hands as if surrendering. "They're back—the Double-Trouble A's."

There was so much to talk about. Since the Montgomerys wouldn't miss me for a few hours, we got in my car (they were both very impressed with Leah's cool wheels) and headed for our favorite hangout, Grumpy's Grill.

When Alyce watched me slop through the Giant Grumpy Burger, oozing sauce all over my hands and licking it up, she joked that there was no doubt I was the real Amber.

Of course that led to questions about Leah. Since I was in her body, why wasn't she in mine? Where was she? Would she ever come back?

"I have no idea," I admitted with a twinge of guilt. "When I saw my real body, I hoped to find her there and that we'd switch back. Only it didn't happen ... and now it can't ever."

"There's always hope," Alyce insisted, chewing on a fry. "And you had a very nice memorial. It was cool to hear people say all those nice things about you. I took notes so I could tell your family everything people said."

I grinned—she was such a great friend. Who else would take notes at a memorial and rush after a thief to save a mostly worthless bracelet?

Looking down at my wrist, I wondered if the bracelet really was lucky. Well, I had my friends back—which was a great start.

Alyce kept staring at me, as if she was still getting used to my borrowed body. But as we talked, joking about shared experiences like nothing was any different between us, it all felt so normal.

Dustin was still worried about my staying with the Montgomerys. "You need to move out of there," he insisted.

"We already discussed this and agreed it's best to wait.

Don't forget the GPS system in my car. I don't want to be picked up by the police again."

"Tell your parents—your real ones," Alyce suggested. "We'll make them believe, and then you can move back home."

"Even if they believe I'm their daughter, Mr. Montgomery won't let me leave." I glanced at Leah's pink leather watch and frowned. "I'll have to go back soon."

"Not so soon!" Alyce objected.

"I guess you have to," Dustin admitted. "But it won't be long. We'll call when we find a way to help you."

"I'll keep Leah's cell phone close," I promised. We got in the car and I dropped them back at school.

The Montgomery house was quiet when I stepped through the door. I smelled something coming from the kitchen and guessed Luis was busy cooking dinner. Otherwise, no one was around.

Shrugging, I went upstairs and tackled the computer again.

I managed to get into some of the programs this time, and found some games to play, but I still couldn't read any of Leah's personal email. One of the games looked cool, so I created a character and went off to slay some bad dudes.

Luis showed up a while later with a hot dish of food. "Your parents and brother haven't returned from the lawyer yet," he explained. "I thought you'd like to eat in your room. I'm headed to my apartment but if you need something just call on the intercom."

I nodded, sniffing the hot covered plate appreciatively. "Thanks, Luis."

Dinner was delicious and since no one was checking on me, I skipped my evening exercise. When I tired of game playing, I shut down the computer and watched some TV until my eyes grew heavy and I drifted off...

A dog was barking.

I opened my eyes and found myself somewhere else...with clouds rather than walls and a foggy sense of unreality. I turned my head—and there was Cola, bouncing toward me with his tongue hanging out and his tail wagging.

"Cola!" I exclaimed. "And you're happy to see me this time!"

He barked, and in my head I heard, *You're my mission.*

"I am?"

I'm your escort.

And then the scene changed. Cola was still there, but I was walking on air or bubbles or clouds. I wasn't really sure. I knew I hadn't died again, so this must be a dream.

An awake dream, I heard Cola explain in my head. *Come.*

I followed him from light clouds to a dark sky twinkling with endless stars. And there was Grammy Greta. I didn't see her arrive; she was just suddenly there, smiling with those knowing eyes I loved so well.

"Amber," she murmured as she enfolded me in her arms. "It's so good to hold you again. I'm sorry it's taken this long."

"Am I me?" I asked, looking down at myself and hoping for chunky legs and a big booty. Instead I saw long athletic legs and perky boobs. Damn.

"Don't be disappointed," Grammy told me gently. "You're meeting me in a dream state, so just imagine anything you want to appear differently."

I concentrated a moment, and then looked down again.

"I'm Amber! And I'm wearing my favorite butterfly pocket jeans."

"It's doesn't matter how you look—I can always see you clearly."

"Then why haven't you helped?" I complained. "I tried to switch back and nothing happened. Cola was at the hospital but wouldn't even help me."

Cola hung his head and tucked his tail between his legs.

"Now don't blame Cola," Grammy chided. "He had a job to do and no time for you. When he returned here, he told me you needed my help."

"But I also wanted to tell you about the Dark Lifer."

Grammy gasped. "You've met a Dark Lifer?"

"Yeah—the hospital security guard, Karl." I thought about mentioning my suspicion of Mr. Montgomery, but it just seemed too crazy.

"I'll notify the Dark Disposal Team," she told me. Then she apologized for not contacting me sooner. "But I've been busy with the Leah Montgomery situation. The switching of souls is a complicated affair, especially when suicide is involved."

"You mean…Leah's really dead?" I asked, afraid.

"No, thank God—and I do mean that literally. She decided to live. We don't have time in this dream state for lengthy explanations so I'll make it simple. Leah committed suicide, but thanks to your mistake, she was given a second chance."

"My mistake saved her?" I asked incredulously.

"Yes. Instead of recycling into a new life, she went into a cocoon where she could consider her options. Ultimately, she asked for another chance at life. But that caused problems."

"I don't understand."

"My job as an Earthbounder Counselor involves something called Temp Lifers. These are souls who temporarily step into someone's body when they're in crisis. When you switched into Leah's body, you accidentally did what Temp Lifers do on purpose."

I just looked at her.

"Okay, I can see you're still confused, so here's an example," Grammy continued. "There's this young girl, Jamie, who witnessed the drive-by shooting of her father. She was so traumatized that she needed a break from her body. So a Temp Lifer lived her life for a while."

"Where did Jamie go?"

"Into a relaxing cocoon sleep. When she returned to her body, she was stronger. Her replacement had gotten her through the toughest moments—with enough memories merged so she can remember some of the experience."

"Is that what's happened to Leah? Is she sleeping?"

"Well... it's different for suicides. But because you stepped into her body, fulfilling the same duties as a Temp

Lifer, Leah didn't die. Good for her, but not so good for your body, which was left at risk. I managed to delay the organ harvesting by causing your hand to move. But getting clearance to transport Leah's soul into your body was more complicated. Finally I succeeded, and your parents received the good news a short while ago."

"You mean my body isn't ... dead?"

"Breathing on its own with a sleeping occupant."

"Wow! That's like a miracle!"

"You're my miracle. You have a natural skill for Temp Lifer work. Mostly we use non-living souls who need redemption. But occasionally Temp Lifers are living people who generously lift out of their body to help someone else."

"How is that possible? People can't just leave their bodies."

"You did," she pointed out.

"Thanks to my bad sense of direction," I said, sighing.

"The Temp Lifer program is highly successful. You'd be great at it, with your natural talent for helping others. If you ever want a job, let me know."

"Any time," I said, flattered. "I'm happy to help out."

"I may take you up on that." Grammy touched my cheek fondly. "I know you thought I'd abandoned you, but I never did. I've been working hard to fix your problem."

"Can I go back to my real body?" I asked hopefully.

"Soon," she promised. "I've calculated your local time, and it should happen tomorrow around six in the evening. But for this to work, you must be near your real body."

"No problem," I assured her.

Then I felt something tugging, pulling me away from Grammy and Cola. I struggled to stay, but the pull was too strong. My last glimpse of Grammy was of her waving to me.

Jerking upright in bed, I shook off the grip someone had on my arm.

"What? Who? Hunter?" I blinked at the shadowy figure by my bedside. Gradually my eyes adjusted; only a small night-light lit the room. "What are you doing here?"

"Sorry for waking you," he said. "But I had to talk to you in secret."

"Um ... all right. What is it?"

"Dad says you talked him out of sending me away. I didn't think you would, but you really did keep your promise. Thanks," he said softly.

"You're welcome. It wasn't much."

"It was to me ... except now I feel bad for stuff I did to you when I was really mad."

"Huh?" I asked groggily. "What did you do?"

"Sorry, I took this." He shoved a book at me. "I won't steal from you any more—or anyone else. I promise."

Then he mumbled thanks, again, and scampered out of the room.

I snapped on my bedside lamp and looked at the book.

It was a journal.

Leah's.

31

Forget sleeping. I propped myself up against the bed pillows and opened the journal.

Unlike Leah's other journal, this one was crammed full of writing, slips of papers, and cards tucked among the pages. Leah must have freaked out when she realized it was missing. Did she guess that her little brother stole it?

I held the book carefully so that the loose papers wouldn't escape. Then I started reading:

The first page had no date or heading—just random scribbles of Leah's name looped with Chad's, and clusters of tiny hearts:

Leah and Chad, Chad and Leah, Leah Rockingham, Leah Montgomery-Rockingham, Chad Montgomery.

Without a date, I couldn't tell if these romantic jottings were recent or history. Leah clearly loved Chad when she wrote this—maybe she still did. Although what she saw in him, aside from hot looks and great kissing, was a mystery to me.

The next page was a shopping list: shoes, shirts, lingerie, earrings and jeans, all ultra-chic name brands. Many of them were now in Leah's closet, and I couldn't deny that I'd gotten a rush when I'd tried some on.

Still, shopping lists were boring. I wanted personal "Dear Diary" confessions. Skimming through more pages of random scribbles and lists, I stopped when I found a poem with no title.

> *I whisper in fathoms of darkness*
> *So soft no one hears,*
> *Not even me.*
> *When I raise my voice,*
> *False reflections cast lies,*
> *Until I no longer know myself.*
> *I*
> *Do*
> *Not*
> *Exist*

I shifted on the bed as uncomfortable emotions stirred inside me. Deep sadness and despair echoed in every word of Leah's poem; the sort of thoughts that could lead to suicide.

Uneasy, I flipped to the next page. A colorful, red, heart-shaped card fell out—a Valentine from Chad.

Marking my place in the journal, I opened the card.

Babe—U R really pretty and special 2 me. I want 2 B with you always. Luvya, Chad.

Okay, he wasn't a poet but the card was sweet and almost romantic. Tucking it back into the journal, I returned to where I'd left off.

At least a dozen pages fluttered by with nothing more than random events, such as *Valentine's Dance, Jess' birthday, Social at Club—formal, wear leopard shoes,* and *Rally in the quad.*

Then I came to a very different kind of list, one that reminded me of fashion designer sketches. There were two rough drawings of T-shirts, with writing inside. On the one labeled *Front of T-Shirt,* it said:

My parents spent a fortune for the Perfect Daughter, and all I got was this great body.

Chemical Peel	*$741*
Rhinoplasty	*$8,890*
Breast Augmentation	*$4,043*
Tummy Tuck	*$4,825*
Liposuction	*$2,746*
Octoplasty	*$2,168*
Cellulite Massage Treatment	*$130*
Microdermabrasion	*$190*
Surgeons fee	*$4,250*
Anesthesiologist	*$937*
Facility Fee	*$1,080*
Total cost:	*$30,000*

On the drawing for the back of the T-Shirt, it said:

Can a person be valued in $$$$$?

I wasn't sure whether to smile at Leah's dark humor or sob at her lack of self-esteem. I couldn't fit this into my memory of her striding confidently through the Halsey High halls like she owned the world. If she was so unhappy, why didn't she do something about it? I could have loaned her a dozen self-help books with advice that could have helped solve her problems. I only wish I'd had the chance.

A glance at the bedside clock showed me that it was almost morning. Too early to get up, but too late to go back to sleep. Not that I could relax into sleep with so much stuff crowding my mind. Besides, there was still half a journal left to read.

It was odd how the more I learned about Leah, the less I knew her. She wasn't any one thing: not simply pretty, popular, cruel, kind, sad, or confused. She was so much more...and a little less, too. Would I have liked her if I'd had the chance to know her?

Probably not—but I would have been willing to try.

I found more reasons *not* to like her in the next few pages. Instead of a shopping list, she had a "dirty secret" list—not any of her own secrets, but those of her closest friends. Kat, Jessica, Tristan, Moniqua, Chad, and other names from school were there—even a few teachers. Across from each name, she wrote the sort of personal things friends told each other in confidence. Kat had a sister who'd run away and starred in porn movies; Tristan hired someone else to take his SAT's; Jessica's mother had an affair with her yoga instructor; Moniqua lost her license twice but still went out driving, and—

I did a double take as I read the next entry.

When Leah had been busy at one of her father's events, Chad had hooked up with Jessica. Jessica Bradley? *Leah's best friend!*

Did Jessica know Leah knew? And what about Chad? Had Leah confronted him?

Probably not, since Leah still hung out with Jessica and dated Chad. But why did Leah put up with the betrayal? Instead, she'd tucked away all her discoveries in her journal. Leah knew enough secrets to ruin everyone at Halsey High.

Did she keep these secret to herself or use them as blackmail? Did knowing things about other people make her feel powerful? Give her a sense of control when her life was tumbling into chaos?

I was still puzzling over this when I found one last poem tucked in the back of the journal.

Beginning…
Hands moving,
Mouth open,
Eyes closed,
Mind drifting…

Thinking of…
Shopping for shoes.
Pink, black, or gold?
An Essay Due in English Lit.
Rocky road ice cream in the fridge,

Can't decide which outfit for tomorrow.
Where C and I will go after school
Gift ideas for Jess' b-party
Pink nail polish out.
Blue-frost polish in.

Ending…
Standing
Smiling
Lying
Crying.
Done.

Chills prickled through me. I wasn't sure what this was about, except it left me with a bad feeling. If Leah was being forced to do something awful, why didn't she just say no? Walk away. Leave. Ask someone for help.

Oh, Leah—what kind of hell were you going through? I closed the book with a sigh.

That was one secret I'd probably never know.

Hours later I woke abruptly—startled because I hadn't expected to fall back asleep.

Someone was tapping at my door. The journal! I had to hide it. Shoving it under my pillow, I called out, "Who's there?"

"Who else?" Angie said impatiently as she strode in waving a sheet of paper. "I brought your schedule. It's almost time for your morning swim."

Schedule?

Alarm raced through me as I realized what would be on that printed sheet after the routine things like swimming, exercise, and lunch. There would be a notation about tonight's society reception—where I had promised to dance with Congressman Donatello.

But I couldn't go. In my dream conversation with Grammy, she'd said I had to be close to my real body, in the hospital, at six o'clock. Not at some fancy event. Or Leah would never get her second chance, and I'd be stuck in her body forever.

"I'm not feeling well today," I faked to Angie.

"You don't look sick." Angie regarded me skeptically.

I nodded, sinking into my pillow. "I ache all over," I said with a dramatic groan. "Could you tell my father that I won't be able to go out tonight?"

Angie frowned. "I'll tell him—but he won't like it."

"I know … sorry." I coughed for effect. "But I can't help being sick."

"Jessica shouldn't have pushed you into helping her yesterday." She switched her suspicion to concern. "You needed more time to recuperate. I'll have Luis fix you up some hot chicken broth."

While I waited for her to return, I watched old reruns of *The Brady Bunch* and *Family Ties*. The happy families reminded me of my real family. It would be so wonderful to go home and leave the Montgomerys forever. If the switch worked, I felt sorry for Leah having to come back here.

Thinking about this gave me an idea, so I pulled out the journal again and wrote on a blank page in the back.

Leah,

In case you forget, you need to know some things.

1. *Your little brother looks up to you. Be kind to him.*
2. *Your mother is incredibly brave. Cheer on all her successes.*
3. *Angie can be rude, but deep down she cares about you. Smile at her.*
4. *Luis rocks! Watch soaps with him and enjoy his cheese popcorn.*
5. *If you respect your friends, they will respect you. Talk honestly to Chad and Jessica.*
6. *Do not let your father tell you what to do with your body. It's just wrong. You do not have to dance or do anything else with his friends.*
7. *Read self-help books. Contact Amber Borden for suggestions.*

I skimmed the list again, smiling as I imagined Leah reading my words and (hopefully) taking them to heart. Grammy said that Leah had already spent some "heavenly" time reflecting on her life. I hoped she'd figured stuff out and would treat her friends, family, and herself better.

As I shut the journal, another paper fell out. Not one paper, but several stapled together. The cover sheet had business letterhead from Congressman Donatello. I expected it to be a letter to Leah, but it was to Mr. Montgomery. Nothing exciting. Only a blah-blah boring "thank you for your generous donations" letter. The attached papers looked like the ledger I made in accounting class. I'd always liked how the debits and credits made tidy rows and balanced out figures. But these figures were confusing: rows of percentages, amounts and long number sequences connected by dashes.

The numbers triggered a memory, but I couldn't place it. The oddest thing was that on the top of the second page was the name "Leah Ashland," followed by a series of numbers. I knew from Leah's driver's license that her middle name was Ashland, but something about this bothered me.

There was a sound at my door.

Quickly, I tossed the papers back into the journal and hid the journal under a pillow—just as Mr. Montgomery strode into the room.

His scowl was my first clue that he wasn't happy.

"I heard you're sick?" he asked suspiciously.

I nodded, coughing and trying to look ill.

"Rather convenient timing, don't you think?"

"I don't know—" cough, "—what you—" cough, cough, "—mean."

"Nasty cough." He bent over the bed, studying me. "You don't look sick to me. You look lovely... positively glowing with health."

"But I feel awful." I added more coughs and rolled my eyes as if I might pass out.

"Sounds serious. So serious I think we should bring in a doctor."

Doctor? Oops... not part of my plan.

"I-I just need to—" small cough, "—rest a while. But I'm sorry about the dance. I don't think I'll have the energy to go."

He reached out to touch my chin so that I had to look in his eyes. "Oh, I think you will."

Afraid and dizzy, I stared at my white knuckles clutching the blankets. My chin throbbed where he had touched me, and when I rubbed the sore spot, my fingers came away with a sticky cream-colored smear. Makeup.

"Ohmygod!" I gasped at his hand's shadowy aura. "You really are a—"

"A what?" He sounded amused.

"A ... a Dark Lifer. You're wearing makeup to hide your hands."

I expected him to lie, but he merely shrugged. "So what? It's your fault, you know. Your glow brought me here. I was enjoying the lecherous body of a security guard at the hospital when I sensed your delicious energy. I became your father to get close to you."

"Well, get out of him!"

"Not quite yet. When I switched into this body, I tapped into your father's memories. He's not a very nice man—which I'm enjoying."

"You're not my father!"

"Who would believe you?" he asked. "I can make your life miserable if you don't obey me. So be a good girl and let me touch your sweet glowing skin. I thought you had stopped glowing, but it's back again ... so irresistibly."

"Stay away!" I tried to hide behind my pillow. "Don't touch me!"

"You can't stop your dear old dad," he threatened. "I control you."

I couldn't get to the door without getting by him—and

his cocky smile showed that he knew this. He was playing with me, like a spider spinning a web around a trapped fly. Suddenly he lunged for me. I rolled across my mattress and jumped up—but found myself in a corner. Nowhere to go.

Trembling, I clasped my arms behind my back—and with all my heart—I touched my rainbow bracelet, turning it twice, then once, whispering the lucky chant, then kissing it.

"Come kiss your dear old dad." The Dark Lifer reached out ominously. "Come closer, sweet Leah. I'm tired of games and can't wait to—"

But before he could finish, there were two bright flashes. Two translucent figures solidified into a man and woman in business suits. They appeared ordinary, except for the fact that their feet didn't touch the floor and ropes of silver draped over their arms.

The Dark Disposal Team! Thank God (and grandma).

"Stay Away!" the Dark Lifer posing as Mr. Montgomery shrieked.

"We've been searching for you for a long time," the woman said, smiling.

"Noooo!" The Dark Lifer threw up his hands protectively. But the two figures advanced, casting coils of silver ropes like a lasso, circling Mr. Montgomery's body in mummy fashion until I saw nothing but silver.

There were more flashes, then the silver ropes fell away. The man and woman vanished. All that was left was Mr. Montgomery—who blinked as if waking up from a long sleep. I couldn't say exactly why, but I knew that this was the real Mr. Montgomery.

"Leah?" he spoke uncertainly. "What were we saying?"

"Uh … how you're okay with me staying home tonight, since I'm sick."

"Is that so?" He stared at me coolly. "That's not how I recall our conversation."

I thought he'd be nicer without the Dark Lifer possessing his body, but he seemed even more intimidating.

I started to go into my story about being sick, but he cut me off.

"Save the excuses." He waved his hand. "Here's how this is going to play out. You may skip your exercise regime and rest in bed until evening. I will not contact DeHaven unless you continue your delusions about being sick."

"But I am sick!"

He waved his hand again, slicing off my complaint. "We made a bargain. And if you fail to live up to your part of it, then I will retaliate. You will find yourself confined to your room at DeHaven, where the fashionable clothing is a straitjacket. And Hunter will go to Camp Challenge."

"You can't do that to him! You promised."

"And you gave me a promise, too—which you will fulfill. Do you understand?"

Tugging the blankets close to my chest, my heart thumped a beat of terror. I tried to think of something to say. But there wasn't a way out—except to surrender.

"All right," I whispered.

"Excellent." He smiled with smug satisfaction. "You should wear the blue Lexie gown tonight. It'll go nicely with your eyes."

Then he turned and left.

32

I could have called Dustin or Eli or Alyce, but I didn't. Not because I didn't trust them—but because I couldn't trust myself. If they offered to rescue me, I'd be tempted to let them, abandoning Hunter. Besides, I was too ashamed to tell anyone what I'd promised to do, as if Mr. Montgomery's demands made me less of a person.

The day lingered on, as slowly and painfully as torture. I alternated staring at the ceiling and watching mindless TV reruns. I only ate a few bites of lunch, then went back to staring at nothing.

Later, Angie came to help me get ready for the Reception. Her dark eyes were surprisingly kind as she set out a blue low-cut gown, silver heels, and a sapphire necklace. "Do you need help getting dressed?"

"No, I'm fine." I shook my head.

I shouldn't be here. I should be on my way to the hospital. I was letting everyone down—Mom, Dad, Dustin, Alyce, Eli...and Leah. Especially Leah. I couldn't save her this time. What would happen to her? Maybe she'd stay with Grammy and work as a Temp Lifer. I could trust my grandmother to take care of her. Unfortunately, I couldn't trust myself to do anything right.

Always going the wrong way...

But what choice did I have? Dark Lifer Dad may be gone with the DD Team, but the real Mr. Montgomery was still here. He owned this body, paid for through bribes and threats. He'd never ever let me leave.

At least with me here, Hunter would be safe. I'd help Mrs. Montgomery stay sober. And in the future, Leah would score higher than any of her teachers expected in math.

Math...

Numbers, dashes and names tickled my memory.

And I lit up with an insight as explosive as fireworks.

"Ohmygod!" I cried out, sitting up in bed. "That's it!"

"What's it, Leah?" Angie immediately rushed to my side. "Are you all right?"

"Better than all right," I said with a nervous giggle.

I'm sure she thought I was crazy, but I'd never been saner.

Watch out Mr. Montgomery, I thought. *Amber Borden is taking you down.*

I did *not* put on makeup, fix my hair or slip into that amazingly gorgeous blue Lexie designer gown.

What I did do was call Dustin and fill him in. He checked a few things for me online, confirming my suspicions. Then I turned on the computer scanner and made some highly important copies, which I printed out.

After that I looked for Luis, but couldn't find him. So I asked Angie instead, and was surprised, pleased, and relieved when she agreed to be a messenger for me.

Then I was ready. Trembling with nerves, I slipped on casual jeans and a plain T-shirt and went to face my enemy.

My smile faded with each step toward Mr. Montgomery. I second-thought and mentally double-checked what I planned to say. Suddenly there were lots of holes in my scheme. What if I was wrong? But no... I couldn't let myself think negatively. Positive thoughts brought positive outcomes.

My life—and Leah's—counted on this.

"Leah, why aren't you dressed?" Mr. Montgomery was looking in a mirror, straightening his striped gray tie.

"Uh...I...um..."

"Well, what is it? I hope you're not still pretending to be sick."

"No...it's not that."

He tapped his fingers on the dresser. "Then hurry to your room and get ready."

I lifted my shoulders and exhaled. "I-I'm not going," I said.

"Leah, Leah..." He sighed wearily. "We've already been through this."

"No we haven't."

"Don't cross me," he warned. "You know what I'm capable of doing."

"But you have no idea what I could do to you." I matched the warning in his tone with one of my own. "I know about your payoffs to Congressman Donatello."

"What?" He chuckled. "Don't be ridiculous."

"It's true, and you know it."

"You have no grasp of my complicated business dealings."

"I do," I said firmly, feet planted, gaze steady, hands tight around the papers.

"This is not amusing."

"I wasn't amused either when I found my name on your papers."

"Don't be ridiculous."

"I'm totally serious—and I have the documents to prove it." I held out the papers. "These are proof that you made excessive donations to the Congressman in an account under my name: Leah Ashland. My first and middle name. There's also an account under Hunter's first and middle name, too."

"My business is not your concern." He reached out for the papers but I jumped back.

"I checked the numbers and contribution laws, and

it's obvious you've contributed more than the legal limit to the congressman's accounts. Coincidentally, the pay-offs happened when a bill came up for a vote on regulating radio stations' song selection—a bill that Congressman Donatello ended up voting down."

His jaw dropped, but then snapped shut and tightened. His gaze narrowed at me and his hands knotted to fists. "Give me those papers."

"If you insist." I shrugged and handed them over.

His grabbed them—then ripped them up, white shreds trailing to the carpet. "So you think you're so smart?" he sneered. "Stupid little girl—you should know better than to defy me. You'll never win. And after the party tonight, I'll deal with you."

"No, you won't," I said simply. Instead of being afraid, I felt more powerful than ever. He wasn't a Dark Lifer. He was only human, and not nearly as smart as he thought. "You will never touch me or order me around again."

"You don't issue the orders here."

Instead of arguing, I asked, "Do you really think I'd just hand over the papers?"

"What?" He looked down at the floor, then back at me.

"You ripped up a copy. The original papers are safe with a friend—who is very politically connected and will post the information on blogs around the world unless I tell him not to."

"You're lying," he accused.

"Do you really want to find out?"

His blustering anger made him red in his face, and if I hadn't stepped back I'm sure he would have hit me. Instead, he took a deep breath, and seemed to consider his options. His frown deepened.

"Leah, I'm very hurt by your behavior," he said sadly. If I didn't know better, I'd almost believe he was sincerely hurt. "But if you strongly don't want to go out tonight, I won't force you. Since I'm doing what you want, will you give me the original papers?"

"I don't have them. My friend does."

"Ah … the friend." He regarded me cautiously. "Well … fine. But don't do anything rash. I'm sure we can come to an agreement. You wouldn't want to cause any embarrassment for your family."

"That's right," I agreed. "I care about both of my families."

"Both?" He was puzzled.

"You wouldn't understand."

"There are a lot of things I don't understand—about these last few days and especially you. You've changed so much you seem like you're a completely different person." His shoulders slumped. "So, what should I do about tonight?"

"Surprise everyone," I said with heavy sarcasm. "Take your wife."

I reached into my pocket and pulled out Leah's car keys. Then I left the Montgomery house.

Forever … I hoped.

The hospital room was just as I remembered—except this time I wasn't alone. Dustin, Alyce and Eli closed around me for support while I knelt by the bed where my real body slept peacefully.

I wasn't sure how Dustin got permission for all of us to visit. I was just grateful for his help—especially when a few hours earlier he'd met Angie outside the Montgomery house to pick up the highly explosive papers.

When I met with him and the others in the waiting room, Dustin said he was glad to see me but sort of disappointed that my plan had worked so well.

"I was ready to blast the Montgomery papers across blogs everywhere," he added. "But I'd rather have you than fame."

I smiled and squeezed his hand, grateful to have loyal friends who rushed in to help with unconditional support. I'd even found support from an unexpected source. When I'd arrived at the hospital, Security Guard Karl came over with a smile.

"I'm not sure why, but I have an overwhelming urge to say thank you." His hands no longer misted with dark grayness. "So, thank you." Then he escorted us through the "No Admittance" doors and up to Room 311.

"It's almost six," Alyce announced, pointing to the wall clock.

"Just three minutes and twenty-two seconds." Eli came over and put his hand on my shoulder. "Just enough time for this…"

He pulled me close and pressed his lips against mine.

They were soft and sweet, with a taste of nutty humor. "That was good-bye to Leah," he said.

"She doesn't know what she's missing," I whispered. "Your brother could learn from you."

Eli laughed. "Now that's a first."

"The first of many," I said with promise.

Then he glanced at the clock. "Just one minute."

Tensing, I stared down at the hospital bed where my real body slept peacefully, breathing on her own without any machines. I took my own hand and thought of all the things people said at the memorial. Some of it was crap, of course, but most of it genuine. I never realized I had that many friends, but I guess I did. No matter who I looked like, I would be okay.

"Something's happening," Alyce cried out, sounding a little afraid.

The room seemed to brighten, as if a sunny window had been opened, but the blinds on the hospital window were closed. I held tightly to my body's hand, closing my eyes but still seeing the light. Expanding, wonderful warm, loving light. And through my closed eyes I saw Leah coming closer, hand-in-hand with my Grammy Greta. In this surreal realm, she looked like Leah and I looked like Amber. The strangest thing was that nothing seemed strange at all. Being together, the three of us, seemed natural.

"I'm ready," Leah told me. Her hair shone and she glowed with a beauty that came from the inside.

"I'm ready, too," I said.

"Thanks for everything," Leah told me. "Your grandmother's explained what you've done. I don't even know you . . . but I guess you know a lot about me. I'm sorry."

"Don't be. Just read your journal when you get back."

"Grammy says my body—the one you've been living in—will remember some of what happened while I was gone. Thanks for taking care of me. I couldn't handle it on my own."

"I'm glad to help," I said, and I sincerely meant it.

Grammy Greta touched my cheek. "That's part of what makes you so special." In this strange, dreamlike place, we faced each other. "You're so good at helping others; you're the right person for Temp Lifer missions. Don't be surprised if you're called on to help when you least expect it."

"Really?" I asked, flattered. "You'll let me help?"

"Count on it. It could happen sooner than you expect, but if it does, don't worry. Rest assured I'll watch out for your real body. I'm always close by for you."

"I know that now," I said giving her a hug.

Then all the bright light swirled around like a shaken snow globe. I saw Leah waving and felt my grandmother's touch slip away.

I thought excitedly about my body, eager to be me again—and to kiss Eli "hello" for *real*. It would be so cool to hang out with him at school, holding hands and saying all the corny stuff couples said to each other. I felt myself falling, spinning, diving forward to the life I loved.

Somewhere nearby, a dog barked.

Then everything faded . . .

. . . to black . . .

M y eyes flew open.
I stared up at a heavy metal poster plastered on the
ceiling.

Huh? I wondered. What was a poster doing on a hospital wall?

Something felt ... odd.

I lifted my head, wisps of straight hair tickling my face.
Not curly hair? I reached up and realized that my hair was
shoulder length. And the hand that flashed by my face had
thin fingers with square French-tipped nails. This was not
a hospital room.

Fear shot through me. Where was I?

But that wasn't the most important question.

Grammy Greta—what have you done to me?

Slowly, I sat up from a twin bed I'd never seen before. I stepped across discarded clothes I'd never worn before. And I stood before a mirror to ask the dreaded question.

Who was I?

The face staring back at me was familiar—but we'd never met. She had dark spiky hair, wide blue eyes, and rounded cheekbones. She was older than me—at least twenty-one—with an edgy aura that hinted at dark secrets.

I'd seen her face only once before—in a photograph on Eli's wall.

My new name was Sharayah Rockingham.

I was my boyfriend's sister.

The End.

Amber's List of Self-Help Books

1. *Positive Persuasion*
2. *The Cool of Confidence*
3. *Networking Works!*
4. *Becoming Your Destiny*
5. *Create Happiness Through Happen-Ness*
6. *Celebrities Are People, Too*
7. *The Bait of Debate*
8. *Grab Life with Both Hands*
9. *Leaders on Board*
10. *Chill Out, Charge Forward*

Disclaimer: None of these books exist, although they may be found in Charles de Lint's fictional dreamlands in Mr. Truepenny's shop of books that were never written.

About the Author

Linda Joy Singleton lives in northern California. She has two grown children and a wonderfully supportive husband who loves to travel with her in search of unusual stories.

She is the author of more than thirty books, including the series Regeneration, My Sister the Ghost, Cheer Squad, and, from Llewellyn, Strange Encounters and The Seer series. Visit her online at www.LindaJoySingleton.com.

A sneak preview of Dead Girl Dancing,
coming in Spring 2009!

I could not believe I was in the wrong body—again!
Memo to self: Never make a promise to a dead grand-mother.

I'd just been talking to Grammy Greta via an out-of-body-experience, and she'd said I had a talent for helping people and I'd make a good Temp Lifer. On the Other Side, my grandmother has this important job of Earthbounder Coun-selor—she gives humans in crisis a time-out from their lives by sending in temporary replacements. I was so flattered by her praise that I'd promised to help her anytime. But I hadn't expected her to switch me into someone else's body right away—especially the body of my boyfriend's sister, Sharayah.

Standing in front of a full-length mirror, I stared at

spiky dark hair, curved cheek bones, an eyebrow ring, and shocked eyes. Transforming from a high schooler to a college girl didn't sound bad in theory; being mature and of legal age for a few days could be a cool experience. But being my boyfriend's sister was sooo going to ruin my love life. Eli and I hadn't seriously kissed yet—and now even thinking about kissing him was illegal and immoral.

I mean, how could I make out with my boyfriend when I was his sister?

And where was Eli's sister? I frowned into the mirror at the pierced eyebrow and the blue eyes—not brown—staring back at me. Since I was here, did that mean Sharayah was in my body? Was she in a coma or waking up to the shock of her life? According to Grammy, Temp Lifers only replaced people who couldn't deal with their problems and were in crisis mode. What was Sharayah's crisis? And how was I supposed to help her when I didn't know how to help myself?

Seeing everything through a stranger's eyes tilted my equilibrium, distorting my senses. Nothing smelled the same and my skin fit uncomfortably, closer to the bones without the cushion of extra pounds. Swiveling my hips away from the mirror made me feel like a floppy doll yanked by puppeteer strings. I steadied myself on a dresser, my elbow brushing a digital clock that flashed 4:57 A.M. Nearly morning? But it seemed like I'd only been sleeping a few minutes. If the clock was right, then not only had I lost my body—I'd lost an entire day.

At least it was easy to guess where I was—in Sharayah's college dorm room. If the reflection in the mirror hadn't clued in me, there was the framed photo of the Rockingham family: Sharayah, her parents, and brothers Chad and Eli. The room was only slightly bigger than a closet and clearly divided in two personalities. One side was all girly pink and organized, with matching satin pillows on the pink quilted comforter of a neatly made twin bed. A sharp contrast to the other side of the room—Sharayah's half, I assumed, since that was where I'd awakened. Her twin bed was tangled in blankets with piles of clothes and random stuff abandoned on the floor. There was an odd smell, too: a mix of sweat, perfume and alcohol. When I inhaled, my stomach reeled and my throat ached with bitter dryness. I ached all over, too, like I'd jogged for a whole day (and I hate exercise). When I looked down at myself, I realized the baggy shirt I was wearing over a lacy red thong was a guy's shirt.

Who was the guy and how did I end up with his shirt?

This was not good.

What had Eli told me about his sister? I remembered his hurt expression as he'd talked about her sudden personality change: dropping friends, shutting out her family, and acting wild.

Exactly how wild? I worried.

I spotted a black leather handbag on the end table beside Sharayah's bed and started for it—then yelped when I bumped my foot on an empty wine bottle, which rolled under the bed and clinked like it had hit another bottle. Someone had been doing some serious partying…and I had a sick feeling it was me.

Did Sharayah's crisis have to do with too much partying? Or was she having romantic problems with her (shirtless) boyfriend? I couldn't even begin to guess until I found out more about her. So I opened the leather handbag and found a hair brush, an earring shaped like a skull, cherry lip gloss, an iPod, keys, a cell phone, and a wallet with Sharayah's driver's license showing she was born in April twenty-one years ago. There were also two credit cards, a college ID, postage stamps, a restaurant receipt—and twelve hundred dollars in cash.

"Wow!" I exclaimed, flipping through the crisp green hundred-dollar bills.

Ordinarily, lots of money would inspire whoops of joy from me—instead, my worries multiplied. Why would a college girl carry around so much cash? Unfortunately, I doubted it was for anything worthwhile like textbooks or tuition. And my thoughts darkened. I hated to suspect Sharayah of anything illegal—she was Eli's sister, after all—and if she got in serious trouble he'd be devastated. The crisp green bills seemed to burn my fingers. I dropped them back into the purse.

Picking up Sharayah's cell phone, I punched in Eli's number, envisioning him sleeping peacefully. My head throbbed so much there wasn't room for any guilt about waking Eli. This was an emergency and I needed him; that was all that mattered. Hurry, answer! I urged, listening to the ringing as I walked over to Sharayah's family portrait and ran my finger along the unruly curl of hair that waved across Eli's forehead. Another lifetime ago (actually only a few days ago), I'd looked at a copy of this exact picture in Eli's room. He wasn't athletic or cover-model pretty like his brother Chad, but when I looked into his eyes I saw loyalty, humor, intelligence … and I missed him.

"Huh?" Eli said groggily after about eight rings.

"Eli!" My heart jumped at his voice. "I'm glad you're there!"

"Who is ... ohmygod! Sharayah! Is it really you?"

"Uh ... sorry but no," I said in a lower-pitched, melodious voice I'd never heard before. "I'm not her."

"What are you talking about? Do you want to talk to Mom or Dad?"

"No! I called to talk to you."

"What is it? Are you in trouble?"

"Not exactly—but I'm afraid Sharayah is."

"Huh? What do you mean?"

"Eli, I'm not—" I sucked in a shaky breath. "I'm not your sister."

"No matter what you've done, Shari, you'll always be my sister. Nothing can be that bad and you know we're always here for you. Are you okay? Mom and Dad are worried sick. I mean, you didn't come home for Christmas! What were we supposed to think?"

"Eli ... I know I sound like your sister ... but it's Amber." I braced myself for his reply, knowing that being in the wrong body was unbelievable—but it wasn't like this was the first time. Only yesterday I'd been a wealthy, gorgeous, disturbed girl from school named Leah Montgomery. Eli knew to expect the unexpected with me. It was one of the many things I liked (maybe even loved) about him.

"Amber?" he repeated. "Amber Borden?"

"How many Ambers do you know?" I sighed. "It happened again."

"This isn't possible. You can't be Amber—she's still in the hospital. I was with her yesterday until visiting hours ended, hoping she'd wake up, but she never did."

"That's because I'm not there anymore. I think Sha-rayah is taking my place. I was shocked when I woke up in your sister's dorm room—and her body."

"No way!"

"It's true. I can hardly believe it myself."

"But you can't be my sister!"

"Only on the outside," I told him. "Inside, I'm still the same directionally challenged, chocolate-obsessed math geek. The last time I saw you—yesterday, I guess—we were in the hospital waiting for the magical switch from Leah's body to mine. After we kissed, I saw this dazzling light and talked to Grammy. I thought everything was going to be okay—until a few minutes ago."

"What went wrong?" he demanded. "Leah acted like she was herself again, but you just kept on sleeping and no one could wake you up—even the doctors couldn't figure it out."

I took a deep breath. "I'm a Temp Lifer."

"Huh? A what?"

"Temp Lifers are like body doubles—stepping in for the rough scenes when someone can't deal with their life role," I explained. "Only instead of working for Holly-wood, Temp Lifers report to the Other Side." It was hard to describe something I didn't fully understand.

My grandmother had said Temp Lifers were usually souls who had passed over, except in rare cases when a living person (like me) helped out. As with anything good, there was a bad side, too: Dark Lifers. These renegade Temp Lif-ers hijacked human bodies to avoid returning to the light.

I'd had a creepy encounter with one and never ever wanted to go through that again.

"Let me get this straight," Eli said, as if trying to be calm even though I could tell he was upset. "Instead of returning to your own body, you swapped with my sister?"

"Yes."

"So while I was waiting for you to wake up, holding your hand and saying...well, things I would never say to my sister...it was her and not you?"

"Um...yeah." I bit my lip. "But I doubt she heard you. She might not even be there. I don't really know how this all works. I swear I didn't know this was going to happen when I offered to help my grandmother. I didn't think she'd really switch me."

"You didn't think at all," he said bitterly. "Finally we hear from my sister and you're not even her."

"This sucks for me, too. I'm alone in a strange place instead of with my real family. I hoped to be back with them by now...and with you, too. I really miss you, Eli. I was looking forward to being in my own body and spending a lot of time with you."

"I wanted that too. Only now we can't...well...anything."

"Yeah. I freaked when I looked in the mirror and saw your sister. I mean, *your sister*. How could Grammy do this to me?" Tears swelled in my eyes. "Everything is so messed up. I just want to be me again."

"Ask your grandmother to switch you back."

"Don't you think I would if I knew how?" I wiped my eyes and gold flashed from the elegant bracelet on my wrist.

It looked expensive, the sort of bling I dreamed of affording someday when I became a famous entertainment agent. But now I'd give anything to wear my cheap "lucky" rainbow braided bracelet. Grammy had said that if I was ever in trouble to say a "magic" chant and twist the bracelet to contact her, but I didn't even know where the bracelet was and without it, I was lost—literally.

"Isn't there anything you can do?" Eli asked me.

"Wait to hear from Grammy, I guess. She told me she's never far away. At least this is only a temporary job, so once Sharayah rests a few days and is strong enough to deal with her problems, I should change back." I hope.

"Only a few days?" Eli sounded relieved. "That's not too bad … it could turn even out to be a good thing."

"Good?" I asked skeptically.

"Good for my family. My parents are really hurt because Sharayah won't visit or even talk to us."

"You said she didn't come for Christmas, so her problems started over three months ago?"

"At least," he said angrily. "A few weeks after Thanksgiving. We blame her boyfriend—some older guy named Gabe. She wouldn't tell us anything about him, but everything changed when they started going out. She switched roommates—dumping Hannah, who's been her closest friend since preschool. We heard from her other friends, too, wanting to know why she wasn't returning calls. The only time we heard from her was when she needed money."

"About money," I said with an uneasily glance down at Sharayah's purse. "Does she … uh … have a job?"

"I doubt it. She's majoring in pre-med and her college

load is too heavy for anything except volunteering at clinics. But she's changed so much that I have no clue what she's been doing. Let me know what you find out. Now that I think about it, I'm glad you're there. If my sister is so stressed out she needs a temporary replacement, who better for the job?"

"Yay, me," I said with zero enthusiasm.

"You won't be alone. After I work out some details—like borrowing a car from my parents—I'll drive there."

"Really? You'll drive all the way to ..." I paused, realizing I didn't even know what city I was in.

"You're in San Jose," he said, chuckling.

That wasn't too far—only a few hours' drive. I suddenly felt much better. "I'll be here waiting. It's not like I can go anywhere else. I doubt I even have a car."

"Actually, you do—if you can call that pint-sized Geo a car. Dad about had a heart attack when Shari bought that car instead of getting something from his dealership. That was only the beginning of my sister's problems."

"She'll be okay," I assured him.

"But will you?" he asked so sympathetically that I felt like crying and had to swallow hard to stay calm.

I didn't know how to answer, reluctant to admit I was scared and worried I'd screw up Sharayah's life as well as my own. I wanted Eli's respect, not his pity, and the self-help books I studied advised stuff like "nothing is sexier than confidence" and "never show fear." So I assured him everything was fine, that I would do a great job as a Temp Lifer and successfully solve Sharayah's problems.

For a moment I actually believed I could do this—like

I was Super Amber and could achieve anything. But I guess my super powers didn't include talking with guys, because there was this awkward silence between us—as if we were both waiting for the other to say something romantic. But who knew if there was even an "us"? We hadn't gone out on a real date, since I'd spent most of our time together in someone else's body.

"Well … um …" I finally said oh-so-not-brilliantly.

"I better … you know … go," he said just as brilliantly.

"You should … I guess."

"I guess … but Amber?"

"Yes? Yes?" My heart fluttered.

"I just want to say …"

"What?"

"That I … I …"

My cell phone beeped, flashing an incoming text message. I swore at the stupid timing of the stupid call, then realized Eli might think I was swearing at him and started to apologize as I hit the "stop" button to prevent another stupid beep from interrupting our conversation. Only the phone was a newer model, one I'd ever used before, and instead of shutting off the beep, I hung up on Eli.

Damn! Not the romantic way I wanted to end our conversation. I considered calling him back but didn't want to go through that whole awkward good-bye thing again. Besides, he'd be here in a few hours and then we'd talk—really talk.

The text message indicator kept flashing, so I hit a few buttons until one seemed to work. There was no name of the sender, only an unknown phone number and a short message:

I M WATCHING U.